INNER

SANCTUM

Book One

DARLENE OAKLEY

LANICO MEDIA HOUSE
Words that make power, ennoblion and life!

A division of Lanico Enterprise

Arkansas • Texas • Louisiana

Dear Elinor,
Enjoy the journey!

ISBN: 978-0-9862057-2-9

Publisher is Lanico Media House, an imprint of Lanico Enterprise.

Printed in the United States of America

This book is dedicated to my two boys, Chris and Brent, who challenge me every day in ways in which I didn't know I could be challenged …

… and to new beginnings.

ACKNOWLEDGMENTS

I don't know how many of these things I have edited. It's entirely humbling to actually be sitting here writing my own. It seems odd that a writer has a hard time putting her thoughts into words – after all that's what I do for a living. But to have something like this come together so quickly after a lifetime of effort to get to this point … words just don't seem adequate to explain what it means to have this book in my hand … and to know that it's in yours!

The problem with these things is you're always afraid you're going to leave someone out.

First, thank you to my family immediate, extended, adopted/online, and my church family at Southgate Community Church in Kemptville. Thank you all for all your support, encouragement, prayers, and especially hugs! The last 5 years in particular have been an extreme challenge and I wouldn't have made it without you.

Secondly, thank you Pat Thomas and Ken Breadner for your opinions and words of wisdom that really helped transform Inner Sanctum into its current form. I cannot overstate how important it is for writers to have good editors and knowledgeable friends at their disposal.

Thirdly, thank you so much to Lacresha Hayes and Jesse Kimmel-Freeman for being so willing to take this on, for your hard work behind the scenes. You have truly made my dreams come true!

Lastly, but most importantly, I give praise to our Heavenly Father and Almighty God for his faithfulness and love and ever-present guidance and support. You have truly carried me through many things and none of this would mean anything without You in it.

CHAPTER ONE

"So, what do you think?" Den Maron's eyebrows scrunched together as he arched his neck to examine the rock formation around him.

"It's the only spot left, Den." Aurora Cassle stepped up next to him, her neck craning in the same direction as his. "The ground is too soft and wet in the south. The quality of the rock in the west would make it too difficult to excavate. And City Council decided they didn't want any residence units built behind the industrial section in the east. So that leaves only one spot, this one."

Den sighed. "I know. I know." He walked away from her, farther into the center of the open space – virtually the only open, unoccupied space in the city. He stopped halfway between the back rock face and the entrance of the catacomb.

"I still can't believe this area is unoccupied and that no one appears to know why," Den continued as he waved a hand at the spot before glancing again at the city layout map in the other hand.

"Me neither." Aurora joined him and traced the outline of the arched ceiling on the map. "Perhaps it was just one of those things where people get used to it being there and don't question it, or perhaps it was the planners' way of accommodating more people when it became necessary." Aurora shrugged. "Still, after 400 annums you'd think someone would have suggested using it for expansion before now."

With a rustling of paper, Den switched from the layout map to the building plan City Council had approved for the site. It was done in anticipation of this location being deemed suitable, so that construction could begin right away.

"It's the same building plan as it was for the other sites we considered, Den. Besides, Egerton's completely underground and built into the rock, there's not much room for variation."

Den glared at her. "I know that, Aurora."

Uh oh. First name, not Rori, his nickname for her. He only resorted to her real name when he was annoyed with her like her mother used to when she misbehaved as a child.

Aurora raised her hands in apology and took a step back.

She turned on her heel as she looked up at the ceiling. Her gaze wandered from the common area in the center of the city to back beyond where they were standing.

"Do you suppose it'll be difficult to extend the lighting web back this far? Do we even have enough cabling and lights for that?" Aurora asked the construction foreman standing next to them hoping to deflect Den's temper. "I'm also curious how the generators will manage the increased power usage for them."

The lights were everything to Egerton. The people's waking and sleeping schedules depended on the lights coming on - light cycle - and the lights going off-night cycle - with twelve hours of each. It had been that way since the First Ones who'd decided to maintain the living cycles they were used to when they were sent down into Egerton.

"There'll be no problem with that," the foreman replied. "There's always enough power. Another web of lights won't hurt it at all. The city planners designed the plasma gasification systems well."

Aurora nodded.

"It'll be a challenge to get the geothermal and air particulate regulating systems back here, though."

Aurora shivered a bit and rubbed her arms as if to demonstrate the foreman's statement. In the other parts of the city with a working heating and cooling system, her denim like pants and woven fabric shirt, common garb for most of Egertonians, would have been sufficient, but here in this neglected section, she wished for something heavier.

Den turned to the foreman as he continued to explain, "We'll actually have to dig into the floor" – he tapped the stone ground with his foot and swept a hand from end to end – "and run joining ventilation and heating lines back here like the other catacombs."

A chill coursed down Aurora's spine as she nodded, then looked at Den. To her eternal frustration, Den turned away and started examining the construction schematic.

What was taking Den so long to make up his mind? He knew City Council expected construction to begin today. The mayor was adamant that the expansion couldn't be put off any longer. Plus, it was past mid-light cycle and she was expecting to have to deliver a few babies and certainly Den had other work he had to do. He also had to be as cold as she was.

"And you'd be able to start today?" Den asked the foreman.

The foreman nodded his head toward his crew that was standing by at the mouth of the catacomb. "As soon as you give the word, Mr. Maron."

"All right, let's do it."

Aurora nearly clapped in excitement.

"We'll get started right away." The foreman turned and headed toward his waiting men.

Aurora followed Den out of the chilly catacomb toward the warmer center, her body shivering again at the temperature change.

"For a moment there, I thought you were going to say no."

"How could I say no, Aurora? As you said, it was the only place left and the mayor wants this started immediately. I just had to be sure that what we planned to do with that space would work."

"So, what did you mean about 'maybe' the expansion might have been needed earlier than now?"

Den opened his mouth to respond, but two little boys, about four or five years of age, darted across the path in front of them chasing a ball. Aurora smiled as the boys scuttled on.

"Gosh, it's been a long time since my two were that young. Morgan and Mayley, Selleck's two children, are just about that age, and Caytor's second is not quite two yet."

Den smiled and nodded. "Yeah. It's been a long time for mine, too." Den's gaze looked uncertain when he turned to her. "Did you ever wish you could have more?"

She stared at him, her mouth agape. "You serious?" She asked once she'd found her voice. "Did you, the mayor's assistant, just ask me, the Family Control Officer, if I ever wanted to violate one of the main tenets of our society, of our survival?"

"Well, it's not like we have a choice." Den shrugged. "It's just something I've been thinking about the last little while, probably because of this" – he waved a hand in the direction they'd just come – "expansion project. All this thinking about families and our growing city.

"I know the First Ones established that families only have two children to avoid unmanageable overcrowding, which was necessary given our underground circumstances. But, Rori, we start having babies at sixteen and by the time we reach twenty-one, that's it." He swiped his hands out in front of him. "No more. Then the rest of our lives is spent on societal work and projects and raising our kids so they can have kids of their own when they're sixteen."

"The survival of our society depends on everyone living within these boundaries, Den. Even if we wanted to permit more than two pregnancies to replace children or adults who die unexpectedly, there's no way to reverse the sterilization procedure which is mandated for every woman once she reaches 21 annums." Aurora looked at him sideways as they started walking again. "This is the natural order of things for our society, Den. It has to be this way."

"It's natural for people to die before they reach fifty?" Den stopped walking again and touched her shoulder.

Aurora was taken aback by the forcefulness of Den's tone. They'd grown up together and knew each other almost as well as they knew their spouses. In all that time, Den had never spoken so vehemently, passionately about something. He was the mayor's assistant. He had reputation in the city of doing a lot of the mayor's official duties. He was normally somewhat soft-spoken, but had a calm, confident demeanor that people almost instantly trusted and respected.

She'd never heard him talk like this before and wondered if there was more behind it. Why did he feel so passionate about the subject? Even if he had reason to feel that way, there was no way he could have voiced it to the mayor or anyone else but her. Before she had a chance to ask anything else he continued.

"I mean, imagine, Rori. In fifteen years, we'll both be gone and likely fifteen years after that, our grandchildren will likely never even remember we existed. Have you also noticed all the empty residence units? Kinda odd, don't you think, that we're expanding at all when it's clear our numbers are getting smaller not bigger like the mayor claims?"

Aurora sighed. He was right about the empty dwellings. There were three of them just immediately around her and Merrick's unit, not to mention a curious number of singles who'd never married. Curious because from the very beginning it was assumed that everyone would marry someone. It was necessary to keep the population growing and stable. If what Den was inferring were true it would mean that these singles weren't necessarily single by choice, but because there weren't enough people.

"Think about it for a second, Aurora. It doesn't make sense for the mayor to be pushing ahead with this project."

Full name again. What was fuelling these ideas? They were so unlike him.

"What do you mean?"

He stopped walking again and looked around, then continued in a lower voice, "Rori, do you remember ever doing a census?"

"I ..."

"You're the Family Control Officer, right?"

"Right." *Where was he going with this?*

"So, have you, as the Family Control Officer, ever done a head count? You're supposed to be in charge of keeping the population numbers and making sure that people are following the two-child-only law for that reason."

"To your first question, no, I've never done a headcount, and to your second question, yes, that's my job."

The look in his eyes was so intense they'd darkened from their usual hazel to almost the color of the soil the gardeners used to grow the city's supply of super potatoes. His black hair and matching brows, which had been drawn together in his fervor, squarish features, and line-set mouth

6

only increased the effect. The power of his gaze went to a part of her soul that only one other person had reached. She found that she couldn't look him in the eye and broke her gaze away.

"Den, where is this all coming from?" She shook her head.

Den sighed. "All I'm saying, Rori, is that your job is so much more than what you're doing. The mayor was the one with the population projection numbers, not you, and as far as you know, it's always been that way."

Aurora nodded.

"You track the births and the deaths…"

Again, Aurora nodded.

"… and yet you've never done a census to confirm the population totals the mayor is telling us we have."

Aurora shook her head. "No. So far as what I was taught the mayor does all the 'official' numbers. It was passed down to me from the person who did it before, just like it is with the mayor's job and yours and everyone else's."

"And we've been instructed to build new dwelling units when we've got I don't know how many empty ones and the only reason we're doing it is because of what he's telling everyone."

Again, the passion in his eyes forced Aurora to look away. "Why are you telling me this, Den?" He was supposed to be upholding and defending the mayor, not subverting him. Although she could see the sense of his argument, she was growing more and more uncomfortable about what he seemed to be suggesting; that the mayor was doing something so wrong that was worth challenging him on – something Aurora couldn't remember having been done in her lifetime. All mayors were held in such high esteem by the population. But still, she couldn't discredit Den's implied conclusions, and she further wondered how any action taken would involve her.

She sensed more than saw him shake his head. "I'm sorry. Just everything about this seems wrong. We're not being told the truth. I've spent the last ten annums working as close to the mayor as a person can get and I still get the feeling that there are things I don't know, things he's not telling me."

"And that's a bad thing?"

"Ordinarily, no. I would agree with there being some things only the mayor knows. But perhaps it's just a gut thing that says this expansion project isn't all it seems to be."

"But City Council …"

"Yes, City Council backed the project, but would you expect any one of them not to if they're given the same information that we've been given?"

"I suppose not. But, if we've noticed the vacant residences, certainly some City Council members have as well, and yet they still decided to support the project."

"Exactly."

Aurora walked away from Den then turned and walked back as her mind worked through what he was talking about.

"It's a lot to process, Den. Four hundred annums of tradition …"

"That's another thing about this. I don't think it started out that way."

"What started out what way?"

Den had worked himself into such a state that she watched him visibly school his emotions back under control as if he had reminded himself that they were still out in public.

"The survival of the city requires strict family control policies, genetic screening procedures at first signs of pregnancy, during annual physical examinations, and at death."

"Yes." Den's lowered eyelids and tipped-down eyebrows told her how upset he was that he had to explain to her something he thought she clearly ought to know.

"So why is it that just as strict and meticulous census taking isn't done to confirm our city's population is safely being maintained or growing as the mayor claims? I think in the beginning it was because it was just as important as all those other processes."

"What do you think changed?"

Den shook his head. "I don't know. It's really just a hunch."

"*Just* a hunch. That's more than a hunch, Den. That's almost an accusation."

Den nodded. "I guess it is."

"What do you plan to do about it?"

"I don't know. Even if I were to confront the mayor or approach a few City Council members, I really have nothing to back up what every fiber of my being is telling me."

"But if you suspect the population is actually declining … ."

"Just drop it, Aurora. I'm sorry I brought it up."

Aurora suddenly wanted to be back in her office. *What was with him?!* "Gosh. You're in a positive frame of mind, today."

"Sorry." Den looked at the ground seemingly ashamed of his uncharacteristic outburst.

"But, I have to agree with you that it doesn't seem like we get to enjoy our families for long, does it?" Aurora hoped changing the subject slightly would settle Den down. "I wonder if the First Ones lived longer?"

They started walking again, closing in on Center Hall.

"I don't know if they lived longer, but I do know they were taller."

"How do you know that?"

"Well, the individual residential units on the expansion plans are 1.42 meters high, nearly a half-meter shorter than the originals we're all living in."

Aurora didn't know what to say to that. She just kept track of births and deaths. The End of Life – EOL - scans she completed upon peoples' deaths before their bodies were released and recycled to produce energy for the city included a height measurement. In all the EOLs she'd done during her term, she didn't recall seeing anything startling. Although, if Egertonians had actually grown shorter since the time of the First Ones, it would likely be more evident in the scan results her predecessors had conducted over the 400 annums they'd been underground. But, at this point, it would be just curiosity that prompted such an examination of records and it would take more than curiosity for Aurora to commit to rooting through so many records.

"What do you think has changed?" Den flipped her own question back at her, interrupting her musings.

Aurora shrugged, her mind briefly drifting to consider Den's question about age, and then to memories of her father's death two years before. No one really wanted to say good-bye to a loved one. People dying at or around fifty annums had just become normal for them. It was accepted as a fact of life that they couldn't do anything about. But she didn't think anyone could deny that it would be nice to have more time with their parents and grandparents.

"I don't know. I don't recall anything really strange coming out in any of my EOLs, but then I wasn't really looking for anything. Perhaps it's because the human race didn't start out living underground like this." She waved her hands at the ceiling. "Perhaps shorter lifespans and shorter statures are a consequence of living underground for 400 annums."

"Perhaps."

They'd reached Center Hall by this time, a two-story dome-like structure in the center of the city. City Council chambers were on the top floor reached by a spiral staircase located at the back of the main floor. Aurora's office was on the main floor, to the left as she entered the hall. Den's was attached to the mayor's office, which was behind City Council Chambers.

"Well, I guess I'll see you later." Aurora waved and Den waved back with a "See ya" as they parted.

She wasn't at her desk long when her pager alerted her to ready mom-to-be. So, she grabbed her medikit from beside her desk, inspected it for the requisite delivery and sterilization materials, and dashed out the door.

CHAPTER TWO

As she scurried the five minutes to the southeast catacomb residence, Aurora entertained Den's earlier comments. It was a testament to their long-standing friendship that he felt comfortable telling her those things despite their respective city executive roles. The fact that the mayor's assistant was expressing a point of view contrary to the very laws that he was sworn to uphold and act upon further made her wonder again about exactly what was behind his comments.

Even though they both worked for the city, she and Den really didn't have much contact with each other, not like they did when they were younger. In the last ten annums, after they'd both assumed their current positions, they'd actually spent relatively little time together, and she realized she didn't know that much about Den's family. This expansion project had brought them together for the last few months as he liaised between her and the mayor and they'd worked great together. It felt like their friendship had picked up right where they'd left off when they'd each married their different spouses.

Many of their friends had thought that she and Den would actually marry each other, and although she had considered dating him, Merrick was the one who had swept her off her feet about the same time as Melle had done to Den and that marked the end of any potential romance between them. But their friendship connection still simmered in the background, and Aurora knew that, despite to whom each of them was married and regardless of which turn their individual lives took, that friendship would always be there.

But in all the time they'd worked together on this project, she realized that he hadn't really told her much about himself or his family, or even talked about his kids that often. In fact, the only time he'd come close to saying anything about his personal life was just this after mid-light cycle as he stood staring at the ceiling in the north catacomb.

As she replayed that exchange in her head, she became more certain than ever that Den's passionate and uncharacteristic outburst had been the result of something that happened during his marriage. It was really none of her business, but something about it just seemed weird to her. Perhaps it was her previous feelings of friendship that fuelled her concern about him. Perhaps it was that which prompted Den to express the thoughts he did even if he couldn't say outright what had happened.

And what of his comments about the mayor not telling everyone the truth? She had to admit that it didn't seem logical for the mayor to push ahead with a building project instead of making use of the empty dwelling units. If their population were truly growing, there should be no empty units. *Why would the mayor do that? And what had caused those units to be empty?*

She had told Den the truth that all the EOL scans she'd done were relatively ordinary. Nothing alarming had come out of them and all the people had died of natural causes – well, natural for them anyway.

But, as she arrived in the doorway of the residential unit, she shoved further related thoughts aside. There was nothing she could do about it now, anyway, and she had a job to do.

From a secret doorway directly beneath the mayor's office, Barna peered into the center of town and noticed Aurora Cassle hurrying in her direction.

Barna waited until the other woman had turned the corner before she pulled the hood over her head and stepped out, heading in the opposite direction. The Family Control Officer wasn't the only one with a job to do. Moments before, the mayor had paged her with a message that the Thompkins baby had tested positive for a genetic defect, and that she was to go and terminate the pregnancy. If the baby had tested negative, the family's file would have been passed on to the Family Control Officer for follow up and delivery. Barna had to admit that her schedule in the last ten years had grown considerably busier, but only she, the mayor, and the Chief Medical Officer knew it. It wasn't that no one knew what she was doing. It was hard to keep anything a secret in a closed community, but after 200 years, pregnancy termination had just become routine and no one really knew how many Barna had been doing, although she had to admit she'd actually lost count. The mayor was the only one who knew the precise total and how these pregnancy losses were affecting the overall civilization.

Aurora looked after every baby being born in Egerton and that's how it had been for the Family Control Officers before her, too. Barna and her predecessors looked after the babies that couldn't be born because their bodies carried something that could pose a threat to the survival of the city.

Truth be told, she hated her job. As much as she understood the necessity of keeping the blood lines in Egerton free of genetic defect for the sake of the survival of their society, it did come at the price of a life – hundreds of lives, actually. Couples who'd had this procedure could always try again, though, even if it was a second pregnancy just as long as it was started before the mother's twenty-first birthday.

Barna could remember one of those word-of-mouth stories that became legend and eventually disappeared telling what happened when, at one time, the idea of allowing more births beyond annum 21 if a couple was unable to conceive by then had been proposed. The mayor and city council at the time had upheld the law even though the amount of terminations even then was increasing. The mayor's refusal 200 years earlier to allow additional births to sustain population numbers meant that, even though Egerton's gene pool was free from physiological issues that could compromise the health of the people, the civilization would eventually die off with not enough births to offset the number of people dying.

Those who paid even passive attention to such happenings within the city – again, it was a small community with plenty of nosy neighbors – probably noticed more and more couples with only one child, and more and more vacant dwelling units and drew their own conclusions about the state of Egerton's population numbers. But only a select few knew how grave the situation was.

What was starting to happen more and more often, Barna realized was that couples who tried again and managed to get pregnant a third time before the mandatory sterilization age often had to have the procedure carried out again anyway. It had happened too many times now for her to just dismiss it. It was almost becoming the norm, which meant that their population was becoming less and less sustainable and she wondered how long it would be before all babies started testing positive for some form of genetic defect.

Like every couple, at the first signs of pregnancy at about between four and eight weeks, Janie Thompkins had presented to the Chief Medical Officer's office to report the suspected pregnancy and have it confirmed. A full genetic screening had been carried out by sixteen to eighteen weeks with the results reported to the mayor by about twenty weeks. Pretty standard, actually. The genetic screening was performed at a time when all the baby's systems had developed sufficiently to determine whether things would continue to progress normally. If yes, the pregnancy became the FCO's responsibility and the couple could celebrate. If no, Barna would get the call to go out and terminate the pregnancy.

Barna announced herself as she stepped into the residence unit.

"Hello." A man looked out from the kitchenette.

"Mr. Thompkins" – it was always strange calling a seventeen-year-old 'mister' – "the mayor sent me. We've received the results of the screening."

She never introduced herself by name.

"Oh, yes! Come right on in." He left the kitchenette and led Barna into the sleeping room. "Janie is just in here resting."

Barna looked down upon the sleeping mother as Mr. Thompkins touched his wife's shoulder and gently called her name. It took her a second to realize Barna was there, and then she came fully alert.

Barna nodded. "Hello, Janie. I'm from the mayor's office."

Janie sat up straighter. "You have the results."

"Yes." Something inside Barna wanted to lie and tell Janie that her baby was fine and would be healthy and live a long fifty-year life. Instead, Barna said, "Your baby has tested positive for a bone deficiency. I'm afraid we have to terminate."

Janie dissolved into tears.

"I'll be out in the living area while you prepare yourself." As Barna waited, she tried to ignore the conversation happening in the sleeping room, to afford the young couple a little bit of privacy. This was their first baby. Late for a first baby by Egerton standards with both mom and dad, in this case, nearing their eighteenth year. Most couples had had at least one baby by now and were trying for the second.

Mr. Thompkins stepped out of the sleeping room. "We're ready."

With her job at the Thompkins' done, Barna stepped back out onto the walkway that would lead her back to Center Hall. Five minutes later she'd passed Center Hall and the plant growers' tents at the entrance of the east catacomb on her way to the medical bay.

"Good afternoon, Dolan."

Dolan Markus, Egerton's Chief Medical Officer glanced up from the patient he was tending to. He checked the instruments by the patient's bed and said something to the family members gathered around before approaching her, Notepad in one hand.

"Good afternoon, Barna."

Dolan always had a quirky smile on his face or some other facial expression that made her laugh. She assumed it was his way of dealing with the seriousness of his duties. He took her elbow and walked with her to the cremation room.

"I've been seeing an awful lot of you lately," he quipped.

"Is that so awful?"

His smiled widened. "No, not at all. Although it would be better if I knew you came just to see me."

Dolan was one of the growing number of people in Egerton who was single, and he had a reputation for being a flirt, but everyone accepted his flirting as harmless and part of his way of lightening the mood.

"Sorry." She waved her medikit in front of him. "I've just come from the Thompkins' dwelling."

Dolan nodded knowingly. "Any problems?"

Barna shook her head. "No, everything went well. They're almost eighteen though and no baby yet. And you have to know they're not the only ones."

They'd reached the cremation chamber.

Dolan nodded again. "No, they're not."

"And those people in there?" Barna jerked her head in the direction they'd come.

"Nothing I can do. We aren't equipped to treat such things. The First Ones assumed everything that would medically threaten our society was eliminated through their genetic screening process. I'm assuming they had a cure on Upper World Earth or at least the technology and know-how to treat the condition. It's a slow, agonizing death if we don't euthanize. We can manage to contain any infection. The city's air filtration and purification system takes care of that, but there's nothing I can do to give them their health and life back. But they will give life back to the city when they're cremated."

"I expect that's a small consolation for their families."

Dolan shrugged. "It's either that or watch their loved one deteriorate in front of their eyes."

"Such a sad business we're in, aren't we?"

Dolan's broad smile returned. "That's why I'm so glad you came to see me."

Barna rolled her eyes. "You're hopeless."

Dolan opened a hatch in a metal tube connected to the crematorium.

Barna placed her biodegradable medipac pouch inside and Dolan closed the lid. He tapped the screen of the Notepad and Barna knew the tapping that followed was Dolan entering the name and date details of this cremation. When he was done, he pressed a green button below the hatch and the machine carried the bundle into the plasma gasification unit. They headed back out to the main medical bay.

"So, when will I see you again?" Dolan asked as they reached the entrance.

Barna almost laughed, and shook her head. "You never give up, do you?"

Dolan chuckled. "Nope."

"Well, I can't say when I'll be by next. Hope it's not too soon."

Dolan raised a hand to his heart and jerked backwards. "Oh! You sure know how to break this guy's heart."

Barna waved and with a "Bye" walked toward Center Hall.

CHAPTER THREE

Den sat at his desk, head tilted against the back of the chair so he could stare at the stone ceiling above him, replaying his conversation with Aurora. He hadn't meant to say as much as he did. He couldn't even say for sure what prompted it all to come tumbling out.

He'd held these feelings inside for longer than he cared to remember, since early on in his tenure with the mayor when he came to the full realization of the mayor's incapacity and just how much of the day-to-day workings of Egerton would fall on him. The only thing the mayor remained adamant about keeping control of himself was the population numbers.

At the beginning, Den had just accepted the responsibilities and Mayor Goodwin's quirkiness, but as time wore on and day after day as he listened to the mayor muttering nonsensically in his office next door, Den begun to understand just how misguided the population was to put their trust in this man. Surprisingly, his boss managed to pull himself together to chair council meetings, which was about the only thing Den couldn't do since he wasn't an official councilmember.

Each mayor was selected by City Council from one of the sitting members, and would hold the position until his death. Traditionally, and from the very beginning of a young one's schooling, they were taught to revere and respect the mayor, and many young girls and boys aspired to be a member of City Council with the hope that one day they would be chosen. While it was true that everyone was eligible to become a councilmember and thus a potential mayoral candidate, the council was mostly made up of members from the same families and the mayoral title rotated amongst those families – so many children's hopes and dreams were dashed. Still, he, or she, was the figurehead of their community and their decisions rarely questioned.

Den couldn't recall the last time someone spoke out against the mayor, or recall a story being told of someone who had. And, Aurora was right. He was accusing the mayor though he wasn't in a position, yet, to outright challenge the mayor and his decisions. He'd secretly hoped that he could convince Aurora that the irrational decision to pursue the expansion project was very obvious evidence that the mayor's mind was not where it should be. He had no idea whether Aurora would pursue any action against the mayor, but she certainly couldn't do it simply based on his feelings.

The expansion project and the mayor's fervor about it, had been the last straw, and he longed to tell someone. He'd had so many opportunities in the last few weeks to tell Aurora his thoughts and feelings about it, but the time just never seemed the right. She continued to blindly investigate potential expansion sites obviously never considering the empty units. Obviously, she was part of the traditional mindset that one didn't question the mayor even when evidence is staring one in the face that something's not right.

Like the many couples who only had one child and the growing number of couples who had none. As the Family Control Officer, Aurora should have been well aware of those numbers and yet hadn't appeared to really consider the societal implications of this until he mentioned it. Though, he supposed he couldn't really blame her. Their schooling system was focused on training the next generation to take over the various positions and responsibilities needed to run the city. They were taught about the laws and city workings established by the First Ones and, as children grew and started showing special skills or interest in a particular role, training continued in that specialty until they were ready for children themselves. Neither the men nor the women would start working the positions and roles they'd trained for until their children were of age to start school. They were taught never to question and that the city and the various people in it needed everyone to do their part for the betterment of everyone else.

All of their history – and the vast majority of all their teaching – was oral. There were no lessons per se except for that which was passed down over the years through the various teachers. The children would be taught and trained to a certain point. Then adults would learn the intricacies of their roles and responsibilities from the person for whom they would take over the position – tricks of the trade, as it were, that only people in those roles would know.

Curiously, none of their lessons included why the First Ones had come underground. They were told that there had been an Upper World Earth or UWE, and how the First Ones had been chosen after rigorous genetic testing those stories having survived generations of retelling, but that was it. Nothing about how Egerton got its name. And even more curious, to him anyway, was why no one seemed to care or want to know why. He was never able to find out from teachers or his parents how Egerton came to be or why the north catacomb had been vacant all these annums. He wasn't sure if it was because the story had been lost over time and they truly didn't know, or if they were deliberately keeping the explanation from him in their impatient, "Not right now, Den."

As for his dilemma with Mayor Goodwin, Den knew the respect that was supposed to be reserved for the mayor by the people had fallen on his shoulders since he was the one the public saw. But that didn't mean the people didn't respect the mayor's position in the city, either. If he had raised any of his questions to anyone other than Aurora, he would have lost his position, and what would happen to the mayor then? What would happen to the city then? A new mayor's assistant would have been assigned from the pool waiting behind him and then they'd be right back at square one with empty residential units, a dwindling population, and a mayor's idea that everything was fine and Egerton was flourishing.

Everything within him knew that the people needed to be made aware of the extent of the situation, but that was going to be tough given how many of them were raised with the same schooling that you don't question anything, you just continue doing what citizens have always done because that's what will keep everyone alive. Certainly, he couldn't have been the only one to notice these changes. If it was obvious to him, it would have obvious to others. Though, like Aurora, they might have just dismissed it as part of how life goes in Egerton.

He probably would have been one of those dismissive types, too, if it hadn't been for Melle losing two babies. If he'd had any doubt about what was happening to the people, he couldn't ignore the reality of what it meant for him and Melle. What was surprising was how many others around him experienced the same thing. That's what had fuelled his thoughts and brought everything to a head with Aurora this morning.

He and Melle had desperately wanted more children, but they hadn't been able to conceive again before Melle turned 21. Their marriage never really recovered from that. As soon as Peggie was old enough to be on her own, Melle moved out and until then they'd tried to keep up appearances, but he could never give Melle what she really wanted even in his position with the mayor – and that was another baby. His helplessness and her depression that seemed to worsen with every passing year until she moved out also prodded him into thinking against the traditional teachings. Other couples accepted the reality and went on with their lives, though he wondered how many of the secretly carried regrets and wishes for the children they would never be able to have.

When he'd first started working for the mayor, Den thought he would eventually be able to convince him to change the Family Control Law and increase the sterilization age. He couldn't precisely say why, but he thought families just needed more time than they used to. Their bodies had slowed reproductively and couples were unable to provide children within the same short timeframe as past generations, and that reality could be mitigated by a simple change in the rules.

But the longer he stayed with the mayor, the more he realized the man's incapacity to deal with the realities of his city. The mayor would never outwardly display any signs of inability that Den saw on a daily basis. Den often heard him blurt out statements that made absolutely no sense.

The mayor had never prepared himself for council meetings, that had always fallen to Den and, having observed his boss in chambers, it was obvious – to Den, anyway – that without his preparatory work, Mayor Goodwin would have just sat quaking and yattering in his seat. Not that there was much business for the council to consider since their laws had been established from the beginning and there was no current or recent history memory of anyone who'd attempted to challenge or disobey those laws. The only reason for the council meetings was to review the various systems and jobs that made the city work to ensure that everything was working as it should and to address any problems that had come up since the last meeting. No new resolutions or laws were required.

In any event, Den's hopes for trying to convince the mayor to change the law evaporated with each passing day until he, too, was caught in the trap of say nothing, do nothing.

That is until Aurora re-entered his life. She had grown even more beautiful since their school years. Her body had handled her two pregnancies well, while not hiding the fact of them. Her hair had deepened from the light brown of the rocks around them to the color of the mud beneath Egerton's underground water source, which she still kept pulled back in a knot high at the back. He couldn't tell how long it was, but it was the strand or two she kept alongside her face, along the cheek he longed to trace with a finger, that showed it was much longer than when he'd seen her last.

Truth be told, he'd been about to propose to her when Merrick stepped into the picture seemingly out of nowhere. About the same time, when it was clear he'd missed his chance, Melle appeared. She was smaller in stature than Aurora, who was still tall by Egerton standards, and had dark brown eyes that didn't quite catch the sheen of the overhead lights like Aurora's blue ones, but Den found himself falling for her in a way he never had with Aurora and which made it easy for him to let go of her. He hadn't thought of Aurora again until they bumped into each other a few days after they'd started their positions. He was still married then and he'd never had a chance to really talk to Aurora until the past few weeks because of his responsibilities with the mayor.

Unfortunately, even though he was single, she was still married and, from what he'd observed that morning during their walk across town, quite happily so. Den smiled at the vision of her walking with him and how he'd so much wanted to hold her hand, but he would never come in between her and Merrick.

Still, it hadn't taken long for their friendship to basically start off where it had ended once they did start working together. His comfort in her presence had provided the opening he needed to let some of his long-held thoughts out and he was fairly certain that he'd piqued her curiosity enough that she might pursue it. He really didn't know why he felt he needed her to believe him and why she might be the only way to get things to change. Perhaps it was because, as Mayor Goodwin's assistant, he had to think and speak as the mayor would. There was no room in his role and in his relationship with Mayor Goodwin to express his own ideas or opinions. Aurora, on the other hand, was free to voice his concerns so long as he could make her see and understand and want to react to the reality around her.

He heard a rustle at the door and the unmistakable sound of the mayor's grunting way of breathing. As his eyes snapped open, the vision of Aurora morphed into the mayor slanted against the wall. It always amazed

Den how the man actually arrived anywhere without hurting himself and couldn't imagine the physical effort it took to appear normal when he walked, however briefly, in public. In the security of the office, however, no such pretenses were required, and Den bore the full brunt of the mayor's condition. Mayor Goodwin's head bobbled uncontrollably.

"Goo', ur ba."

Den's mind translated the mayor's garble into, *Good, you're back.*

"Yes, not too long ago, sir." Den rose and tried to usher the mayor into a vacant chair in front of his desk, but the man balked and Den backed off. "Sorry, sir. Just wanted you to be comfortable."

"An you. 'ot necry."

Thank you. Not necessary.

"'ave you cho' a si'?"

Have you chosen a site?

"Yes, we have, Your Honor, and construction has already begun."

"'er goo'. 'er goo'."

Very good. Very good.

"'ere?"

"The north catacomb, sir. That big open space."

Mayor Goodwin's eyes widened and his jangling head stilled as he raised it to look Den in the eye.

Den wasn't sure what he saw in the mayor's eyes. He didn't know how to describe it. Surprise. Shock. Anger. Rage. Hatred. All Den was sure of in that split second was he was done doing the mayor's work as soon as could be arranged – and that meant helping Aurora with whatever she

26

needed.

CHAPTER FOUR

Aurora bundled the newborn, all clean and measured and weighed, and laid her against the mother's chest, where she immediately began to suckle. Leaving mother and father and baby to bond, Aurora excused herself, and left the dwelling. She hadn't taken two steps when her radio pager buzzed on her hip. She unclipped it from the holster and held it next to her cheek.

"Cassle, here."

"Rori, it's Den."

Had something already gone wrong at the dig site?

"What's up? I thought you were at the office."

"I am. I need to talk to you. When are you coming back to your office?"

Was he still upset about their conversation? Perhaps he'd gathered the courage to talk to the mayor. Given Den's position, the mayor would likely be more inclined to listen to him, wouldn't he?

"All right. I'm heading back toward center. I'll be about five minutes. I'll meet you in your office?"

"No, actually I'll come to you. Page me when you're in."

"Okay. Will do." The radio was only silent a few moments when it buzzed again. A different number: Dolan Markus. "Cassle, here."

"Cass? Markus, here." His voice always sounded cheery, but Aurora knew it was an attempt to make his reason for calling a little more pleasant. They'd known each other as long as she and Den had and Dolan had used the shortened form of her last name for about the same length of time. Most everyone combined his first and last names into Dom.

"Hey, Dom."

"You don't sound happy to hear from me."

"Sorry." Aurora forced herself to smile and hoped it came through in her attempt at a sing-songy voice. "Hey, Dom, how are you? Is that better?"

"Much! I'm doing great, thank you. Mrs. Terrence, on the other hand, is not."

Aurora's heart fell though she'd known it was coming. Mrs. Terrence was the same age as Aurora's mother who had died just before her father a couple of years before. Since each generation was all around the same age, it wasn't uncommon for a bunch of deaths to happen relatively close together. Most deaths were of natural causes. It used to be rare that people in Egerton died of anything other than natural causes, but the scuttlebutt around town had been relaying stories of a growing number of people who had died of unnatural causes. No one knew precisely how many.

That thought brought her back to Den's rather disturbing comments from that morning. Clearly someone somewhere – specifically the mayor – knew that something was happening to their civilization, and yet his advocation and approval of the construction of the new dwelling units presented the idea that everything was fine. If the mayor knew the full impact of the population change, why wasn't he doing more? Were there even any alternatives? Perhaps if they knew why more and more people were developing the illnesses that threatened their civilization, they could do more to prevent the illness, treat it or even cure it.

"You still there, Cass?"

At Dom's voice, Aurora noticed she'd stopped walking and was standing in the middle of the road, but people seemed not to mind as they passed by.

"Yeah, I'm still, here. Are there any others?"

"Not at least for the next few days."

"Okay. I'll be right there." Once Dolan signed off, Aurora switched to Den's channel.

"Den, here."

"Den, I'm going to be a while getting there. Dom needs me to do a final."

"All right. How long do you think you'll be?"

"At least an hour. Dom says there shouldn't be any more today so I'll be free after that."

"Not a problem. See you then."

Aurora sighed, clicked off the radio pager, and clipped it back onto her hip. Without looking around her, Aurora continued up the walkway toward Center Hall. Instead of going in, she headed east into the industrial catacomb from which the city's basic functions were run: laundry, barbers, messengers, food cultivation, and medical. Dolan Markus' office was the first unit on the right.

Dolan was hunched over his desk tapping some notes into a Notepad no doubt making preliminary notes about Mrs. Terrence. Aurora pulled on the string hanging just above her head in the doorway and a little bell sounded. Dolan's head jerked up from his work.

"Hey, Cass. That was quick."

"Yeah, I was already out. The Marshall baby."

"Ah. Well, at least you had some good news, today." He rose from his chair, pad in hand. "I'm sure I don't need to tell you Mrs. Terrence is this way." Dom led her down the hall to the room at the very end, his white medical coat billowing out behind him.

"You've already done the brain scan?"

"Standard policy just after death before the electrical signals have the chance to degrade and disperse." He tapped at the Notepad in his hand. "Sending the results to yours … now." He hit the last button.

Aurora's pad vibrated, indicating message received.

The place had a slight antiseptic smell to it. Dom had likely grown used to it. By all rights she'd been here enough times that she shouldn't even notice it anymore, but every time she visited, her nose crinkled at the odor.

"Still haven't gotten used to my cologne, eh?" Dom joked as she sniffed.

She returned his smile with a turn of her head. "Nope, sorry."

Aurora waited in the doorway as Dom walked over to the bed with Mrs. Terrence on it and rolled the sheet down. She then stepped up beside the dead woman's head.

Aurora leaned back against the wall.

"What's the matter, Cass? This one personal?"

"Mrs. Terrence was a good friend of my mother's. I hadn't seen her much since Mom passed on. She looks just like I remember. No matter how many of these things I do, I don't think I'll ever get used seeing bodies without air in them. How can you joke so much when you see so much death?"

For the first time since she knew him, Aurora saw sadness in Dom's eyes.

"That's precisely why I need my sense of humor. I usually only get to see people when they're hurt because of some kind of accident, sick, or when they've died – pretty negative circumstances. And some of them are my neighbors and family members too. I have to have a sense of humor to survive my job."

"You never married, did you? Was that because of your job, I mean, the amount of time you need to be here?"

Dom shrugged. "Probably most of the reason. Just never found the right one, I guess." He looked at her for a moment, then back at Mrs. Terrance. "Guess it takes a special woman to appreciate the stories of the dead and ailing to whom I seem to be so attached."

"Are there so many of them?"

"I wouldn't say a lot of them, but there's never a shortage of work. With so many people being born around the same time and a fifty-year life span meaning a bunch of people dying around the same time, there's a pretty steady stream of customers."

Aurora shook her head at Dom's last statement. He just couldn't help it. Even when talking serious, Dom's sense of humour poked through.

Dom took a deep breath and straightened his shoulders. "Speaking of customers, time to put Mrs. Terrence to rest."

Aurora consciously shoved the sadness from her mind and slipped into her FCO final examination mode. "Right."

"I'm sure you have other more lively and happenin' places you'd like to be."

Aurora inwardly groaned at Dom's joke, his effort to talk up the pleasures of his job.

Dom grinned knowingly at her quirky smile. "Good to know I haven't lost my touch at making you smile."

Aurora sighed. "Nope, you haven't. And as for more lively and happenin', there's nothing more happenin' than the expansion site." Aurora leaned over Mrs. Terrence's face as Dom tapped on his pad and prepared to jot down her observations of her visual examination.

"You've chosen one?"

"Yeah, the north catacomb. Did you know that space has always been empty?"

"Kinda forgotten about it. I don't get out that way much."

Aurora dictated her observations starting from the crown of the head and systematically worked her way down. There was nothing extraordinary until they reached her abdomen and two inches below the belly button was a scar about three inches long. It was so faint and in such a spot physiologically that it was hardly noticeable.

"What do you make of this, Dom?" Aurora pulled the stomach taut with her gloved hand so that the scar was easier to see.

Dom leaned over the body, then looked up at her. "A caesarean section scar? I read about them, of course, as I prepared to take over as CMO, but I've never actually seen one."

"Neither have I on an EOL, anyway," Aurora said.

"How many children did she have?"

"Two."

"And both were born normally?"

"Yes, as far as I know. It was before my time. I would have been ten years old when she was sterilized."

"Are you sure she only had two?"

Aurora glared at him.

"Don't look at me like that."

"Of course, I'm sure she only had two." Aurora doused her temper. "At least I was sure until I saw *that*. And the FCO at that time would have died a while ago. If she only had two children and they were both born vaginally why does she have a caesarean scar? Unless she had a termination in between or before the first one."

"Yeah, it's possible. Terminations would have been done by caesarean at her time. Now we use a kind of laser curettage procedure. It's cleaner and less invasive for the patient. In fact, I just saw Barna, this morning."

Aurora nodded. "I wonder what was wrong with the baby?"

"What?"

"Mrs. Terrence's baby."

"Oh." Dom tapped on his Notepad. "Let's see what I can find out. Genetic profile scan showed chronic calcium deficiency in bones resulting in soft bones, particularly in legs and rib cage. Something we just can't treat."

"What do you mean? Why not?"

"Cass, this kind of deficiency can only be caused by one thing and that is vitamin D deficiency."

Aurora's eyebrows crinkled. "Somehow, I'm thinking I'm supposed to know what that means."

Dom leaned back against the wall.

"You know that everyone is required to come in every year for a physical, right?

"Yes."

"And part of that examination includes a full genetic work up including blood tests to make sure nothing is developing, and to ensure that if anything is developing that we catch it at its earliest stages."

"Right. And …"

"Well, from the very beginning of Egerton, each person at their annual physical would receive an injection of vitamin D as a supplement."

"Why?"

"I was always told it had something to do with the environment. The city's laser lighting system was designed to provide a certain amount of ultraviolet B rays, which our skin actually processes into vitamin D, which the body uses to absorb the calcium and phosphorus in our diets which our muscles and bones need to stay healthy."

"Okay."

"Do you ever remember having one of these injections?"

Aurora was a bit surprised by his question. "No. But you say they were given to everyone at one point?"

"Yes, they were. The story that was passed down to me was that a couple hundred annums ago, supplies of the supplement were starting to run out, so it was decided to stop the annual injections and use what supplement supply we had left to maintain levels in those who started to show signs of vitamin D deficiency, but that supply ran out about a hundred annums later."

"So no one is getting them now."

"No. Not for a long time."

"So, whether this was a first pregnancy termination, or done in between babies one and two, why did the screening results come back with a defect on this one and not the two that were born?"

Dom shrugged. "No one really knows why. All I know is it's not just unborn babies. Half my ward, in there" – Dom waved a hand in the direction they'd come – "are people who can hardly walk, and are achy and fatigued. Some are in such pain, but I really can't help them. Our pain medicines have to be rationed very carefully, as well, and what I'm giving them isn't nearly enough."

"But if our lights were designed to help our bodies produce this vitamin, why are there still deficiencies?"

"Well, the body only processes the UVB rays when they actually touch the skin. It won't work through clothes."

Aurora looked down at her own arms, which were fully covered by her knit shirt – the same kind of knit shirt that everyone wore.

"What about the face?"

"Yes, it works if the rays hit the face, but not enough. And even with our climate control and air filters, I don't think any of us would be comfortable going topless."

Aurora groaned at his quirky smile. "No, I don't think any of us would be comfortable doing that. But a warmer climate might mean that we could at least wear something with shorter sleeves." Aurora looked at the ceiling. "I wonder what provided those rays before the First Ones?"

"That I don't know. I'm sure someone at one time knew. Probably whatever light source they had."

Aurora looked back down at Mrs. Terrence. "I wonder how many other babies have tested positive for this."

She slipped her cellular scanner from her pocket to collect details about the internal systems of a person's body.

"You mentioned Barna was in earlier."

"Yes."

"With a terminated pregnancy?"

"Yes."

"Did that one test positive for the same thing?"

"Yes."

"If you had the medical resources to treat the bone conditions, would the pregnancies have been terminated?"

She sensed rather than saw Dom glaring at her as she lined up the scanner just in front of Mrs. Terrence's scalp.

"It doesn't seem like these kinds of conditions would be life threatening or dangerous for the rest of the population."

"Not the skeletal condition, no, but children with this condition are more susceptible to respiratory infections, which even with our air filtration systems we can't afford into our society. It's not only treatment that's required, but prevention, but some of these cases are so severe it's unclear if even supplementation, if it were available, would be effective."

She and Den had already talked about the curiosity over everyone's height being less than the First Ones'. Changes in skeletal structure resulting in physically shorter denizens was hardly life threatening, but what if there were other changes that could pose a threat if passed on to the next generation.

It was reasonable to assume that these physiological changes would not have appeared all of a sudden, but gradually over a period of time since the time they stopped the annual vitamin D injections.

Dom agreed with her when she voiced her thoughts. "From a medical perspective, it sometimes takes a while for these things to develop so that they actually appear on a scan."

"Like how long?"

"Annums. Generations. You understand genetics as well as I do. You know how family traits get passed from one generation to the next. That could happen with these kinds of things as well."

"Like height and bone structure?"

"Yes."

When Dom shot her a questioning look, she explained Den's observations about the height of the new residential units versus the originals.

"Yes, precisely," Dom affirmed when she was done.

"And what could those changes mean?"

Dom sighed. "Well, being shorter might not be life-threatening. But that doesn't mean that other genetic changes won't be such as heart or brain or defects to other parts of the body."

"But why would these changes happen at all? The First Ones were all genetically screened to keep out such things, weren't they?"

"Yes, they were and I don't know, Aurora."

Uh-oh, first name. And Dom's voice had lost its usual joviality. She waited for him to continue, since there seemed to be more to the story, but he didn't. *First Den. Now Dom. What was going on with people today?* It was becoming clear that there were secrets that she wasn't sure she wanted to learn, but her gut told her she would eventually anyway. She couldn't quite put her finger on why, but the same gut instinct told her that all this – the expansion project, Den's curious comments, and Dom's medical findings were connected.

In the meantime, she had a job to do.

She pushed her suspicions aside and pressed the "Go" button on the scanner. A green light spread across Mrs. Terrence's head. As Aurora moved the scanner steadily down the body, the beam widened to include the width of the shoulders and torso, and narrowed again as it passed the hips. Once the scan of the feet was done, Aurora clicked the scanner off.

Dom rolled the sheet back up to cover the body and slid it back into the freezer.

"It'll take several hours for the results of the scan to be complete. You want me to let you know what I find?"

"Absolutely."

"I will do that." Aurora slipped the scanner back into her pocket and met Dom's gaze. With a final glance at Mrs. Terrence's covered body, Aurora said, "If the family has already said their good-byes, you have my clearance for the cremation as soon as can be arranged."

Without saying anything further, Aurora left the medical bay, her mind abuzz with questions about what she'd just learned.

CHAPTER FIVE

As Aurora walked back toward center, she glanced up at the main clock and decided she would get the analysis started on Mrs. Terrance before letting Den know she was back.

Once she reached her office, she retrieved the genetic processing unit from her cabinet.

When the GPU was done processing all the information collected from Mrs. Terrance, the results would appear on its digital readout screen, which would then be recorded in the "Deceased Ledger," along with all the other measurements and observations. The CMO would receive the results as well and pass them on to the mayor.

Aurora plugged the hand-held scanner into the GPU and waited for the "Processing" confirmation message to appear before placing the computer back in her cabinet and locking the door.

That taken care of, Aurora paged Den who said he'd be right down. While she waited, she opened a drawer in her desk and withdrew a stack of Notepads containing the records of past centuries of births and EOL results. Her discussion with Dom over Mrs. Terrence and the conditions of her terminated pregnancy and the vitamin D deficiency symptoms made her wonder precisely how many people they had lost in the last hundred annums or so not only due to deaths by unnatural causes and conditions they could no longer treat, but also due to the terminated pregnancies. It was also reasonable to assume that there'd been miscarriages likely due to the heart, brain or other defects Dom had mentioned. The birth records wouldn't show her those except in cases of later-than-normal pregnancies where there hadn't been a termination. Just her basic mental math told her that without every couple having two babies each, there wouldn't be enough births to offset the number of deaths. She'd just finished sorting the pads from oldest to newest when Den stepped in.

"Hi. That was fast."

"Well, I said I'd be right down." Den plunked himself into a chair in front of her desk and leaned forward across the desktop. Aurora leaned a little closer herself, sensing that Den didn't want anybody to overhear what he was about to tell her.

"The mayor's not happy."

Aurora jerked back. "What do you mean the mayor's not happy?"

Den frantically flapped his hands up and down to shush her.

"Sorry," Aurora whispered. "What do you mean the mayor's not happy?"

"He asked me which site we'd chosen and I told him the north catacomb. He started going on about how of all the sites why that one and when I told him why it was the most suitable site, he started muttering something I couldn't understand and stormed off to I don't know where."

"But that doesn't make any sense. He knew the north catacomb was one of the approved candidates, there was obviously a chance we would pick that one. If he didn't want that one to be chosen, why did he not try to take it off the list or something?"

"I don't know, and he wouldn't tell me. Maybe he just hoped that we'd choose one of the other sites."

Den's radio-pager squawked on his hip.

"Tannet Nalos, here. Construction crew in north catacomb."

Den unhooked the pager from its latch and brought it up to his mouth.

"Den Maron, here, Tannet. What's up?"

"We've found something, sir, that I think you should see."

Den's curious gaze met Aurora's. "What is it?"

"Ah, I really think you should come and see it for yourself, sir."

Den sat back in his chair with a sigh. Aurora nodded as she stashed the sorted pads in a safe place, then picked up her current one from the desktop and stood.

"I'm in the FCO's office, right now. We'll both be there shortly."

"Wonder what they found?" Aurora said once they left Center Hall.

Den shrugged. "I don't know, but I have a hunch it has something to do with why the mayor was angry that we chose that site for the expansion."

"I've been doing a lot of thinking about what you said earlier about the head count and the numbers."

"Oh?"

"Yes, plus the fact I've just come from seeing Dom and conducting an EOL on Mrs. Terrence. I discovered that she had a pregnancy termination and that the reason for the termination was that the baby had tested positive for a medical condition that we can't treat or prevent." Aurora explained what Dom had said about vitamin D deficiency.

"And, I get the feeling," Aurora continued, "that that's not the only thing we have to worry about."

"Like what?"

Aurora shrugged. "Honestly, I don't know. I just have a feeling there's a lot more happening to Egerton than anyone really truly recognizes. Illnesses caused by living down here that we can't treat are just one thing that's affecting so many. As the FCO, I'm also well aware that pregnancies can be lost on their own before any genetic screening can be carried out or verified. Whether or not those miscarriages are due to the effects of our surroundings, I don't know that I'll ever be able to verify that medically."

Aurora stopped talking as they entered the north catacomb and met up with Tannet in front of the back wall, the other construction team members milling about along the sides out of earshot.

"What's up, Tannet?"

"Glad you guys were able to get here so fast." He flashed a high-beam light against the back wall. "We were just getting a feel for what was already here and how we were going to start when we found this."

As he waved the beam in an arc-wise fashion from floor to about head height, the light revealed a very distinct line running from the floor into an arc and then back down to the floor. Den gasped.

"It's a door," Aurora breathed and started feeling around the illuminated shape. As her hand passed over the right hand side of the door, she thought she felt a divot in the rock. She placed her hand over the divot where there was just enough space for a couple of fingers. When she pulled, something clicked inside the rock and the door opened inward a crack, dust raining down on their heads.

The three of them shoved on the door and it swung open the rest of the way to reveal a set of stone steps going upwards.

Aurora turned and looked at Den, speechless. Was this why the mayor was so upset about them choosing the north catacomb because he was afraid they'd find the door? The only possible destination for these stairs would be the surface. Why would he be afraid of that?

Aurora stepped onto the landing and looked up, followed by Den, and then Tannet with the light which he shone upwards in front of them. Aurora tentatively set her foot on the first step and then next and then the next. Before long, the light from door below them had disappeared as they headed up.

They stopped when Tannet's beam showed no more steps ahead, but something solid and hard above their heads. Tannet rapped his knuckles against it and was rewarded with a deep, metallic rumble.

"Well, I guess that's the end of that." Aurora said, her voice muted by the rock walls around them.

"Look at that," Den said, as Tannet panned the light beam around the door. Den squeezed in and swept a hand along the left hand side of the door until it landed on a bump. He felt around a bit more. "It's a lock. Looks like it could be locked from either side. We'll need Fransen Tines for this."

Aurora let out a disappointed sigh. Fransen Tines was the city's locksmith and lock maker. It was slightly odd that Den hadn't mentioned asking the mayor, who'd be the more obvious keyholder. But, given what he'd just told her about Mayor Goodwin's reaction to their selection of this catacomb, Aurora decided not to say anything at that moment. Besides, there was a work crew waiting for them and probably wondering what happened to them. And who knew what they'd already told others after she and Den and Tannet had disappeared through the door. The climb had probably taken a good portion of an hour long enough to pique their suspicions.

"Let's head back down."

"What do we do now?" Tannet asked when they'd reached the bottom of the stairs again and emerged into brightness of Egerton.

Aurora stepped back from the door and stared at the hole, shaking her head.

"Obviously, we can't begin construction," Tannet said.

Aurora shook her head, still unable to put words to all of her thoughts. All she managed was, "No."

When Den closed the door, it blended perfectly into the wall. No one, except them would know it was there.

"Honestly, I don't really know what to do from here. Thank you, Tannet. I guess we won't be needing your crew after all," Aurora said finally. "Let's keep this between ourselves, please. I know it's going to be very difficult to keep the men from talking, but let's make sure they do stay quiet about it for now, until we figure out what to do next."

"Yes, ma'am." Tannet tipped his construction hat in an old-fashioned gesture and left to instruct his crew.

"Wow," Aurora sighed when Tannet was out of earshot.

Den just nodded.

"Did you ever think … ?"

Den shrugged.

"You mean, you knew?"

Den shrugged again. "No, I didn't know. Another one of those hunches."

"You seem to be having a lot of those lately. Where did this one come from?"

"I really don't know. I've been fascinated with the idea of going to the surface since I was little. Not because of anything in particular, just childhood curiosity. I've examined every possible nook and cranny of this city and hadn't found anything. I assumed the door was extremely well concealed so that someone didn't accidentally stumble upon it."

"You obviously didn't look here."

"Believe it or not, that thought had never occurred to me. Although looking at the length of this catacomb …"

"Not to mention the fact it's stood empty for as long as anyone can remember and for which there've been records."

Den tilted his head to one side. "That too. It makes a perfect entry way to the city, and probably explains why it hasn't been filled in or used for something else. It needed to stay empty, either out of reverence for the First Ones – a practice that was lost over time, or in the instance it was needed again."

"I would have thought, though, with you being so curious that you would have found the door before now."

Den smiled. "You'd think. By the time I explored every other alternative, I was old enough to understand that my hunting would bring suspicion since every part of Egerton, besides here, was occupied and I was getting into places that I wasn't supposed to be getting into at that age. So, I stopped looking. At least, physically looking. The thought and curiosity never really left me. It just kinda got shoved to the back of my mind cause then I met Melle and then Peggie came along."

Den stopped almost abruptly. Aurora waited for him to continue, but he didn't. Again, not revealing much about his family, but enough to pique her own curiosity. He only mentioned one child. She recalled his comment about having more children and the ferocity of his argument. *Was that it? Because he and Melle were only able to have one child?*

She was about to ask, when Den said, "Well, I need to get back. I have a few things I need to get done."

Seemed like a pat excuse to retreat back into his office, almost like he regretted revealing so much about himself, but Aurora decided to go with it. It wasn't as if she didn't have anything to do either.

"Okay. Let's walk back then. Perhaps we can figure out what our next step is going to be."

They walked in silence for a few moments.

"I don't see how we're going to get around telling City Council about this. They're going to need to know that the project can't go ahead, and they're going to have to be told why."

"I know. I don't even know what to tell them. Right now, all we have is the presence of a very real door. Everything you've said about not actually having a population growth is just a hunch because only the mayor has those exact numbers."

"Every fiber of my body is telling me those numbers are not actually growing."

"I'm inclined to believe you given what I've just learned from Dom. But, again, we're only going on hunches and don't have anything really to counter what the mayor is trying to make everyone believe."

"The only way to do that, without doing a census – which I really doubt the mayor would approve – is going back through your birth and EOL records."

Aurora nodded. "I would at least be able to verify how many

families have had two babies. From the time of the First Ones, with one thousand people, or five hundred couples, that would mean one thousand babies born each year. And, eventually the first one thousand people would die off, so we'd have enough births to offset the number of deaths.

"Normally, the computer tallies these statistics automatically at the end of 100 annums. I started after the last count was done, so it would be easy to track the numbers from there."

If even just a few of the women of Egerton only had one baby that could spell disaster for the survival of their civilization – and Aurora suspected that she would find more than a few single-birth families, and that it was probably more the norm now than having two. Like Dom's vitamin D deficiency patients, the pregnancy terminations and, Aurora was sure, a whole host of other medical and health-related things – it had been gradually worsening over a long period of time, along the generations. Their civilization was shrinking at a much faster rate than anyone could imagine. There simply were not enough people in the gene pool to keep the population going.

That brought her back to the question of why the mayor wasn't doing anything about it when he had those numbers in front of him. Building new dwelling units wasn't going to solve the problem.

Would allowing couples to have more babies solve it? She suspected this particular issue had been raised before when it had started becoming more obvious that people weren't able to have two babies. But, the law had remained as it was. She knew it would solve the numeric issue, but would it solve the medical/genetic problem? With more births, it was likely that there would be more healthy births to account for those which were unviable due to medical conditions. That would be something else to look into.

But finding the door also presented the question of going to the surface. Even if they did return to the surface which would eventually take care of the vitamin D deficiency, Aurora had no idea how going to the surface would help the other conditions. They still wouldn't have medical supplies and facilities they needed for treatment and prevention. Though, Aurora supposed, if there was anything left of the people on Upper World Earth, particularly those who had had enough technology to build Egerton, perhaps they'd left records behind about how to make those things.

She still wasn't convinced that was the only option, or the best option available. She needed more information.

"Give me a few light cycles," Aurora said. "That will give me enough time to go through my records and pull the data we need."

"The council's next meeting is in three light cycles. They don't have to know anything until then."

And Aurora knew that they likely wouldn't be pleased with her report.

CHAPTER SIX

Aurora sat back in her chair with a yawn and rubbed her eyes as she laid her head against the headrest. They burned and felt like they were going to pop out of her skull.

The overhead lights had cycled down hours ago, and she'd been left with her windup desktop lamp which provided just enough light for her to see the screens of her stacks of pads, but little else. She'd spent many nights with this light since babies arrived whenever they decide to arrive, whether light or night cycle and recordkeeping was required regardless.

This night cycle, however, she was record keeping for a different reason. On the floor to her right were several piles of Notepads containing birth ledgers and death ledgers – 400 annums' worth of numbers and names, and she'd just counted them all. What Den had suggested was true. Egerton's numbers were, in fact, *not* growing – the full accounting and comparison of numbers from the First Ones down to Baby Marshall clearly showed that.

The amount of births was no longer offsetting the number of deaths. Not only that, but most couples now had only one baby, not two, and there was a growing divide between the number of girl babies and the number of boy babies being born, so much so that it was impossible for each person born to find a mate with which to help the population along. It explained why there were so many singles like Dom, and so many empty residence units.

With her numbers done, she felt confident she could convince City

Council that their population was shrinking, but she still couldn't tell them why. That part of the mystery could only be told by annual medical scans and EOLs. She doubted she would be able to look at any of the results of the annual medical scans. Her position as FCO allowed her certain freedoms with information sharing, but not the annual medical scans. Although, if she could find sufficient reason through the results of the EOLs, she might be able to convince Dom to look back at those specific people or families to look for trends. She wouldn't have to describe which families had which trends to City Council. She just needed to know what kinds of things had been developing over the generations that posed a threat to their society.

She still didn't have answer for her question about whether allowing more births would ultimately improve the health situation for Egertonians, or if going to the surface would provide any increased benefit aside from the vitamin D deficiencies. Going to the surface would give them the space they needed to accommodate bigger families, but that didn't mean the resources – food, shelter, medical supplies – for dealing with the increased population and burden would be there. And there was no telling how long it would take before their bodies started reaping any benefits to being on the surface. Like it took generations for the effects of lack of vitamin D to appear – and Aurora assumed other medical conditions she hadn't uncovered yet – it would likely take generations for the society's genetics to work these conditions out of the population. The deterioration hadn't happened overnight and it wouldn't be solved overnight either.

She'd have to find pretty significant evidence that going to the surface would be the right and best option to counter the possible arguments that they'd be no better off than if they stayed in Egerton when it came to managing the medical and genetics conditions already affecting them. To do that, she'd have to prove that living underground as long as they had that resulted in the increased incidents of these ailments.

That thought brought forward another question – what had the plans been for the First Ones? When the builders contemplated, planned and built Egerton, had they intended for people to live in it for 400 annums? The only way she'd be able to answer that question would be go back through the city's history in the archives. She suspected the answer to these two questions would form the heart of her argument.

Aurora's eyes shot open. *When had she started seriously considering the option of going to the surface?* Perhaps it had something to do with Den's revelation that as a boy, he'd gone looking for the door. Even though they'd hung out together as children, she never knew of his searching. She certainly had never thought of going to the surface. At the moment, all the surface had going for it was the solution the vitamin D deficiency.

There could be a whole host of other unpredictables that the surface could present, particularly re-establishing a civilization up there. *What had happened to send them all into the inner sanctum of the earth? What had happened to the people of Upper World Earth since? Were there people still living up there? Would they remember Egerton? Would they welcome them if they suddenly appeared after twenty generations? Would any of the families from which the First Ones were chosen still exist?*

As her fatigued mind played with all these ideas, it became clear to her that having more babies and going to the surface would need to be done together. If the UWE light source provided the nutrients they needed to keep babies and adults healthy, that's what they needed to do. And clearly more births were necessary to bring their population back up to sustainable levels. But, it was also clear that her research wasn't over.

She had half a mind to go home to bed, now. She knew she would need a clear mind to take in all the information she was about to unearth. And she knew there were a few babies due in the next few days, as well as a few finals.

She closed her eyes again. Perhaps just a few moments here. She didn't know how long she'd been asleep when a triple-beep emanated from the cabinet. *Mrs. Terrence's final genetic scan results.* Aurora was suddenly wide awake. It took a few moments for sensation to return to her legs after sitting for so long, but she made it to the cabinet, unlocked it, and retrieved the genetic scan unit. She returned to her desk and set it on top. With a deep breath of anxiety mixed with anticipation, she sat down and flipped up the digital display:

Name: Sharon Terrence (nee Solomon)

Age: 50.3 annums

DOB: Night Cycle hour 5, Week 25, Annum 351

DOD: Light Cycle hour 2, Week 37, Annum 401

Hair color: Brown; no anomalies found

Eye color: Blue; no anomalies found

Hearing: No anomalies found

Brain: No anomalies found

So far, pretty standard.

Bone density T-score: -2.0; diagnosis preliminary osteopenia; minimal but increasing risk of fracture

That one was interesting.

With her middle finger on the touch pad, she moved the cursor to hover over the word "osteopenia" and a bubble popped up: "Beginning of bone loss; precursor to osteoporosis." Aurora skimmed the list of associated medical factors that would put Mrs. Terrance at risk for developing this condition and only one applied – early menopause, which in this case was caused by the sterilization procedure. Since all women were sterilized at an early age, Aurora wondered how many other women had started showing the early signs of osteopenia before her time as FCO. What they'd been doing to sustain the civilization appeared to be one of the sources of a condition that could compromise the quality of life of Egerton's women. Since the information was in their database, the knowledge had to have been passed on by the builders of Egerton and the First Ones would have had access to this information when they were developing the city's laws.

Most of the legislation established by the First Ones was supposedly independent of any influence of similar laws and procedures practiced by the city's designers, such as the type of time measurements they used. It was conceivable that the First Ones established the sterilization protocol on their own even knowing what it would eventually do to women's bodies. Why Aurora wasn't sure she'd ever know. It would also have seemed logical to allow more babies to be born in the beginning to reach a sustainable population level faster. But the law, so far as she knew, had always stated two babies.

At this late, sleep-deprived hour, her mind was having a hard time connecting all the dots, so Aurora decided to let those dots simmer in the back of her mind while she finished reading Mrs. Terrance's results.

She moved the cursor back down to the bottom of the screen, the pop-up window disappeared, and she kept reading. Bone calcium and phosphorous levels were chronically low, which was consistent with what Dom had told her about vitamin D deficiency. Heart and other organs showed varying degrees of increased stress. How much of it was due to living underground or lack of vitamin D or other minerals and nutrients, Aurora wasn't sure, but it didn't take much of a stretch to conclude that, once one of the body's systems had been compromised or affected, other systems would suffer as well.

The scan also confirmed the presence of the caesarean section scar, which really wasn't much of a mystery anymore. The report finished with leg length and feet measurements, which were both normal, aside from signs of osteopenia.

She wasn't entirely sure why, but once she uploaded the results to her EOL Notepad, she decided to search through the current and past EOL database records to review results for things she might have originally passed off or not paid attention to. Without Dom's explanation, she likely had dismissed similar findings in previous EOLs. Plus, she wondered what other conditions she might have missed or dismissed because they didn't seem important. She decided she would make note of anything that didn't come back as "normal." Perhaps if she traced a particular family of someone who'd died of "unnatural causes". Mrs. Terrence had been relatively healthy. Others, like the ones currently in Dom's medical bay, were not. She also suspected that some conditions might be easier to hide or minor enough for someone not to report them. She chose a few names of families in which someone had died of natural causes and unnatural causes. Then, just on a whim, she tossed the mayor's family name into the search parameters. Considering his odd behavior lately, perhaps something would come up on re-examination of EOLs on deceased family members.

While the computer ran the search, Aurora picked up the birth ledgers, again this time counting the single-baby families. By the time the overhead lights cycled on, Aurora had a total, and had also confirmed how many women were older than normal when they had their first baby, and those families with a larger-than-normal age gap between babies one and two.

She had only two full cycles to put the rest of the curious pieces together before appearing before City Council.

CHAPTER SEVEN

"You look terrible!"

"Thanks a lot, Dom. You really know how to cheer a person up." Aurora flopped into a chair in front of his desk.

"Well, lucky for you I've just brewed some tea." Dom filled two well-used granite-wear mugs and set one in front of her.

She took a grateful sip and warmed her hands on the mug.

"So, what brings you here, this early in the light cycle? I assume you have some news on Mrs. Terrence?"

Aurora sat up and realized she'd almost drifted off. She took a bigger sip of tea and tried to focus her mind on her findings.

"Yes, I do. Not just on Mrs. Terrence, but a few others as well."

"A few others?"

Aurora explained the EOL results on Mrs. Terrence and her decision to search for more information.

Dom nodded as he rested his chin on the back of his hands, elbows sitting on the desk. "What did you find?"

Aurora mentioned the families she'd decided to search and that the re-examination of the EOL scans had returned with virtually everyone showing signs of vitamin D deficiency in varying severities and gradually worsening from generation to generation going back over one hundred annums.

"And while we haven't had a death from it yet, scans also showed that certain families are becoming predisposed to cancer – lung cancer, particularly – one of the most severe effects of the condition, something that, according to the medical database is something we really can't treat. It's horrible what that disease does to a body.

"Anyway, lungs, bones, hearts, blood, skin. It varies from family to family, but all these systems are affected. Then there's the mayor."

"The mayor?" Dom sat up straight in his chair.

"Yes, I threw the mayor's family name into the search, just on a whim, and previous EOLs didn't show anything, but the final brain scans did."

Dom's raised eyebrows said, *Oh?*

"Yes." Aurora decided a little explanation was in order. "Den came down to talk to me when I returned to my office after Mrs. Terrence's EOL. He told me that he'd told the mayor that we'd selected the north catacomb as our expansion site. Den said Mayor Goodwin became very upset, started muttering and stormed off. We thought this was very strange behaviour since it was the mayor who'd been pushing for this expansion even though there didn't seem to be any need for it, and he hadn't spoken out against the north catacomb being one of the options. If he hadn't wanted that site to actually have a chance of being selected, why had he allowed it to remain on the consideration list? Then ..."

"Then? There's more?"

Aurora nodded. "Then, Tannet paged us while we were talking in my office and told us there was something in the north catacomb that we ought to see. It was a door."

"A door?"

"Leading to a stairway going up."

Dom rubbed a hand over his face. Aurora wasn't sure what she read in Dom's expression. *Confusion? Concern?*

"The north catacomb was the way the First Ones came down. That's why it's been empty all these annums. Respect for what that area represents, even though most of us have forgotten that part of our history."

"So, if the site was important, why did the mayor allow it to be considered?"

"I don't know. It doesn't make sense. Plus, I don't think that was why he was so upset. I think it was because of the door. I don't think he wanted anyone to be presented with another option."

"Another option?" Dom's eyebrows crooked down almost meeting in the middle.

Aurora couldn't explain where the extra energy came from that drew all her stray thoughts from the past light/dark cycle together into the words that tumbled from her mouth.

"Initially, when I decided to look through my records, I was just going to verify Mrs. Terrence's age when she had her two children, but then, it occurred to me that the defects you mentioned yester-cycle could have also meant that other women might have miscarried before the genetic screening test or before the results came back, which would also mean that they were older when they had their first child or had to wait longer for baby number two."

"And?" Dom tilted his head down then looked up at her.

"And there've been many miscarriages or pregnancy terminations, particularly in the last 200 annums. A disturbing number of them."

Dom sat back in his chair and tapped his stylus on the desk.

"And what does that tell you?"

Dom's nonchalant posture and demeanor confused her. He didn't seem surprised at all by her findings, as if he wasn't hearing anything he hadn't already heard. And, he wanted her to voice her own conclusions rather than offering his opinion, almost like he suspected or knew what she would find.

"It tells me that Egerton is dying. There should be 4000 people living here assuming the two-children-per-couple accounting proceeded uninterrupted, but there's less than 3000. The current population is no longer sustainable. Something is happening to our bodies that is making it more difficult to produce healthy babies and carry pregnancies to term. Plus ... ."

"Plus?" Dom raised his eyebrows.

Aurora nodded. "Plus, there are numerous empty residential units."

Dom's downcast gaze told her he'd noticed it too.

"To my recollection and learning, there hasn't been a census taken in about 200 annums. For as long as I can remember, and as far as what I was told in FCO training, all the EOL information has always gone to the mayor. Only the mayor knows the precise count of the population of Egerton. He was the one who brought forward the reasoning for the expansion based on population projections."

"And?"

"And," Aurora continued, growing annoyed with Dom's attitude, "don't you think that kind of thing would fall to the responsibilities of the FCO, not the mayor? The mayor, of course, would need to know the numbers and be aware of them, but he shouldn't be doing the counting."

Aurora couldn't sit any longer. She set her remaining untouched tea on the desk as she stood, then started pacing in front of Dom's desk. "I have a feeling that something happened about 200 annums ago that prompted the change in how the information is managed.

"What's also intriguing, or disturbing depending on how you look at it, is that if his numbers show exactly what mine do, then why is he pushing for this expansion? He knows the population is shrinking. So far as we all know, it's not as bad as it seems, until you look at the actual numbers and see the number of people suffering from conditions like this vitamin D deficiency that you can't treat, and the only treatment left available for this condition is the light source of Upper World Earth."

"Upper World Earth?"

"I'm getting to that."

"Okay."

"I think that the mayor was upset with our decision because he knew about the door, because he knows our population is shrinking, he knows society-wide our health is deteriorating, but he also knows, and most people accept, that the only thing we can do is continue to terminate pregnancies where deformities or conditions would threaten our society, and continue to live down here. The discovery of the door presents us with another option – of returning to Upper World Earth. That's what he was upset over."

Dom just nodded. Again, his lack of response nagged at Aurora. *This was so unlike him.*

"Aren't you going to say anything?"

Dom shrugged. "I'm just waiting for the rest of the story. Taking it all in."

The words demonstrated a smidgen of his sense of humor, but were devoid of his usual bubbliness. She had just told him their civilization was dying. As Chief Medical Officer, he should be more than just taking it all in. He should be showing at least a bit of concern. Perhaps it was just her fatigue making her think he should be just as upset as she was.

Aurora decided to continue her report.

"So, we've put the expansion on hold so I can find out what's going on. So far, I've found out that, numerically, we don't need the expansion now, anyhow, but City Council needs to be told why. And that means finding out what's causing the defects and how we can stop it. I have two more light and dark cycles before I have to stand in front of them with a report.

"And, although the members of City Council probably don't want to know, I need to find out why no one seems to know what's happening to our population and overall health. It seems odd that in such a closed environment no one has noticed anything or tried to do something other than the status quo of terminating pregnancies and watching our loved ones die so much earlier than they could otherwise with proper treatment."

"Fear is a powerful deterrent, Aurora."

Uh-oh. Full name again.

"Fear of what?" Aurora's fatigue-clogged mind churned through all the information. "Or, fear of whom?" Even as the words came out of her mouth, Aurora couldn't believe them. She set that train of thought aside for a moment. "With all this curious behaviour from the mayor, I added his name to my search list and found out that time-of-death brain scans of various members of his family showed disruptions in electrical activity within the brain consistent with what the database calls 'schizophrenia' with a list of symptoms or characteristics that pretty much explains the mayor's odd behaviour: disorganized thinking and speech, saying things that seem incoherent, paranoia – if my hunch about his reasons for being upset about

61

the north catacomb is true – delusions, considering the obvious evidence that our population is shrinking not growing."

Dom rose from his desk and paced as far as he could in his small office.

"The only thing is, while this seems to be genetic and I've discovered is getting worse along the way in several of the family lines that I dug into, the medical database didn't really give me a cause, or reason why this condition would develop in the first place. I suppose I have to do some more digging to find that out."

Aurora shook her head against the onslaught of thoughts and emotions and connections that her brain was too tired to make any sense of. "I just know that, while terminating pregnancies might have seemed like the way to go at the time given our dwindling medical resources, it's obviously not helping. That and the two-babies-by-twenty-one rule is killing our society. I don't really know why, but something tells me that allowing families who are capable to have more babies would be of more help than killing those that have a deformity. Perhaps the ingenuity that comes from caring for someone with a deformity or disability will help solve other problems. I just know there has to be another solution, another option and the mayor knows it. And that's what I have to present to City Council."

She looked at Dom who had stopped pacing and met her gaze.

"You said fear is a powerful deterrent. Perhaps, following the mayor's way of thinking, he was the one who was afraid. Afraid because he didn't know what else to do but to keep the city humming along as it always had." Aurora paused as she considered a more sinister reason. "Or, he was afraid of losing control, which seems more consistent with what I've read about this schizophrenia."

Her shoulders drooped and she couldn't divert her eyes from the floor. She felt like the entire weight of the world were on her shoulders, adding to the fatigue from a sleepless night of disturbing revelations that seemed to be leading to more disturbing revelations.

Aurora looked up at Dom who was leaning against a wall. He was watching her with much more intensity than he had earlier and she assumed that she'd finally told him something he'd hoped she'd never find out.

"It also occurs to me that that's why Den, and other mayor's assistants before him, have taken on most of the mayor's responsibilities. With this kind of mental incapacity, the mayor is unable to perform his duty to do what's in the best interests of the city." Aurora stopped rambling, rested her back on a wall and tilted her head up to look at the ceiling, but closed her eyes.

"My brain hurts," she said after an exhausted sigh.

"No wonder. I don't think I've ever heard you talk so much."

Aurora's eyes snapped open and she looked at Dom who wore a crooked smile.

"No, I guess you haven't. Sorry about that. Guess I was on a roll."

Dom was silent for a long time. So long that Aurora began to worry about his reaction. Perhaps she should have kept her thought about the mayor's incompetence to herself. Perhaps she should have gone to Den before coming here. She'd only come here first because she thought he would want to know about the results of Mrs. Terrence's scan. She had never intended to tell him so much. In fact, she hadn't even really come to any of these conclusions about the mayor and returning to Upper World Earth until right that moment. But, as she reflected on all she had found so far and where that appeared to lead, she knew her gut reaction was right.

"Say something, Dom."

Dom sighed. "Going back to the surface. You really think that's the better option?"

Aurora suspected Dom wasn't asking because he doubted her. After all, he was the one who had said the light source on Upper World Earth possibly held the cure and treatment for the conditions from which most of them were suffering.

"Yes. I haven't worked out everything yet. I need to consider the risks before I bring that recommendation up to City Council. I have to know for sure that it will do what I hope it will, and show them why we need to do this and why we need to allow families to start having more babies. There are lots of empty residence units, so there's room for more people. So I have to present the argument as well, as to why going to Upper World Earth would be better than staying down here. City Council approved the mayor's proposed expansion because they were going on numbers that he gave them. I'm sure they've seen the empty units like everyone else has, and there have got to be a few that will support this idea once I present them with all the information and evidence. But, I imagine a bunch of them aren't going to be happy about it."

Dom's crunched eyebrows said he wasn't happy either.

"I know, it's disturbing to think our society can't survive as we've always known it," Aurora continued. "But we won't survive at all if we don't do something. And you know, if the people who sent the First Ones down here were intelligent enough to have built this place, then they were probably intelligent enough to know what living down here would do to us and I have a hunch that we've been down here a lot longer than they intended. That's why we no longer have the capacity to treat these conditions and supplies are running out or have run out. We weren't supposed to be down here this long."

Dom sighed again. "It is disturbing. But, you make a good case. So, there's only one question I have left for you."

"Which is?"

"What are you going to do next?"

Aurora's pager went off. She checked the display. "First, I'm going to go deliver a baby," she said. "Then I'm going to do a little more digging in the archives to see what I can come up with about the reasons why the First Ones were sent down here and if there's any record of what happened 200 annums ago that made us start the pregnancy termination practice. Was the option of going to the surface presented or even considered back then? And what about the option of extending the childbearing age and allowing more babies to be born?"

Aurora stood and started to leave, but stopped and leaned against the door frame. She felt Dom approach and sighed when his strong hands began massaging her shoulders.

"Okay, Cass. But, as Chief Medical Officer, I must make you promise that you'll get some rest."

Aurora nodded.

"And you'll keep me posted on what you find out."

She looked at Dom and smiled. "Of course, thanks for the tea."

CHAPTER EIGHT

Aurora's pager went off just seconds after she handed the newborn to her mother. It was another few minutes before she could read the display, excuse herself and respond to Den on her radio.

She stifled a yawn as Den's voice came over the speaker.

"Yeah, Rori, just wanted to follow up on yesterday and see if you've managed to turn up anything."

Aurora had planned to fulfill her promise to Dom and go straight home for a nap before continuing her research, but she couldn't see any way of stalling Den any longer and certainly didn't want to discuss it out in the open.

"I'm actually on my way back to you now, Den. I'll see you shortly."

As Aurora wove her way through the wandering residents, each intent on their own duties, she pondered more about her meeting with Dom and all the information she had collected thus far. Certainly, she didn't have all the information yet, and she knew Mayor Goodwin would be pretty upset if he found out that she had discovered his family history of mental illness and that she was going to present the recommendation of going back to the surface to City Council.

No one would be very happy about the prospect of returning to the surface regardless of the medical evidence that the society would die if they didn't. It would mean completely changing their way of life, revealing to everyone that the mayor couldn't be trusted, and going to a place that was completely unknown to them and may, in the end, prove just as deadly to them as staying here.

Dom had asked what she was going to do next. As soon as she could she knew she needed access to the city archives although she didn't know how she was going to do it. Only city councillors or the mayor had access to those and she had no idea which ones she could trust. Plus, asking them would mean having to reveal why she needed to go down there, and she didn't want to tip her hand before the next council meeting.

By the time she arrived at Den's office, she could barely stand under the weight of the stress and had to support herself on a shoulder against the wall.

"What's wrong?"

Aurora looked up, meeting Den's concerned gaze.

She shook her head, trying to bring her mind back to her purpose for being there.

"Sorry, Den. Worked all night. And haven't been to bed yet. I stopped to tell Dom about the EOL results on Mrs. Terrence and other things I found, and just came from delivering a baby." She tried to chuckle, but it sounded more like she was choking. "No rest for the weary."

Den took her arm and guided her to a chair. "So, what did you find?"

"That you were right."

Den's expression didn't change as he took his seat behind his desk.

"You don't seem all that surprised."

Den shrugged, then smiled. "No, I guess not. Just one of those hunches I knew wasn't just a hunch. Tell me."

At those two simple words, a torrent of words spilled from her mouth, recounting all the information she'd unearthed and her visit with Dom. The only thought recurring in the back of her mind as she related her story was whether Den would support her in front of City Council. This investigation had gone further than she ever expected it to, and, she suspected, further than he expected it to as well. In the meantime, she would take his sympathetic ear and mind for what it was worth – and worry about the council presentation later.

"So, decreasing population plus increasing medical ailments and a crazy mayor," Den summarized in a hushed voice as he pushed against the back of his chair. "Where does that leave us, then?"

"In terms of the expansion or—?"

"In terms of survival, Rori."

Aurora examined Den's face before responding. While Den had never been jovial – not like Dom, anyway – Aurora had never seen her friend this melancholy. Clearly, he understood the full societal implications of this information.

She took a deep breath. "I intend to recommend to City Council, tomorrow, that we change the law and allow couples to have more than two children. I'm also going recommend that we delay the sterilization procedure to allow more babies, and for couples who are having trouble conceiving more time. And, to address the other health issues, I'm going to recommend that everyone move back to Upper World Earth."

Tomorrow. What a scary word. Aurora knew her blood pressure had just soared at that reminder.

"Wow, Rori."

That seemed an understatement to her, but Den's tone indicated he almost as overwhelmed by this influx of information as she was.

Aurora nodded. The weariness of a night of research and the amount of preparation looming ahead of her meant it was all the response she could muster.

She sighed. "Yes. But I need to do some more digging. I need access to the historical archives. I need to learn as much as I can about the First Ones and why they were sent down here in the first place. That will give me a good indication of what challenges we might expect encounter if we move the whole civilization back up. I'm also hoping to find records of the original decision to start pregnancy terminations or if someone raised concerns about vitamin D deficiency and other illnesses before. I suspect someone did, and the stories of whatever happened to them have been forgotten. I feel like the mayor is preying on a fear that's so ingrained in us we forget what started it and has just become normal for us.

"You commented that the mayor is doing things that, logically, should have been conducted by the FCO. Has it occurred to you, as well, that the reason you're doing most of the mayor's work is because this mental illness means he's no longer capable of doing his job? Some of the city councillors have also shown signs of the same mental illness."

"Which is likely why they didn't oppose the expansion project." Den rose from his desk, and propped a hip against the corner. He was so close her head started to swirl.

"I know it seems strange after what we've just discussed, but we really don't know if the surface is any safer. Part of my childhood fascination with finding the way to the surface was also the question of why the First Ones were sent down here if not for some terrible catastrophe up there. I was never able to find out why, but it made sense to me that whatever the reason, it was bad enough that creating Egerton was the only form of survival available – otherwise, we wouldn't be down here. While I don't think the plan was for us to be down here this long, I do think that Egerton was supposed to be a long-term solution for something. It wasn't meant to be something temporary.

"So, if Egerton were part of some kind of survival plan for the First Ones and the society they came from, what were they supposed to be surviving? And could it still be a threat if we move everybody up there?"

"Egerton is 400 annums old. Do you still think whatever threatened them could still be a threat to us?"

"It's possible."

"It is also possible that because we've been down here 400 annums that even if that reason is no longer a threat, any bacteria, viruses or germs on the surface could also pose a threat because we don't have any immunity to those things."

"Hmm. Quite a dilemma. Do we stay here knowing the quality of life our current ways have produced and will produce for our children and grandchildren and the great-grandchildren we'll never see? Or do we go to the surface and take the risk that what's waiting for us up there won't present us with a new, and just as life-threatening, situation?"

Aurora glanced at him. "That's a rather negative way of looking at it. But, yes, it's the dilemma I have to consider from every direction before I present to the council tomorrow. What time is that council meeting anyway?"

Den sat forward and tapped on his Notepad. "It's scheduled for 08:00."

Aurora sighed, again. Her shoulders hunched a little more. "That gives me about 18 hours to find all the information I need." She rubbed her dry, burning eyes.

Den rounded the desk. "Look, it's just after mid-light cycle. Why

70

don't you go home and get some sleep? I'm sure Merrick is wondering what happened to you. Meet me back here around 16:00 and I'll have arranged access to the archives for you."

"Thank you, Den." She felt more relieved than she sounded. Merrick. Her husband. What would he say if he knew what she was working on? She hadn't even considered that until now, she'd been so focused on Mrs. Terrence's report and delivering babies. "Going home to bed sounds like a wonderful idea. I'll see you back here at 16:00."

"Well, look who's home!"

Aurora smiled and gratefully surrendered to Merrick's arms. The fatigue in her body completely taking over.

"You've been delivering babies?"

"Yeah, a couple." They sat at the kitchen table.

"I haven't seen you in almost two cycles and you've only delivered a couple babies? Last I saw you, you were off to get the expansion started with Den." Merrick turned to their small pantry and withdrew a couple of super sweet potatoes, which were genetically altered to provide proteins and other vitamins, nutrients and minerals. After setting them on the counter between the sink and the small stove top, he withdrew a small cast iron pan, drizzled it with a little soy oil, then proceeded to cut the potatoes into chunks.

"Yeah."

"Well, how did that go?" Merrick tossed the chunks into the pan, seasoned them with a little pepper and swirled them until well coated in the oil. He set a lid over them, then turned around to face her, waiting for her answer.

Aurora hesitated. After twenty-five years of marriage, it should have been easy to tell Merrick everything. She should be able to guess what he'd say or how he'd react or even anticipate his personal thoughts about the survival of their society. To her recollection, she and Merrick had never talked about it, but then there'd never really been a reason to until now.

"Merrick, have you ever wondered about not being able to watch our grandchildren grow up?"

Merrick shook his head and stared at her.

"What's happened, Aura?"

At the use of his pet name for her, her heart melted and she didn't stop until she'd recapped everything including her last visit with Den.

"Wow. No wonder you're exhausted." Merrick leaned back in his chair, then stood and paced about the small kitchenette and living area before stopping in front of the stove to check the progress of the sweet potatoes. "You really think Egerton is dying?"

Since he was turned away from her, Aurora couldn't see his expression, but she knew his tone. He wasn't asking out of concern or interest, but out of skepticism. She immediately regretted telling him, although it was not like she had any choice.

"It certainly appears that way. From what I've learned from the records, our society is slowly and inevitably dying. We can't continue living the way we've been doing. So many people are sick and so many babies have died because someone decided that was better than finding an alternative that would correct the underlying problem."

"But you said we might not be able to survive on the surface either." Merrick sluiced the softened sweet potato onto a plate and set that and a fork in front of her.

"That's a possibility."

"This is the only home we've ever known. Some people won't want to give that up even if it does mean dying here."

There it was. Merrick's opinion and, basically, ultimatum. Daring her to choose because he'd already made his choice. Somewhere deep down, when the thought of returning to the surface first came up, she'd known eventually she would face this kind of challenge, though she hadn't anticipated that it would come from her own husband. That he would choose to be apart from her instead of taking on the challenge of a new life somewhere else. He was content to keep things as they were. He wasn't interested in a different or better way. She nearly choked on the sweet potato for the ache in her chest.

"I realize that. I know I might not be able to get council to agree and I know there's no way I'll be able to convince everyone to leave. And, ultimately, I can't force anyone to do anything. If people decide to stay, then there's nothing I can do. But I have to see this through and let the people of Egerton make the choice for themselves."

"Tell me, Aurora, what do you think will happen to families where not everyone will support and agree with what you're telling them? What if one family member wants to go, and another doesn't?"

Aurora was surprised at Merrick's curt tone. She looked at Merrick and saw thinly veiled anger in his eyes.

Aurora shrugged as her heart plummeted and set her fork down unable to stomach another morsel.

"I honestly, don't know, Merrick. As I said, I can't force anyone to go. That's their own personal decision."

"And what about the people that would be left behind?"

The weight-of-the-world feeling returned, and Aurora's shoulders hunched with pressure. She never really thought that Merrick would be opposed to the idea of going to surface even when faced with all the evidence and information, and what she suspected she would find in the archives. What she said was true. She knew she wouldn't be able to convince everybody, she even doubted being able to convince City Council at all, but she never imagined Merrick not going with her. Her reasons for doing this went far beyond their own family and affected the lives of everyone in the city.

But she understood his question. Once she set things in motion with her presentation to City Council in the morning, every family in Egerton would be faced with the same decision and dilemma. People would be left behind. Some families would likely split because of her. But she had no choice but to go with the people who decided to leave.

"I don't know, Merrick. I can't just dig all this up, make my recommendations and then not follow through with it." She directly met his gaze and spoke with an intensity that she didn't know she still had. "Don't you see this is bigger than you and me? This is about saving Egerton, about bringing our children and grandchildren a better quality of life, of treatment for a range of conditions that we can't treat ourselves anymore, but the light source of Upper World Earth can. I don't know how the mental illness of the mayor and others factors into this or whether having more babies will help with that, but I will find out and I do know that, at the very least, Egerton won't survive at all if we don't do something."

Merrick scowled at her.

"You're willing to break up our family--"

"I'm trying to save our family, and everyone else's. I'm trying to make sure that future generations will have a better quality of life and that Egerton as a society will live on and not die out if we sit here and continue doing things the way they've always been done."

"Why change anything at all? If this is the way Egerton's meant to be maybe that's the way it should be. Why tamper with it? We weren't supposed to live forever. You may have become unhappy with the status quo, but some of us are quite happy with it."

"You're happy that hundreds of babies are killed in each generation from conditions that could be treated on Upper World Earth?"

"You don't know that."

"Know what?"

"That going to Upper World Earth would do anything of the sort."

"You're right, I don't. All I'm going on right now is Dom's word as CMO that we can no longer treat these conditions and they're gradually getting worse, and there is no absolute guarantee that going back to the surface will solve anything, but I believe I have a responsibility to the people of Egerton to present them with the information and let them decide for themselves."

"Sounds like you've already made your choice."

"It doesn't seem right that if I bring these recommendations forward and people decide they want to leave that I stay here."

"Den put you up to this, didn't he?"

Her breath caught in her throat. "What?"

"Den put you up to this, didn't he?" Merrick had stopped pacing and now looked straight at her with an expression in his eyes that she'd never seen before. *Jealousy?* "You and he always had something going on when we were young. I thought I never had a chance with you, but he never stepped up. I wondered how long it was going to take working with him day after day for this to happen."

Aurora was too shocked to say anything. Of course, she couldn't tell him that there wasn't anything between her and Den, he probably wouldn't believe her anyway, or deny that Den hadn't put the idea in her head because he had.

The silence hung over them with the weight of the stone ceiling.

Eventually, Merrick hung his head so she couldn't see his eyes.

"You'd better get some sleep," he finally said.

The surety of Merrick's tone felt like a knife to her heart that twisted as she watched him leave their dwelling.

CHAPTER NINE

"You were supposed to get some sleep," Den said when she arrived at his door.

Aurora moaned as she rested her head against the rock.

"I tried, really I did. But babies don't really listen to when I need to sleep. Whatever's going on here, I'm still the Family Control Officer, and babies still need to be delivered."

Den nodded and smiled sympathetically.

"But I did get a couple of hours in," Aurora amended with a sigh.

"Are you ready to dig into some paperwork, then?"

"As ready as I'll ever be, I guess."

"'I guess'?" Den drew her into his office and leaned her against the wall, his voice barely above a whisper. "Last I saw you, you were raring to go look at files and I had to convince you to go home and get some sleep. There's none of that fire now. What happened? I know there's something more going on than just lack of sleep."

Aurora sighed again and couldn't stop her eyes from welling up with tears. Den was right. It wasn't just the fatigue talking, although that was probably playing a role with her emotions right now.

"Merrick's not going to come with us."

"What?"

"When I arrived home, I told him everything, kinda had to. He was not happy. He didn't discourage me or disagree with my findings, but he didn't support my ultimate suggestion that the citizens of Egerton leave and re-establish on the surface. He thinks that as citizens of Egerton we should stay here and live out the existence we were meant to rather than leave the society and only home we've known and risk dying somewhere else." Aurora couldn't lift her eyes from the floor. "He wasn't there when I left."

Den nodded again. "I suspect he's not the only one that's going to think that way. Unfortunately, there's not really much you can do once a person's mind is made up. They're entitled to make their own choices." He paused. "What about your kids?"

Aurora looked up at him then. His blue eyes bore into hers. His musky scent cuing a spiral down to her stomach. She was too tired and too emotional right now – not to mention still married. With much effort, she pushed herself away from the wall and, most importantly for the moment, away from Den. Stress, grief, rekindling of their past friendship, it was all too much right now.

"I haven't talked to Caytor and Selleck, yet. Caytor's always been kind of a daddy's girl, though, so I imagine she'll probably go along with what Merrick says. And Selleck, I don't know. He's always been one to make up his own mind about things."

Aurora sighed again. "I never imagined doing what's right to save our society would mean the breakup of my family." She couldn't stop the flow of tears that took over for a few silent moments. To Den's credit, he didn't try to hold her or comfort her or talk, he just let her cry.

"What about Melle? Have you talked to her?" Aurora managed when the ebb of tears subsided.

Den's face turned sad as he shook his head. "It's been over for us for a while. She's living with Peggie, now, and has been since Peggie was old enough to be on her own."

"I'm sorry to hear that." And she really was. With that statement came the realization that she and Den were essentially free to leave. They would obviously have ties to their children, but they, too, were of the age where they had families of their own and would make their own decisions. She and Den really didn't have a choice but to leave Egerton. After all, if he were going to support her motion to City Council as it appeared he would be, and people decided to leave, he couldn't very well stay behind. It appeared that their family situations were really making it possible for them to leave without looking back.

With that thought, Aurora took a deep breath and straightened her shoulders.

"I guess we're in this together, then," she said with a small smile.

Den smiled back. "I guess we are."

"Well, then, time to get back to work. That City Council meeting isn't getting any further away."

"Follow me."

Den led her down through a maze of stairs Aurora didn't even know existed below and behind the council chambers and mayor's office. The lower they went, the older the smell around them became. Clearly, this was a virtually uninhabited part of the city.

Finally, when Aurora didn't think she could take another step, and started wondering if she'd ever survive the trek back up, they arrived at a door at the very bottom.

Den removed a key from his sweater pocket.

"How did you get that? Don't only the mayor and city councillors have the key? You said you had to arrange access for me to see the archives. You didn't … ?"

"Relax. I didn't have to do anything except ask Fransen Tines."

"You mentioned him when we were in the tunnel."

It also gave me a chance to explain about that door so he could work to find a key or create one that would work.

"You what?" Her incredulous tone reverberated off the stone around them.

"Shhh! You're getting shrill." Den waved his hands up and down. "Don't panic. I wouldn't have asked him if I didn't think I could trust him. His wife was also unable to have more than one baby. He and I have talked about the possibility of a way out for a long time."

"Sounds like you have a kind of an underground network."

Den stepped up to the lock door and slid the key into the slot.

"There's more of us out there than you or the mayor realizes. There are too many things going on in Egerton for people not to start questioning what's happening."

The bolt unlocked with a *CLUNK* and Den turned the levered handle. Another *CLUNK* and the door swung open. Den felt the wall around the door for a light switch.

"There's actually power down here? I almost thought we would have had to bring our night cycle lanterns or something."

Several strings of small laser lights lit up the room.

"Well, I don't know that they get much use. I'm surprised they actually work."

In the midst of startled, dancing dust motes stood rows of filing storage containers.

"Where do we even begin?" Aurora asked, overwhelmed by the amount of information before her. There were three rows of metal filing containers, one row for the first 300 annums they'd been underground.

"Well, I guess it would depend on what you're mainly looking for."

"I hate to say it, but I think we need to start right from the beginning. I already have a trend of body measurements going back the last 100 annums. I need to find out when exactly people seemed to start shrinking and confirm the physical condition of the people who were first sent down here. I need to know if the designers knew of any potential threats to being underground long-term. I also need to know why the First Ones were sent down here in the first place and if whatever threatened them might still be a threat to us."

"In that case, I think we need the dustiest boxes," Den said as he walked down to the last row, "which I believe are these right here."

Aurora followed as he continued down the aisle.

"Assuming the very first box brought down here is the one in the deepest part of this alcove, I'm guessing we need this box." Den stopped in front of the stack in the farthest most corner of the room and tapped the bottom box with his toe.

"I don't think I can argue with that logic," Aurora said. "It's almost kind of what I was afraid of. I'm also almost dreading what we might find in these boxes."

"Why?"

"Well, think about it, Den. The First Ones likely weren't sent down here for a good reason. My guess is that they were sent down here because something bad was happening up there." Aurora pointed at the ceiling. "Plus the fact we're basically looking in everyone's family history, and some people wouldn't approve of us snooping around. We may have all come from these same ancestors, but it's kind of creepy looking back at basically our great-great-great – however many greats grandparents, and, perhaps, the very person responsible for Egerton overall – and who may have known that right from the beginning living in Egerton would eventually kill us."

Den was quiet, obviously mulling over what she had just said.

"These voices – ghosts, really – from the past may not say anything we really want to hear, or the people of Egerton want to hear."

"Rori," he took her hands and forced her to look at him, "Whatever is in these boxes, you know you're acting in everyone's best interest and that only the records of the First Ones can answer your questions. If you don't find those answers, no one will be given any choice but to die here."

Aurora's shoulders perked up and she took a deep breath. "What if I don't find anything?"

"You really think you won't?"

Aurora shook her head. "No. I believe I'll find what I need. And, you're right, I have to do this. My gut is telling me the kind of information I'll probably hear, but there's something almost creepy about having someone speak out loud what you've only heard in your head."

Den lifted the first of four boxes down.

"Well, the only way you're going to stop being afraid of what you think you're going to hear is to look at them. Then you'll know."

"You're right, again. Gosh, I hate it when you do that." She glanced sideways at him as she smiled and took down another box.

When they reached the bottom-most box, she looked at Den.

"Why are you helping me, Den? As the mayor's assistant, you could get in so much trouble for this."

"Like you needing to come down here to find out what's happening to our civilization, it's something I need to do. I'd like to say it's just to fulfill a boyhood dream, and it is that, but I also feel that Egerton is doomed if we don't do something and whatever's down here will help us decide precisely what that something needs to be."

"Us?"

"Yes, us."

Aurora smiled again. "Well, thank you. I can't tell you what that means to me." Particularly given Merrick's opposition and withdrawal from her life. "What are you going to do while I'm reading all these?"

"Well, I kind of have to go back to my office. I have things to do to get the mayor ready for Chambers in the morning. I'll come back and check on you in, say, two hours?"

"All right." Aurora wasn't sure how long Den had been gone or how long she stood there staring at that very first box before she made herself as comfy as she could on the stone floor, set her Notepad on her lap, then lifted the lid off box number one and examined the single row of about 12 Notepads inside. It was almost a relief to see the Notepads. Aurora was afraid that the First Ones had used something that would have deteriorated over time. The Notepads were the easiest and safest way of storing information for long periods because of the high-capacity memory and the internal self-sustaining battery, though she wondered if 400 annums had been enough to compromise both.

Assuming the pads were in order from oldest to newest, Aurora chose the pad at the very right, her hands trembling. She took a deep breath, then pressed the power button at the bottom. The screen burst to life and a woman's face appeared. She appeared to be about 50 years of age – confirming for Aurora that The First Ones did have longer life-spans. As it was now, most everyone in Egerton died before or around the age of 50. This woman, however, looked relatively healthy. Of course, Aurora couldn't be certain of her assessments of age and health since her only her frame of reference was how things were in Egerton 400 annums after this woman's recording.

The woman was slim, with a handsome and wise face, and curly gray hair that came just to her ears. She was sitting probably at a desk, but Aurora couldn't see it, and wore a white coat with her name stitched above the pocket on the right hand side.

Aurora rested her back against the stack of boxes behind her as the woman spoke.

"Hello. This is Dr. Imogen Heinan. I'm recording this history of the establishment of the underground City of Egerton. I have no way of knowing who is watching this or why or how old Egerton is now. I can only hope that this recording will help answer some of the questions that have likely brought you to seek me out.

"As a matter of context, at this recording it is the year 2150 as measured by Upper World Earth's calendars. That might not mean much to you, since Egerton was supposed to have created their own time measurements. Anyway … ." Imogen's next words were drowned out by a blast of sound in the background.

The picture of Imogen Heinan shook violently though Aurora hadn't moved her hands.

Imogen sighed. "The concept for Egerton came out of the need to save a portion of our civilization as it became more and more clear that we would likely not live out this century. Upper World Earth had been involved in a world-wide war for five years, and things were really deteriorating. It was out of the concern for the survival of the human race in general that several scientists – myself, a few others, and architect and engineer, Joshua Egerton from the North American Continental Democratic Congress and similar teams from the other three Continental Democratic Congresses – worked to find a solution, and that solution was to build underground cities with each congress designing and building their own. Ours was named Egerton, obviously after Joshua." A picture of Joshua Egerton appeared briefly on the screen. He looked a little younger than Imogen, and wore a round wire-and-glass contraption on his nose.

"We decided that to give the people the best chance of survival, each potential citizen would undergo genetic screening to make sure that we were not sending the people of Egerton underground with any genetic deformities or pre-dispositions to illnesses or anything that could potentially threaten the longevity and quality of life for everyone.

"It took another five years after the decision to create Egerton to find the ideal place within North America. As of this recording, the three other cities have been built and citizens chosen and we're all expected to 'go underground'" – she crooked the first two fingers from each hand in the air – "at the same time.

"Egerton was built in the Canadian Shield as it was the most structurally sound location in all of North America. Plus the underground aquifers from the Hudson's Bay region and all the lakes within the Canadian Shield would ensure a safe underground water supply.

"After all our genetic screening, 1000 people were selected. This message is being recorded on the eve of the First Ones' descent into Egerton. The idea is to bring you all back up after fifty years. There are certain things about living underground that we simply can't anticipate such as what your bodies will do without sunlight even though the overhead lights do provide a certain amount of ultraviolet radiation as well as what will happen to your bodies after long-term exposure to the mineral-containing rock around you. Hopefully, another genetic screening in fifty years will provide some of those answers.

"The only thing we probably won't be able to determine at that fifty-year screening is the effects of inbreeding since any genetic repercussions from inbreeding will only start becoming visible after the population's really completely intertwined."

Imogen's pause gave Aurora a chance process what she'd said so far.

Imogen continued, "Let me tell you about inbreeding since the effects of lack of vitamin D and the link between long-term radiation exposure from the surrounding rock and lung cancer are available in your medical database. Egerton started out with 1000 people. We tried to select people from a variety of cultures, body types and never more than one person with the same basic gene code to ensure that the civilization would survive.

"When a limited number of people marry and have children and their children get married and have children with other people within the same community, over time genetic deformities, behaviors and effects can occur such as impotence on the part of males, infertility on the part of females, facial deformities and other skeletal or bone deformities that can be life-threatening. Even with our careful screening and selection of the people for Egerton, this breakdown in the genes of your children could also happen. It was simply a matter of intermarrying and procreating with people who, over time, have become part of the overall gene pool. Our scientists estimated that the people of Egerton would become completely genetically inter-related within 200 years. Because of the diversity of the original gene pool, it may take longer for the genetic side effects to start appearing, but they will, inevitably, appear."

Imogen looked down at her desk and then looked back up at the screen.

"There's one more thing that I can imagine has encouraged you to seek out this information, human beings were not meant to live underground for long periods of time. Preliminary trials and computer simulations showed that, even with the overhead lights in Egerton providing Vitamin D, without real direct sunlight the musculoskeletal system will start to break down and autoimmune diseases and life-threatening cancers that we so carefully screened out may re-emerge. Also, with inbreeding there is an increased risk of mental illness that can develop without a discernible cause and be passed down and worsen from generation to generation.

"I attach with this recording a visual file documenting what we know about Vitamin D and the element radon which is known to be present in the surrounding rock formation and which could also affect your bodies after long-term exposure, as well as information on inbreeding. I also include several files that contain the entire history of Upper World Earth up to this point. There was a once-held common belief that if you didn't know where you came from, you'd be liable to make the same mistakes. So, please, use this information as an example of what to avoid and how to make humans live and flourish again."

Imogen looked down at her hands again and took a deep breath before continuing.

"I have no way of knowing how long into the future this is being watched. Our intention was for Egerton to be a haven of safety and growth and prosperity until Upper World Earth is safe from the threat of war."

Some more explosions detonated in the background closer than the last one and Imogen ducked. She looked around her as dust dropped in clusters beyond the window behind her.

"The hope was to bring you all up in fifty years' time so we can judge the success of this project before closing the doors behind you until such time as one of my successors thinks it's safe. I'm afraid I won't live long enough to bring you back up and do these interviews myself. I have left instructions in my office about when, where and how you should return to the surface." Imogen took another deep and sad breath. "That is, if there is anyone left," she added.

"I pray that when you do finally come back to Upper World Earth – and you must come back for the sake and survival of everyone in Egerton – that you will live peaceful lives, lives that are respectful of other people and not jealous of what others have and you do not, and that you will believe that everyone is created equal and that no one human being is inferior or less important than another. Much of the conflict you see behind me and which was the cause for the development of Egerton was a result of people who did not hold these attitudes. The ultimate survival of the human race depends on you re-establishing civilizations without these old ways of thinking and living. This is why Egerton was to have none of the religions and political parties and prejudices and attitudes of Upper World Earth."

Another war-time roar rattled the windows, this one farther away.

"Well, I think that's all I have for you right now. Whenever and why-ever you're watching this message I can only hope that it means that, in the grand scheme of things, Egerton has been a success. You are alive. You have survived. And that's what we set out to accomplish. So I guess, since I know I won't be able to see you in fifty years, I will have to be satisfied in the knowledge that you are reading this and the only way that is even possible is because of all the work and effort and planning that went into Egerton.

"This is Dr. Imogen Heinen, signing off."

The picture froze, suspending Dr. Heinan's face in a moment in time. Aurora stared at her until she had memorized every bit of her face. Moments later, a menu appeared displaying the information the doctor had mentioned about Vitamin D, radon, inbreeding and the history of Upper World Earth. Aurora powered up her Notepad and downloaded the files.

When that process was complete, Dr. Imogen's screen went blank and Egerton's very first Notepad powered down.

Chapter Ten

Aurora dropped the Notepad to her lap as her mind worked to absorb all that she had learned. Inbreeding, world war, diseases, lack of sunlight, genetics, the apparent grief of a woman who believed she likely wouldn't live long after the recording and wouldn't live to see if the project she'd worked so hard on had been successful.

Since her time was limited, Aurora decided to keep looking through the rest of the Notepads in front of her. She would have to review this extra information later. She would certainly need it if she were to have a hope of convincing City Council and the citizens of Egerton to return to the surface. She just hoped Dr. Heinan's words would be sufficient to convince people to leave.

"Aurora? You still down here?"

No response.

Den stepped a little further into the room.

"Rori?" He looked down one aisle and then another. "Rori?" He found her between aisles two and three, attention completely fixed on the Notepad in front of her.

"Rori?"

She didn't look up but instead waved for him to sit down.

"You have to see this."

"What is it?" he asked as he lowered himself to the ground beside her.

Aurora paused the recording, set the pad down and rubbed her eyes which were dry and itchy from the dust. She could swear her brain physically ached, too, with all that she had just learned about Egerton's first 200 annums.

"I've found a very curious mayor's journal entry. All the other mayor entries I've found have been a summary of the year's business in council or providing more information about a decision council has made or something official. This one is completely separate.

"I've already come across several Chief Medical Officer's reports finding skeletal deformities and other physiological and neurological conditions appearing in End-of-Life scans, and some babies being born with horrific deformities. These findings are consistent with Dr. Heinan's file on what would start to happen to our people without sun exposure and with all the families intermarrying for so long. There's also an additional threat of long-term exposure to the minerals and radiation that are naturally present in the walls around us."

"Whoa! Hey. Slow down. You're losing me."

Aurora's cheeks puffed out as she exhaled, trying to regain some semblance of control of herself. She recounted for Den what she had discovered on the first Notepad.

"Okay, got it," he said when she had finished. "So, what's up with this one?" He nodded to the pad in her hand and reclined slightly against the boxes behind them.

"Okay. You ready for this?" Aurora hovered her finger over the pause button.

"I'm ready."

The recording resumed. The date stamp on the recording was early in the 200th annum.

"This is Mayor Annis Warton recording a private meeting between myself, Chief Medical Officer Shallon Hillis, Family Control Officer Jella Carmon, and Pudray Gilbert, whose role will become apparent in a moment.

"I have called this meeting to discuss the disturbing medical changes, deformities and ailments that have started to appear in Egerton's population as recorded in previous medical logs by both FCO Carmon and CMO Hillis in their End-of-Life Final examinations. Things like shorter overall body measurements when compared to measurements of previous generations, some lung deformities and some couples being unable to conceive due to one partner or the other being unable to produce sperm or ova to procreate and keep our society alive. Some babies have been born with strange deformities.

"CFO Carmon and CMO Hillis claim that infertility, and increased rates of birth defects and miscarriages are a threat to the sustainability of the population in Egerton. To that end, they have recommended that the Family Control Laws be changed to allow couples to have more than two children to counteract the effect of other couples' infertility, and that the sterilization age be raised to accommodate the extra births. They believe this reproductive compensation will help offset some of the birth defects and deformities that have started happening on much too frequent a basis.

"Further, CMO Hillis has speculated on several occasions in my office that several of these newly-appearing conditions, if left unchecked in our gene pool, will eventually lead to the death of every member of Egerton. The extent of the conditions will continue to get more and more severe as they are passed down from generation to generation, inhibiting the long-term viability of Egerton. Medical resources are also running short and have actually run out in terms of treating vitamin D deficiency and resultant related medical conditions. CMO Hillis tells me we have enough to continue maintenance doses for those most seriously affected, but eventually that, too, will run out and we don't have the medical resources to continue to treat the respiratory ailments and other things that are happening as people's other bodily systems start to become affected.

"The decrease in overall stature is something that our society will just have to learn to live with. So far as we know, there is no way to stop the progression of this. It seems to be affecting everyone, though, so perhaps it's just a natural part of our lifecycles now.

"I feel obliged to mention that CMO Hillis has speculated that these new medical conditions have something to do with Egerton's walls and the limited exposure to the ultraviolet rays from the lighting system due to our clothing requirements. He has recommended that the only way to counteract the continual appearance of these illnesses and progressive deterioration of our society is to return to the surface. I also feel obliged to mention that this is not the first time returning to Upper World Earth has been brought forward.

"However, it is my belief and fear that this could result in dissent and division amongst Egerton's citizens. Plus, we have no guarantee that returning to the surface will be of any additional benefit to reducing future birth defects, fertility and mental health and other medical difficulties that are appearing without any obvious direct cause.

"So, as an alternative to returning to the surface, after taking CMO Hillis and CFO Carmon's concerns into account, I have decided and plan to present to council that genetic screening be carried out on every known pregnancy and should the unborn child show signs of any of these genetic mutations, the pregnancy will be terminated. This genetic screening will be carried out in current and future pregnancies to ensure that any further incident of these symptoms and characteristics will be kept from entering our society. Every new pregnancy will be genetically screened by Pudray Gilbert. Any positive results from this genetic screening will result in termination of the pregnancy which will be carried out by Pudray Gilbert. If the genetic screening comes back clear, the file will be passed on to the CFO to be followed until delivery. Pregnancy termination will occur before the end of the fifth month and be carried out by caesarean section.

"The fetus bodies will be processed through the CMO's office, which will in turn ensure that these terminations are recorded for my benefit, and will still help sustain the city by being incinerated just like our adults who die. Pudray Gilbert will be instructed to avoid, as much as possible, being noticed by anyone in the coming and going of her duties, so as to avoid any panic and dissension amongst the population that may also threaten Egerton's survival as a society.

"Also, any genetic records of forthcoming pregnancies will be deleted as the pregnancies are terminated. The only record of any deformities or physiological ailments will be in the CMO's logs which are still needed to track our history and heritage for future generations.

"Further, all EOLs, death and birth records, including how many known terminated pregnancies and miscarriages will be reported directly to me. I will monitor the numbers coming in and keep track of the population myself."

At this point in the recording, Hillis and Carmon looked at each other with a "he's joking, right?" kind of expression.

"Further, the sterilization age will remain the same and the Family Control Law will remain as-is, as making a change this drastic to the way we've lived so far will create a sense of fear and uncertainty about Egerton's future and that would be bad for the morale of the city."

Den's gaze met hers. *Morale of the city?*

"Since we do not know the source of these deformations, characteristics and symptoms, and can only speculate as to possible influences rather than causes …"

"Wait a minute. You can't … ," CMO Hillis started, but the mayor held up a finger.

"… we cannot prevent these things from reappearing, but we can, at the very least, slow down the process by eliminating potential threats as they become apparent.

"This will be the only record of this meeting. This is Mayor Annis Warton signing off."

Aurora and Den sat in silence for several moments after the screen went blank.

"Wow," Den finally said.

"The morale of the city is better served by keeping everything the same so people don't know exactly how bad the situation is. He decided ignorance was better than giving them a choice. He decided killing babies was the right answer even though the mathematics governing population numbers at that time was already starting to affect the ability of families to procreate. I'm stunned." Aurora paused.

"I have medical evidence going back 200 years of these deformities and medical problems continuing to appear, regardless of this genetic screening and pregnancy termination practice. I also have statements from the city's designer and builder that we were not meant to live underground for as long as we have been and that these medical issues would begin to appear and threaten our survival. And, I have evidence that the return-to-the-surface option was brought forward as a solution to the problem." Aurora paused. "Am I correct in assuming that something of this magnitude would have been passed down from mayor to mayor, kind of secrets of the trade?"

"I would imagine so."

"Then it wouldn't be too much to assume that the mayor's office has known this for the last 200 years, but has never presented that option to the people."

Den settled back into silence for a few moments then said, "That'll certainly add weight to your argument and recommendations to Council. Do you think you have enough from down here?" He stood and brushed the dust off his pants.

Aurora sighed. "Yeah, I guess so." She downloaded the mayor's meeting onto her pad, replaced the old pads back in their boxes, sealed them, and set the boxes back in their rows where they belonged. She followed Den to the staircase where he turned off the lights and closed and locked the door behind her.

As they neared the half-way mark of the stairway, Aurora thought she caught sight of someone crossing the stairs ahead of them, and then the sound of a door opening and closing.

"Did you see that?"

Den shook his head. "No."

Even with the dim light, Aurora knew she had seen something, and couldn't do anything but follow her gut.

"Come on." A couple of steps up, Aurora stopped and felt along the inside wall until she felt a metal latch. When she turned it, the door opened into one of the back alleys of Egerton, and not a few steps ahead of them was a cloaked figure. No one looked as the figure passed, which Aurora figured, given what she'd just read, was the entire point of this person's job ... if her hunch proved correct.

Aurora wove in and around the crowd, not even checking to see if Den was following her. Once close enough, Aurora touched the figure's shoulder. The figure startled and turned.

CHAPTER ELEVEN

"Excuse me?" The figure said.

Aurora couldn't believe she was staring at the woman and couldn't think of a word to say except, "Barna?"

"Aurora. What are you doing here?"

"Yes, s-sorry, for interrupting," Aurora stammered. Den finally caught up to her. "Um, I'm – er, we – are looking into some curious medical conditions affecting some of the citizens of Egerton and wanted to ask you a few questions." Aurora was careful to keep her voice quiet. It would do no good to incite a panic now from someone overhearing their conversation.

"What makes you think I might be able to help with that?"

"Because I know what you do. I know about the deformed babies."

Barna's gaze never faltered. "Everybody knows."

"They may know what you do, but they don't know why you do it."

"Of course they know ... ."

"It's happening more, isn't it?"

Barna sighed and looked at the ground and then back at Aurora. "Meet me by the door on the stairs in half an hour." With that, Barna disappeared, blending into the crowd.

"Well, what do we do now?" Den asked.

Aurora's radio beeped. She glanced at the display. She hit a button and brought the speaker up to her mouth. "Hey, Dom. Cass, here."

"Hi, Cass. Got another EOL for you."

Aurora sighed. She was standing purely on adrenaline after finally figuring out all that was going on, and wondered how she would ever get through this final screening. Not like she had any choice.

"All right. I'll be there in a few minutes." She turned to Den. "Well, I guess I'll meet you on the stairs in thirty minutes."

"Cass! Glad you're here," Dom bubbled without looking up.

"Hey, Dom."

Dom's head snapped up at her tone.

"Wow, you look like death warmed over." He stood and tried to usher her to a chair but she refused with an outstretched hand.

Aurora smiled at his humor. "Thanks, Dom. You always know just what to say to perk a lady up."

"I do my best," he jibed back. "Seriously, though, what's going on?"

"Let's talk while we're doing the EOL. I need to be back to Center Hall in thirty minutes."

Dom nodded. "Let's go then."

As before, Dom led the way down the hall. Aurora waited while he prepared the body for their examination.

"I was right, Dom," she said, as she stepped up to the table.

"About what?"

"About the babies, the terminated pregnancies, that our society is dying, and that the city's builders, or at least those who conceived the idea, knew that we couldn't live down here forever, and that the suggestion of going to the surface was raised earlier, and actually prompted the current pregnancy termination practice. The mayor decided pregnancy terminations and continuing to restrict families to two babies and keep the sterilization age as it was, was more important for maintaining the 'morale of the city'." Aurora carried on without waiting for Dom to respond, fearing she'd lose her nerve. "I know that one of your predecessors, CMO Hillis was the one who made the proposal to head back to the surface to the mayor 200 annums ago."

Dom leaned against the wall next to the body and looked at her.

"I found a recording of a private meeting between the mayor at the time, the chief medical officer, the family control officer and a new person who was given the task of terminating pregnancies. After that meeting, every new pregnancy underwent genetic screening. The clean results were sent on to the Family Control Officer, and the positive ones were given to this new person and the fetuses brought to the CMO to be incinerated and the reasons recorded and passed on to the mayor. Any record of the results of the positive genetic scan was to be deleted aside from what was recorded by the CMO."

"Wow."

Dom's drab tone told Aurora he wasn't surprised at all. *How could he not be upset by this revelation? Unless … he already knew what she would find.*

100

Instead of drawing information out of him, Aurora decided to relate the part of the meeting where the mayor had laid out all the medical things that the CMO had reported.

"The mayor said that the CMO had proposed returning to the surface because living in Egerton was causing these changes, but the mayor decided to go the pregnancy termination route because he didn't want dissent or division in Egerton."

"I can see his point. You do know that's probably what's going to happen once this all becomes public."

"I know."

"You don't even know if it's safe to go back to the surface."

"No, I don't. But I heard it from Egerton's designer that these things could start appearing if we lived down here too long. It's now been too long. It was too long 200 annums ago, and the mayor decided to make us live down here longer still even though it was clear that CMO Hillis and the FCO were not happy with his decision.

"Whether we go to the surface or not, we will die. But I want to make the decision for myself how I live out the rest of my life rather than have some mayor's decision 200 annums ago rob me of that freedom to choose. I think it's highly unfair to expect us all to die down here without at least making us aware that there is another choice and one that at the very least will eventually mean that our children don't have to deal with some of these deficiencies and deformities. Some of these can be prevented."

"Don't mince words, Cass. Tell me what you really think."

Aurora chuckled and smiled. "Sorry, just getting warmed up, I think, for tomorrow morning in front of City Council. So," Aurora said as she looked down at the body in front of her, "Mr. Jackman, I see."

"Yes."

Aurora brought her scanning device out.

"What time's the council meeting tomorrow?"

Dom's question surprised her. "08:00, why?"

"I will be there."

"What?" Aurora straightened and looked at him.

"I believe you. And I want to back you up. I think the people of Egerton deserve to be able to choose for themselves where they live. If living in this city is actually what's going to kill all of us off, we need to give ourselves the chance for our children and grandchildren to live as long as possible."

Aurora smiled as she leaned back over Mr. Jackman. "Thank you. I might quote you on that."

"I just bet you might." Dom scuffed the ground with the toe of his shoe. "I feel I should warn you, though."

"About what?"

"About what happened to Shallon Hillis."

Aurora completed her microcellular scan and met Dom's gaze. He *had* known. All along.

"Why didn't you tell me before now?"

Dom looked down at the ground. "I guess, knowing the story, I wanted to make sure you were certain about pursuing this and that there was stronger evidence than what Hillis brought forward." He looked up at her, his eyes and face riddled with guilt. "As CMO, I'm faced every day with the reality of the choice that Mayor Warton made, knowing that from a medical standpoint, most of what you see in my medical bay can actually be treated and prevented in future generations, contrary to what you've told me the mayor said."

Dom's countenance changed from looking guilty to looking confident and bold.

"And, contrary to what the mayor believed, that was not the only record of that meeting. Both before and following the meeting, Shallon Hillis made log entries detailing what he'd been observing, what he found out through testing – he didn't go through the archives like you did – what he planned to present to the mayor, and his reaction to the mayor's heinous decision to basically do nothing except terminate pregnancies.

"When we take on the responsibilities of CMO, we take an oath to do no harm as far as it is possible. Every letter of Mayor Warton's decision grates at the very soul of what we've vowed, and has limited us for over two hundred annums in what care we're able to give our patients."

"And, yet, no one has said anything or tried to stand up to the mayor since?"

Dom shook his head.

"What happened?" Aurora was terrified to ask.

"CMO Hillis was charged with treason for speaking out against the mayor's decision following that meeting. According to his log entries, and those made by the second-in-command among his medical staff when he was arrested, City Council debated what his punishment would be. In the end, he and his family were exiled to the surface, and the matter basically downplayed by the mayor's assertions that the words of a traitor, someone who wasn't acting in the best interests of Egerton, couldn't and shouldn't be trusted."

Aurora stared at Dom, mouth agape, completely speechless.

"That's why I wanted to be sure of your story and argument for going to the surface because it had been tried before."

"And you're still willing to back me and stand before City Council with me even though you could face the same fate?"

"Yes. I'm tired of this charade. And, believe it or not, there are many others who share the same feelings. Most of my medical staff, for instance, and I know there are a few councilmembers as well. The mayor thought he could stamp out all dissension, but he only succeeding in burying it for a bit until the situation has become so much worse, we really don't have any choice any longer. We have to leave."

Aurora's gaze drifted down to the body in front of her, as she tried to process all Dom had told her.

"All I needed was for someone with the courage to stand up to the mayor to come along. As strong as my feelings are about this issue, I don't think the mayor would listen or those members of city council who still support him."

Aurora looked back up at him. "What makes you think he will listen to me?"

Dom shook his head. "I honestly don't know that he will. But I think the situation is serious enough that once the people are told the truth, *they* will listen and the mayor will have no choice but to let us go. I think the fact that the message is not coming from me, someone with an obvious bias, and coming from someone like you who has upheld this law and can show what's wrong with it and how it needs to change and how the mayor has decided not to, will convince a lot of people. I believe you're the person that they need to hear the message from. The fact that I'll back you will lend more weight to your recommendation than if it came from me directly."

"But, what about ..."

"I have nothing here, Aurora." Dom's voice turned angry. "All I do is watch people suffer and die, or have to euthanize them because there's simply nothing else I can do for them." Dom's eyes had darkened from their normal light gray to the darker gray of steel. "Even if there are struggles on the surface, at least I would have the hope that moving us into the light would bring a future for these people without these medical conditions. Perhaps, it wouldn't solve everything immediately, but it would give us more than what we have now, and I believe that's worth standing up for and fighting for before there's nothing left."

CHAPTER TWELVE

Aurora arrived at the mid-way point of the back stairs of Center Hall with Dom's words still ringing through her head. Whatever fatigue had plagued her body earlier, his support of her had energized her, which was a good thing because there was still an enormous amount of work to do before the city council meeting.

Den and Barna were waiting for her.

"Sorry, I'm a bit late. I was finishing a final examination."

"Let's go in, shall we?" Barna said as she waved a hand toward the wall opposite the door to the outside.

"Go in where?" Aurora asked.

"In here." Barna pushed on the wall and a door slid silently open revealing a room about the same size as the archives. It housed a small desk on one side, and several rows and stacks of boxes, similar to the ones in the archive room. Aurora assumed that these were the medical records of the terminated pregnancies. But, hadn't the mayor said that all records of these pregnancies were to be destroyed?

"What's all this?"

Barna held up a hand, and then a finger telling Aurora to wait. She pointed at the door which was sliding shut behind them.

"How did you find me?" Barna asked.

"We were coming back up from the archives and you passed in front of us. I decided to follow you."

"What were you in the archives for? No one goes down there. That's why my office is here." Aurora was about reply when Barna's eyes widened in realization. "Wait a minute. You said you knew about the babies."

Aurora nodded.

"That's why you were in the archives."

Aurora nodded again.

"How did you find out about the babies?"

"I performed an EOL scan on Mrs. Terrence yesterday." *Had it been only yesterday?* "I discovered a caesarean section scar and confirmed with CMO Markus that the she'd had a termination because the baby had tested positive for a chronic bone condition that we couldn't treat." Aurora recounted, seemingly for the hundredth time, the results of the Mrs. Terrence's EOL and the thoughts and discoveries that led her and Den to stand in the room with Barna, although she left out her thoughts about returning to the surface. All that seemed important right now was the increasing infertility and birth defects.

Barna raised her eyebrows. "Impressive. And, yes, you are right about the terminated pregnancies."

"More and more babies are testing positive for some kind of skeletal or other kind of deformity or medical condition."

"Yes."

"Do you still work for the mayor?"

"I assume you mean the Genetic Control Officer in general, rather than me."

Aurora nodded.

"Yes. I do. Although I try to do my job so that no one really takes notice of me. I'm not supposed to stir up panic. That's getting more difficult, though, because I'm out sometimes several times a day now. Never used to be that way."

"I know. You're supposed to be virtually invisible. Unnoticeable."

Barna nodded. "So what are you going to do with me now that you've found me?"

Aurora didn't have an answer. She shrugged and smiled. "You know what, I have no idea. This was completely unexpected."

"What were you planning to do with all this information about the babies and the genetic implications of the pregnancy terminations?"

Aurora paused, her gaze locked with Barna's. She'd just met this woman though they'd probably passed each other countless times. She had no way of knowing whether Barna could be trusted with her ideas for the future of Egerton.

"I know what you're thinking," Barna interrupted Aurora's musings. "You don't have to worry about me spreading the news. I'm invisible, remember? And it might help to know that don't like my job anyway, so if whatever you're doing will mean that I can find another line of work, I'll probably go along with it."

Aurora smiled at that. "I don't know about another line of work, at least not immediately, but perhaps a change of location. I plan to recommend to City Council and to the people of Egerton that we return to the surface." Aurora related what had happened at the meeting 200 annums before.

Barna's eyebrows creased. "I'm actually well aware of that meeting. It's in the GCO archives and mandatory watching when a new person takes over the position. And I'm glad you found all the evidence you have. It's actually very encouraging."

Aurora jumped back slightly in shock.

"No, really. When you see how many scans come back and you perform all the pregnancy terminations I have, particularly over the twenty-some years I've done this job, I can't help but draw the same conclusions. Maybe not precisely why these things are happening, but they must have something to do with our environment."

"Well," Aurora continued, "part of my presentation to City Council will be how the mayor's office has covered up the seriousness of the population sustainability and medical conditions for 200 annums, and was actually presented with the return-to-the-surface option, but instead decided that pregnancy terminations were the best way of keeping more serious illnesses out of Egerton's population. And, in light of what I've discovered about the mayor's family history of mental illness, I plan to express my opinion that the mayor is no longer fit to make decisions on behalf of the people and that Egertonians be given a chance to decide for themselves." Aurora couldn't hide the disdain in her voice.

"Do you know how I was selected for this job?" Barna asked.

Aurora frowned not sure what Barna's selection had to do with the mayor's decision, but sensed she wanted to tell her story, so Aurora shook her head. "How?"

"I was selected for this because my parents died earlier than expected and I had no brothers or sisters who would remember me. That's why I'm virtually invisible. No one knows who I am. Well, I suspect there are a few who might remember me, but most don't. Do you have any idea what it does to a person's soul to take a baby, even one with a defect, away from his or her mother, let alone hundreds of them? What it does to me every time I have to tell a mother that her baby has to die even if the baby is really deformed? If, as you say, getting out of the rock and into the sun will eventually help bring an end to these, I'm all for it."

"Would you be willing to tell City Council that when I meet with them tomorrow morning, and the people of Egerton later?"

Barna sighed. "I would really like to, but if I go to the surface with you, then the rest of Egerton will certainly die. If these babies are allowed to be born with these conditions red, diamond-shaped eyes and no brains ..."

Aurora placed a hand on Barna's shoulder. She had to be the most unique person Aurora'd ever met. Wracked with grief over her job and yet realizing the impact on the society if she were to stop doing that job.

"Don't you feel that couples should be able to decide whether or not the pregnancy is terminated rather than have someone else deciding for them? If we present to them the hope that going to the surface could mean that no more pregnancies will be terminated if we get out of this rock and out into the sun, I have a feeling many will join us."

Aurora wasn't completely confident of that, but hoped it would at least convince Barna to testify and improve her argument to City Council and to the citizenry.

Barna sighed, again, then smiled. "You're right, of course."

Aurora surprised herself as she hugged Barna, and from the expression on Barna's face, surprised her too.

"What exactly do you want me to say to the council?"

"Just what you just told me. What you know about the genetic screens of the pregnancies you've terminated, that they're increasing and what those symptoms mean for the survival of Egerton overall. It's too bad we don't have the records from the scans, though. We have no way of knowing if the mayor's tampered with them once he receives them from the CMO. They just have to take your and our word for it that it's getting progressively worse."

"What do you mean 'we don't have records'?"

"According to Mayor Warton's meeting, he ordered that the records of the genetic scan be deleted except for the chief medical officer's and his own."

Barna walked behind her desk and flipped a switch on the wall. Three strings of lights lit up the back of the room revealing more archival boxes.

"I guess my predecessors didn't agree with the mayor's decision either. They've kept all the results of the genetic scans. We've also kept a log of them, how many scans came back with which conditions or deformities to track the progressive decline of the population." Barna opened a drawer in her desk and withdrew several pads. "What?"

Aurora shook the look off shock off her face. "I could kiss you! That's just the information we need!"

Barna chuckled and held up her hands. "No, no. That won't be necessary."

"Well, it seems like you ladies are set," Den said. "I need to get back to my office. The mayor's about to leave for the day and will likely have a full set of instructions for me. I'll radio you later."

To Aurora's surprise, Den kissed her cheek before he left. Her cheeks flushed hot as the door slid shut behind him.

CHAPTER THRITEEN

"Thought I might still find you here."

"Huh?" Aurora lifted her head from the table as Barna did the same, and stifled a yawn. Finally Den's face came into focus. "Oh, hi, Den. What time is it?"

"A little after mid-night cycle."

Aurora yawned.

"I thought you'd be hard at work."

Aurora glared at him. "We were, but I guess the sleeplessness of the last few cycles finally caught up with me. What's up? And what's so important that it couldn't wait until light cycle?"

Den dangled a key in front of her.

The remaining sleepiness in her body disappeared.

"Is that ... ?"

"That's the key. Fransen finished it not long ago. I thought you'd want to see it."

"Yes, of course." Aurora reached for the key.

"No, I mean, do you want to see the surface?"

"Really? You think we should go now?"

"Why not? It will answer the question of whether or not the world is safe to return to." Den shuffled a foot. "Plus, it would be the fulfillment of a boyhood dream. I'd like to be the one to see it first."

Aurora smiled. "How can I say no to that? Let's go."

With everyone else asleep except for the few needed to cover the night shift for various functions, it was pretty easy to cross from Center Hall to the north catacomb without being noticed.

Perhaps this was the ideal time to go, when no one was watching. It would give them a chance to scope out UWE themselves without anyone, except Fransen perhaps, knowing what they were doing. But, since they didn't run the risk of being seen, they walked without any flashlights or night-cycle lights. Within moments, they stood in front of the door.

"Wow," Barna sighed. "Is that it?"

Aurora nodded, though she wasn't sure Barna could see her. "That's it."

Den opened the door and they started up the stairs. At one point when they couldn't see the door behind them anymore, Den turned on the flashlight. They continued up until they reached the upper door. Den removed the key from his pocket and stared at it.

"What are you waiting for? Nervous?" Aurora asked.

Den shook his head. "No, not nervous. Anxious though. I've waited for this moment my whole life. I don't want to go too fast. I want to savor it."

Den slid the key into the slot and turned. The lock unlatched and he pushed on the door. It didn't move.

"It's really heavy," Den grunted.

"Or buried," Aurora suggested as she joined him on the top step. They pushed together and the door started to move. Just a little at first, but their efforts seemed to be loosening it and eventually the door opened enough for them to climb the last couple of steps, leveraging the weight of the door further open as they went. It landed with a soft thud on the ground.

"There's no light," Aurora said.

Den craned his neck. "Just those little twinkling things way up there."

"Well, one thing's for sure there's certainly no bombing."

She felt rather than saw Barna nod beside her. "How do we know for sure? What if they're simply sleeping? Seems like UWE is on the same waking and sleeping schedule that we are."

"Somehow I don't think wars sleep, at least not the kind of war we saw in Dr. Heinan's recording." Aurora took a deep breath. "So that's what UWE air smells like." She leaned down and touched a velvety green, diamond shaped thing just barely visible under Den's light. "This is a plant like we have in our growing houses, but not the same kind of plant. But these are definitely leaves."

Den waved the beam around the ground and the path ahead and behind them.

"Let's go this way," he said, and turned to follow the path on the right.

Along the way, Aurora saw tall, rough-skinned things with more leaves, some with three-pointed, virtually symmetrical leaves, and others with spiky leaves with brown, knobby seeds about the size of her hand. She took one off and turned it over in her hand and decided to take it back with her. Further down the path they found smaller plants some with bunches of little round bubbles, and others with pointy leaves with white stripes down the middle that looked something like a head of hair that hadn't been combed.

"I wonder what this would all look like during light cycle." Aurora looked up at the rough-skinned plants towering above her and took in the soft somewhat squishy terrain under her feet – so different from the hardness of the rocks that she knew. She was almost tempted to take her shoes off just to see what the ground felt like on her bare feet, but it was probably better to wait until light cycle. She wouldn't want to step on something dangerous.

Eventually, the large and other surrounding plants gave way to a clearing that was soft under their feet and gave a clear view of an expanse of twinkling lights in the sky along with a bright, round object. Aurora didn't think this was the light source that Dom had said would solve their vitamin D deficiency problem, but it certainly was most beautiful light she had ever seen.

Den had stopped walking clearly in awe of what he saw as much as she was. He reached for her hand and she didn't pull away.

"Is it what you thought it would be?" She whispered.

Den nodded. "It's better. Thank you."

"Thank you for what?"

"For letting me go first and for sharing this with me."

Aurora shrugged. "Where else would I be?" As soon as the words were out of her mouth, heat rushed through her cheeks and she was grateful that it was still too dark for Den to see her, though she knew he was watching her intently. *Where had that come from?* She was still a married woman, technically. Shouldn't she be fighting to stay with her husband? In both cases, Merrick had made it very clear that their marriage was over and that she wouldn't be able to convince him to change his mind. All that was left was for him to serve her with a dissolution of marriage certificate, which he likely would do after her recommendation to City Council became public knowledge.

Truth be told, as much as she loved Merrick, her feelings for Den were different. Beyond friendship, almost a soul mate that despite their deep love, she'd never experienced with Merrick. What she thought was just a slip of the tongue, turned out to be precisely what she was feeling. There was no other place she'd rather be than with Den at this moment. She squeezed his hand. He turned and looked at her then and she knew that if it weren't for Barna being with them and the fact that they knew nothing about the world in which they were walking he would have kissed her. But logic prevailed, and Aurora knew it would have to wait until later.

Aurora tore her gaze from Den's and it was then that she saw enormous black silhouettes rising out of the ground.

"What are they?"

Den shook his head, then released her hand as he walked toward one of them. "There's got to be at least ten of them."

Aurora followed him, Barna's footfalls following behind. In fact, hers were the only footfalls. *What happened to the people and animals from Dr. Heinan's files?* Dr. Heinan had said she didn't expect anybody would survive and perhaps she was right.

"Den!"

He hoisted himself up onto one of the steel structures. She reached him just as he jumped back, startled at what he found inside. He jumped down gasping for breath out of shock.

"Dead?"

Den nodded. "Dead in their seats. Obviously the war was still going on then. It wasn't the war that killed them. I didn't really think I'd find anyone in them. Like Barna said, I thought they'd be empty because people were sleeping."

"Maybe we should check the other ones just to make sure. I don't think I'm ready to declare the war over yet."

They spread out. Most of the steel structures were the same except for a tube-shaped one Aurora found on the farthest most part the green expanse. It seemed like it was half in and half out of the ground with one flat long object that drew to a point and a rounded top in the middle of the tube that was broken, with jagged sharp edges. She pulled herself up on to the flat piece and was able to look into the hole underneath the top. Inside, a figure sat slumped over the stick in front of him. It was still clothed and wore a kind of hard, rounded hat with glasses over where his eyes used to be, but these, unlike Joshua Egerton's, were rubbery around the outside instead of wiry. The ground around it was charred, crunchy like the tube had plowed into it and then exploded, like the bombing in Dr. Heinan's message.

These findings certainly confirmed that the war had been long over, though it didn't look like these people died as a result of the war but because of something else. What else could have killed them and how did it kill these people so quickly that they died in their seats, still in the performance of whatever duty they were doing? And would that something else still be a threat to them? The fact that she and Barna and Den were still alive and these people had obviously died very quickly was a good sign that it was safe now. Particularly with their bodies sequestered away from whatever germs or bacteria existed on UWE, they'd be much more susceptible to any that might be left and would likely experience symptoms pretty quickly. No, there was no longer any threat here.

Aurora took a deep breath partly in relief and partly enjoying the fresh, outside of stone, unfiltered air.

"Aurora?"

She turned as Den approached.

"What's that one?"

"I don't know. Some sort of flying tube, I think. He appeared to die of the same cause as all the rest. Something killed them really quickly. If it were still here, we would be suffering any ill-effects by now."

"That's what I was thinking too."

Barna waved at them where the tall plants and shorter, wavier plants of the opening joined.

"Guess we ought to head back."

"Yep. You have a presentation to give tomorrow."

They traipsed back along the path and back down the stairs, closing the door behind them.

Aurora almost didn't want to go back. The moment they reached the bottom of the stairs and re-entered Egerton, she longed for one more intoxicating breath of Upper World Earth. But she had a job to do first. And the next time she saw UWE, it would be to introduce their people to a new world that would be completely theirs without the trials and attitudes that plagued and destroyed the old one.

CHAPTER FOURTEEN

Aurora's heart raced, her palms were sweaty. She was almost in full panic mode. She was sure that Dom would have to resuscitate her if she didn't calm down.

Den, Barna, and Dom waited with her outside the council chambers. It was 07:59. The doors would open precisely at 08:00. Council members had been trickling in over the past thirty to forty-five minutes.

She jumped at Den's hands on her shoulders, but started to relax as his hands kneaded the stress out.

"You're going to do fine." Den's voice sent involuntary shivers down her spine, but she took the comfort for what it was worth and shook the tension from her body. "Remember, you're doing this for the sake of the people of Egerton. Their mayor and City Council have been dishonest with them and going back to surface is our only option. It's either that or we all die."

Aurora let out a big breath and looked down at her feet. "I know that."

"And you're not in this alone," Barna said.

Aurora looked at each of her supporters. "Thank you."

A lock clicked on the council chambers door, and one of the members stuck his head out.

"Ms. Cassle. You're up." The member's eyes widened as the foursome started for the door. "We were under the impression that it was just going to be you, Family Control Officer."

"I know, Member Neelins. I will be doing most of the speaking, but these three have been helping me with the Expansion Project and I didn't think it fair that they sit on the sidelines."

Council Member Jakob Neelins nodded and opened the door wider to admit all of them.

Aurora had stood in front of the Council before to present her options and suggestions for Mayor Goodwin's expansion project, so the stone circular table didn't really surprise her, but it was a relatively small room, just enough for 12 councillors and a mayor, and, given what she was about to tell them, she almost felt like the walls were closing in on her. She reached a hand behind her and Den took it. She gripped his hand so tightly that she was sure she was hurting him, but he never pulled away. When the room stopped swirling, she let go of his hand and focused on the pad in front of her, which contained the presentation that she and Barna had worked tirelessly on into the wee hours of the night cycle. Aurora'd had just enough sleep to help her get through what was sure to be the most trying light cycle of her life.

As she stepped away from her supporters into the center of the room, within view of all the councilmembers, she found she couldn't look at the mayor directly. That was kind of sad, actually. She'd always liked Mayor Goodwin. She supposed she shouldn't be angry with him for a decision his predecessor made so many years before. Hopefully, he would be objective and listen to her evidence and make the decision Mayor Warton refused to.

Because it was proper protocol, Aurora glanced briefly at the mayor as she addressed Council.

"Mayor Goodwin and honorable members of Egerton City Council. As you are all aware, the last time I stood before you, it was to present to you the proposed expansion location options for Mayor Goodwin's expansion project. Mayor Goodwin wanted this project because, according to him, the projected birth and death rates indicated that Egerton was about run out of living spaces for our future citizens. Because I trusted the mayor was bringing us accurate numbers, I took on the project and thought nothing of it even though it has been obvious to many people that there are more and more empty residence units, more and more single people because there isn't a sufficient ratio of men to women, and it is becoming more and more common for families to only have one baby before sterilization age."

She paused to let City Council digest this last statement.

"I wish I were standing before you, this early light cycle, to tell you that the expansion project is going ahead, but it cannot – at least not in the location we thought and not for the reason we thought."

Murmurs rippled around the table.

Aurora continued with the tale of Mrs. Terrence's EOL scan results and her ensuing investigation into the population numbers and archival search that led to the confirmation of medical conditions that were threatening Egerton's survival. She purposely left out mentioning the meeting in Mayor Warton's office. She had another purpose for that. She wanted to present as clear a picture as possible for council members. As she spoke, she watched the council members' faces change from curious to rage and fear.

"Councilmembers, I'm here to tell you this morning that the mayor's office was warned 200 annums ago, and several times before that, that these medical conditions would continue to arise and grow progressively worse over time, threatening our civilization, and that the decrease in fertility would mean that our population was no longer sustainable."

"How do you know this?!" One council member cried.

Just the reaction Aurora had hoped for though she was somewhat surprised that Mayor Goodwin hadn't said anything yet, but his time was coming.

"From Mayor Annis Warton himself." Amidst the cries of outrage, Aurora pulled out her pad, hit the power button, then sent the recording of the meeting in Mayor Warton's office to each councilmember's pad. When the recording finished, the council members settled into stunned silence.

"Two light cycles ago" – Hard to believe it had only that short length of time – "Mayor's Assistant Den Maron gave the final go ahead to begin construction in the north catacomb. Construction crews began immediately to set up their equipment. Later on in the same light cycle, Tannet Nalos called Den and I to tell us they'd found something. When we arrived, we found they'd discovered a door that led to a stairwell leading up."

There were gasps all around the Council table. Aurora waited for quiet before continuing.

"What is curious is that before getting Tannet's call, Den told the mayor about the decision to go ahead with the building project in that site, but instead of being happy that the project was going forward, Mayor Goodwin got mad."

Aurora cast a quick glance at the mayor's reddening face.

"Why would he be mad about the project continuing? If he were upset about the selected location, why hadn't he voiced anything during Council meetings that he'd prefer a different site? I don't really know. Why did he lie to us about the population numbers? I don't really know that, either. My speculation is, just like Mayor Warton was afraid of losing control of the city, indicated by his comments about his concern about dissension and division and the morale of Egerton, Mayor Goodwin was also afraid of losing control."

"How dare you?!" Mayor Goodwin erupted to his feet, his head bobbling slightly. "You have no right. No evidence!" He sputtered.

His outburst startled her, but she continued before he said anything else and directly addressed him.

"The people of Egerton probably already suspect that you have not been telling the truth about the numbers because they walk by these empty residence units every day, they know that so many families have one child, and many other families don't have any children.

"It is my suspicion that you, Mr. Mayor, were hoping this expansion project would maintain the illusion that Egerton is growing and thriving, when the reality is that if we don't change our situation now, there won't be an Egerton left.

"It is also my suspicion that you, Mayor Goodwin, were well aware of the information that was presented to Mayor Warton and his decision 200 annums ago, and chose to continue the practices that were obviously not helping the situation and actually making it worse. The evidence is so obvious now that our civilization is dying – even without the information from Egerton's designer Dr. Heinan, which I will play for you in a minute – the citizens already know it, but you, Mayor Goodwin continue to refuse to believe it."

The mayor's head was bobbling completely uncontrollably now. It was exactly the kind of reaction she'd hoped to get from him. Not that the physical signs of his condition would be enough to convince Council of his mental instability, but Den had told her that this was a sign that the mayor was starting to lose control, and that's what the councilmembers needed to see. Surprisingly, Mayor Goodwin said nothing. Aurora wasn't sure if it was because he didn't know what to say or he was too angry, and unstable, to say anything.

"I implore you, councilmembers, today, to rule that Mayor Goodwin is not and cannot act in the best interest of Egerton because he is also affected by a mental illness that is genetic and has been traced back through his family line, and a number of family lines of other councilmembers as well, which is consistent with Dr. Heinan's information about the effects of generations of inbreeding. Symptoms include paranoia – that is, suspicious of people around him, irrational, illogical and inappropriate reactions to life around him, speaking in ways that don't make sense." She couldn't have planned it any better. At just that moment a string of words completely unintelligible spewed from the mayor's mouth.

The gasps around the table were louder this time. And Mayor Goodwin's face blanched when Aurora cast a glance his way.

Aurora allowed herself a quick smile. *Gotcha!* "I implore you, councilmembers, to rule that the people be allowed to choose whether to live here or to return and rebuild our civilization on UWE. I implore you also to allow women to bear children past the age of twenty-one and to allow families who are able to have more children to have more children to offset the effects of infertility of other couples to sustain our population."

"I'd like to introduce the members to Barna Kindle, Egerton's current Genetic Control Officer, who is here lending her support and has extensive records going back to Mayor Warton's time that will demonstrate undeniably how bad the situation is. Chief Medical Officer, Dolan Markus, and Mayor's Assistant Den Maron" – another series of gasps – "also support my proposal. It is my belief, as it is of CMO Markus, and was of his predecessor, CMO Hillis, that the deterioration of our bodies is a result of the continual and long-term exposure to the elements in the rock around us, and the lack of natural sunlight exposure."

"And now, ladies and gentlemen … ." Aurora paused and looked at the mayor, daring him to challenge or interrupt her. When he didn't, despite his red face, turned-down eyebrows and head bobbing, she continued. "I would like you to hear from our founder's own words that we were never meant to live underground for so long and that doing so would result in the medical conditions we've documented over the years and that are increasing in occurrence."

"How do you know they're increasing in occurrence?" One member asked.

"Because, Councilmember Killick, contrary to Mayor Warton's instructions, Barna, and her predecessor Genetic Control Officers, have kept the results from the genetic scans and have tracked the occurrence of each medical condition and deformity for the last 200 annums. Apparently, those before her didn't agree with the mayor's decision either and hoped that eventually this information would be needed."

Aurora stepped aside and Barna moved into her place. As Barna described the results of the genetic scans she'd seen and the records she reviewed of past GCOs and the increasing frequency of her visits to couples, Aurora watched the faces of the councilmembers. Some kept their expressions very schooled. Others were clearly shocked by what they heard. Some, Aurora swore, didn't look all that surprised. Perhaps their family had been affected by a terminated pregnancy or infertility. Barna presented a pretty grim picture of reality facing Egerton's families. When Barna finished, Aurora expected to hear protests or cries of false information or questions, but there were none, even from Mayor Goodwin and Aurora was satisfied that Barna's testimony had done its job.

Barna stepped back behind Aurora and Aurora took the lead again.

"At this time, I would like to play for you a statement made by Dr. Imogen Heinan, Egerton's geneticist, the person responsible for us all being here on the eve of the First Ones' decent into Egerton." Aurora sent the recording to the councilmembers' pads and seconds later, Dr. Heinan's voice reverberated through the room.

As with Barna's testimony, no one spoke for a few moments after it ended.

"Thank you, Mr. Mayor and councilmembers. That's all I have for you."

"That's all? That's all?!" All heads turned to Mayor Goodwin who rose from his seat, rounded the table somewhat unstably, and entered the inner circle a few feet away from Aurora. As he shook his fist at her, she wondered if he was going to keep his distance. "I did what I did for the sake of the people of Egerton. As have all the mayors before me. All you people whining over what you've lost and forgetting the life you have down here. All you want to do is tear this apart. How is this going to be good for the people of Egerton?" He waved hands at everyone around him.

"You have no right to come in here and accuse me of not taking care of the people of Egerton and of not taking the right steps to ensure its survival."

"You can't deny the evidence anymore." Dom stepped forward essentially in between the mayor and Aurora. "The mayor's office has been well aware of these changes in our bodies and that they would continue to grow worse. Mayor Warton's decision and the decision of every mayor since to continue what he started, has only made the situation worse. No one is surviving anymore, Mayor Goodwin. We may have grown used things the way they are, but they don't need to stay that way for the next 200 annums. There may not be anyone left in 200 annums. At least on Upper World Earth our children and grandchildren would have a chance they don't have down here.

"We simply can't sustain the population based on the birth-to-death ratios now and it's been that way for the over 200 annums. The only way is to allow couples to have more children and to bring families out of the environment that's causing these defects in the first place."

"Never! I will never let [unintelligible] them leave!" The mayor stormed out of council chambers.

Those left behind sat or stood in stunned silence for a few moments.

"Aurora. Everyone." All heads turned at Dara Killick's calm voice. "Let's continue the meeting. As the co-chair, I'm authorized to lead the meeting in the absence of the mayor, and I think that it's imperative that we continue given what we've just heard and witnessed. You've presented some pretty startling evidence, today, Aurora. I think it's safe to say most of us on this council are overwhelmed at how advanced and debilitating these medical conditions are, that they're only getting worse despite Mayor Warton's pregnancy termination policy, and that the mayor, himself, has played a key role in keeping the true reality of the gravity of Egerton's situation from everyone. I will refrain from voicing my personal opinion on the apparent reasoning behind these actions for the moment. But, given what we've just observed about the Upper World Earth from Dr. Heinan's message, how do you know that going to surface is any safer than remaining down here?"

The council member used her first name. Interesting. Not usual council protocol.

"Because I've been there."

Another round of gasps.

"You've been there?"

"Yes, last night." Aurora withdrew the elongated plant seed that she'd brought back with her. "This is a pinecone according to Dr. Heinan's earth files from a tree that we saw last night. There is no direct threat to the people of Egerton from the armed conflict we saw in the clip. Everyone is dead."

"From what?" another councilmember asked.

"To be honest, I don't know. Whatever it was, it killed them fast. All the people we found were still sitting in the machines they were working in."

"How do you know that same thing won't kill us?" someone else asked, almost panicky.

"Because if it killed them that quickly, it would have killed us too and we wouldn't be standing here before you. Granted, there is also the chance that because we've lived so long underground our bodies will react negatively to any other bacteria on the surface.

"I believe, though, that this is still the best option for our survival. If we stay down here, there eventually will be nothing left of Egerton at all. And the whole purpose of Egerton was to preserve the human race so that when the war finally ceased on Upper World Earth, we could repopulate it, hopefully along with the other three underground cities."

"What about those who choose to stay in Egerton?"

Aurora looked down at the floor, then back at the councilmember.

"I've considered that question from the very beginning of my search for the truth. Despite whatever information I have, I can't force people to leave or stay. That would make me the same as Mayor Warton."

"So, that could mean that some family members would stay and some would go to the surface," the same councilmember continued.

Aurora looked back at Den. "Yes, Councilmember. That is possible."

"And if these families are split, what does that mean for the continuation of the human race on the surface?"

"That's a very good question, but it's one that I cannot answer. The reality is that there are risks to going to the surface that none of us can really anticipate. But, if we stay here in Egerton, we will most certainly, continue to suffer from these diseases and conditions, which will only worsen with each of the future generations. As I said, we can't force anyone to leave or stay, but the people of Egerton deserve and need to make that choice for themselves."

Aurora took a deep breath. So far, things had gone pretty much how she thought they would. She'd anticipated the councilmembers' questions. Now, as she looked from council member to council member, she wondered what each of them was thinking. Did they think she was crazy? Would the mayor go back on 200 annums of apparent tradition and side with her? Would he change his mind at all?

She and her supporters waited as the members chatted amongst themselves.

Finally, Dara Killick stood.

"Ms. Cassle, would you and your party mind stepping outside while council discusses all the information you have presented and considers your recommendations?"

CHAPTER FIFTEEN

Outside the council chambers, Aurora let out the breath she didn't realize she was holding.

"I don't think I've been so nervous in all my life." Aurora heaved great lungfuls of air as she leaned against the wall.

"That went far better than I thought it would," Dom said.

"Did you expect Mayor Goodwin to react like that?" Barna asked.

Aurora shrugged and looked at Den. "I had a little inside scoop on that. I didn't know precisely what he would do, but he pretty much did what I expected him to do."

"But how many of the councilmembers will still vote for what they think he would want. We have no way of knowing where their allegiances are."

Aurora nodded. "You think they'll say no?"

Barna's mouth twitched upward on one side as she shrugged. "My gut says the councilmembers will vote the way the mayor would want them to even if he isn't there, but I think a few of them will privately back you. This isn't over."

"What are we going to do if they say no?"

Aurora shrugged as she looked at Den for moral support.

"We go anyway and save as many as we can," she replied

The group fell silent after that. Aurora paced for a little bit, but eventually drifted next to Den who took her hand, so she just stayed there, her mind whirling with what she imagined the councilmembers were talking about.

She wouldn't verbalize it, but she believed Barna was right. She had known the potential ramifications of bringing this information forward. She had hoped against hope that City Council would decide the right thing and let people choose peacefully, then the only conflict would have been amongst the families of Egerton as they decided what they wanted to do.

She hadn't even seriously considered what might happen if the council voted to keep things as they were. They could all be arrested and sentenced to exile, like CMO Hillis and his family. How would they save Egerton then?

Aurora shivered and Den's hand tightened on hers.

She turned and looked at him and knew from the expression in his eyes that he was thinking the same thing.

Dom and Barna had wandered a little farther down the hall, so Aurora thought it was safe to voice her thoughts.

"I think Barna's right. What if this all goes wrong, Den?"

"You've done what you knew was right and you have exposed the truth. Whatever happens we just have to adapt and look for opportunities to do what we know we need to do. The mayor won't make it easy."

"What if we're arrested for doing so, Den? How will we get everyone out then?"

Dom and Barna had returned by then.

"How do we tell others about what's really going on and coordinate an exit if we're in prison?"

"Perhaps all we need to do is get the word out about our decision to leave. We don't know how many people have already thought or wondered about it. Remember, people may have not known about the specifics of what's been happening over the last couple generations, but they've noticed things, they've known family members or friends who have been unwell and experienced the symptoms of one of these conditions. Pretty much every family has been affected by the effects infertility. I think there is much more dissension than the mayor realizes."

"That's true. But I'm sure Dr. Heinan didn't mean for the civilization to be split. To be able to keep human beings alive and thriving on the surface, I'm pretty sure she meant for everybody to go. How successful is this going to be with only a percentage of the people she assumed would be returning?"

"I don't know, Rori. Perhaps it'll be enough to raise the sterilization age and change the two-babies-per-family rule."

"Okay. But how will we get the word out what we're planning."

"Word of mouth. We're going to have to do it individually, face-to-face. The city's grapevine will take care of the rest," Barna said. "I can start that. After all, my role is to be invisible right?"

"You're also not supposed to cause a stir," Aurora chided.

Barna shrugged and smiled. "Wouldn't be the first time I've broken a rule."

Aurora chuckled. "Well, I think now might be a good time."

"Fransen, Tannet and the construction guys that watched us go in that door, and a bunch of people we probably don't even know. All it takes is a little spark to get it going."

For the first time since she started this search, Aurora felt a sense of hope.

"It will take at least a couple light cycles to visit all of the residential units."

"As soon as we get the word from City Council, we'll have to decide what to include in our message."

At that moment, the chambers door opened and Council Member Neelins appeared and ushered them back inside with a wave of his hand.

CHAPTER SIXTEEN

The council member kept his face devoid of emotion. Aurora couldn't tell if he was happy or disturbed by council's decision.

Mayor Goodwin had returned, obviously recovered from his outburst. Aurora wondered if councilmembers had not only wanted to discuss the matters she brought forth to them, but to also try to coerce the mayor back for the vote. As she returned to the center of the council chambers, Aurora could have sworn the mayor was gloating. His head was still now and his mouth set in a determined line with one corner tipped upwards as if to say, "Nice try, Aurora."

After a few suspenseful silent moments, Mayor Goodwin stood, but didn't move out from his seat.

"Ms. Cassle …"

Aurora noticed that he didn't use her title

"… I want to commend you for your hard work and dedication to the people of Egerton to have brought this issue before City Council. I don't think any one of us could disagree that you did this with the intent of helping Egerton. However, council has voted to not allow anybody to return to the surface."

Anger, frustration, fear, disappointment all clouded her heart and mind. Aurora struggled with her composure, but she knew she couldn't let herself disintegrate here.

"You said yourself that there's no guarantee that life would even be possible or successful on the surface. Why uproot an entire civilization just for the prospect or hope that life on the surface would be the better, long-term option? It's taken 400 annums for these conditions and deformities to get to this point. I believe, and City Council has agreed with me, that our genetic screening and pregnancy termination practices will continue to slow the progress, and we would likely be able live out perhaps another 400 annums. This is the only life that we have ever known. I'm not willing to take the risk of death on the surface when we have a certain life down here."

Aurora looked from councilmember to councilmember and was relieved to see that at least a few of them, as Barna had suggested, didn't appear all that happy with the mayor's words.

"Further, the Family Control Law will remain as it is with the sterilization age of twenty-one and only two children per family. Considering most families now only have one child it seems no one is going to violating that law.

"As for you four, as much as we believe you were acting in the best interests of Egertonians, we can't have you living down here subverting the rule of the mayor's office and City Council. Therefore, it is the council's decision that you all be stripped of your titles and responsibilities as Family Control Officer, Chief Medical Officer, Genetic Control Officer, and mayor's assistant. Your access to documents and records of Egerton is hereby revoked."

Again, Aurora reached behind her for Den's hand.

"The council has also decided that you four be exiled to the surface and you will have no further contact with Egerton."

It was what she feared. What would they do now?

Aurora looked down at the floor desperately trying to keep tears at bay. Until Barna had suggested it, Aurora had really hoped that the council would see things her way or that she would be able to sway the mayor to do the right thing. Apparently, her definition of the right thing and the mayor's were two totally different things. To him, the right thing was keeping Egertonians living and dying in the dark instead of freedom of choice and living in the light.

"You four are all under arrest for subversion and treason," the mayor announced. Egerton's rarely used security officers appeared from behind Mayor Goodwin's seat and quickly tied the four's hands. "You will be kept in detention until the council decides on a date for your exile."

"No! You can't do this!" Dolan shouted as one security officer yanked him toward a different door than the one they had entered. "You need to give people a choice. You can't just sentence them all to die the way you think they would like to die!"

Aurora was too stunned to say anything and didn't fight the security officer.

The metal door clattered shut behind them. The detention cell had a single laser light in the center of the ceiling, was no more than 5 meters square, and had bench- or bed-shaped features carved into the rock presumably for the comfort of any prisoners.

No one spoke. Aurora wouldn't have been able to speak if she wanted to.

Her heart physically ached and almost had her curling up in a ball to assuage the pain. The furthest she got was leaning her hands on her thighs in a sort of half-squat.

"I-I'm sorry, you guys. I really didn't think they'd do this."

"This isn't your fault, Aurora," Den said. "If it's anyone's it's mine."

Aurora snapped her head up. "No--"

Den held up his hands. "Yes, it is. I was the one who put the idea in your head about there being a bigger problem, about the lower ceilings in the proposed dwelling units and the shorter lifespans."

"Hmm. I guess you did do that, didn't you?" Aurora conceded with a smile. "So, now, I guess we just wait."

"Wait for what?" Dom asked.

Aurora shrugged. "I honestly don't know. I think this is one of those situations where you won't know until it appears."

"Aurora? Aurora?"

The voice seemed to come from a distance. Out of a fog.

"Aurora."

It was Den's voice. Aurora opened her gritty eyes.

"Huh?"

"Aurora. Selleck's here."

"What?" Den's face finally materialized and the fog started to lift from her mind.

"Selleck's here."

"Oh." Her son looked like an Upper World Earth puppy she'd seen pictures of in Dr. Heinan's records as he looked at her through the bars. He probably never expected to see his mom behind bars.

"Hello, sweetie. How are you?" Aurora laid a hand on his cheek and kissed his forehead.

"I'm fine, mom. How are you?"

Aurora yawned. "Tired, but I'm okay. How did you know I was here?"

"Dad's staying with Caytor and told her and me about what you were doing. It's a pretty big thing when four of the town's top citizens are arrested. News travels pretty fast."

"Yeah, I guess it would." Aurora couldn't meet her son's gaze.

"I believe you, mom."

Aurora looked up, then. "You do?"

"Caytor does, too, but I think she'll choose to stay with dad."

"Choose? City Council has decided not to let anyone leave."

"When half the city decides they want to leave, there'll be nothing the mayor can do."

Their efforts may not have been in vain after all.

"Have you overheard other people talking about it?"

Selleck nodded. "At least those around us."

"And what are they saying?"

"Most know you've been arrested and why."

"Why is that?"

"They know that you were arrested for wanting to go back to the surface."

"So they don't know why we wanted to go back to the surface?"

"Don't think so. We only know because dad told us."

"How do they feel about going back to the surface?"

"Some are appalled at the suggestion, but most people I've heard think it's about time."

"Yes, it is."

Dom, Barna, and Den all approached the bars at the new voice. Seconds later, Councilmember Dara Killick emerged from the shadows.

"What are you doing here? They'll arrest you too," Aurora said.

"Then let them arrest me. I know there are at least three other members of council who feel the same way. As you know, council decisions have to be unanimous. The four of us initially voted in favor of going to the surface, but voted with the mayor when it was obvious that we weren't going to get the results we wanted, the right results, or to get him voted out as mayor, since we would have been outvoted on that, too. Plus, we wouldn't have been able to help you if we were arrested for ultimately subverting the mayor's wishes.

"As your son has already told you, word is spreading about your arrests and what you were arrested for, but they don't know the entirety of the role the mayor's office has played. You're right. The people do deserve the right to choose."

"So, what do we do?" Den asked.

Dara Killick looked directly at Den. "We give them that choice."

"How?" Barna asked.

"Look, the mayor may think that he runs this place, but the uproar over your arrests will keep him from being able to do anything about it. People are already deciding, without knowing the whole story, whether they'll go to the surface or not. The mayor won't be able to stop them if they decide to go, and most of the public opinion is on your side."

"So, what are you suggesting?" Dom pressured.

"So, I'm suggesting that you all be patient in here. Let the buzz filter through Egerton, say, over the next light and night cycle. And when people are ready to go, it should mean a relatively easy exodus. I need to go. I'll check back in with you tomorrow morning."

"I'd better be going, too, mom. Love you. Don't worry. We'll be fine."

Aurora just waved as her eyes welled up with tears and her throat tightened. Hands wrapped around the bars, she rested her head against the ones in between. To Den's credit he didn't try to comfort her right away. He apparently understood that this was a mother/son moment.

When her tears were spent, Aurora returned to her spot on the ledge. Den was waiting for her there and handed her a handkerchief.

"Thank you." Aurora dabbed away the remaining tears.

"Not exactly the response I expected."

"What me bursting into tears?"

"No, I mean the apparent response to our arrests," Den explained.

"No, me neither."

"Guess you can't stifle the will of the people for forever," Barna said.

"No, I guess not. And the will of this people is to go back to sleep.

It's been a long light cycle," Aurora said with a yawn.

They separated after that, each finding a little bit of space on the ledges and falling asleep just as the overhead light cycled off.

CHAPTER SEVENTEEN

The ensuing couple of days flew by in a whirlwind. As word of their imprisonment and case for returning to Upper World Earth spread, public opinion swayed Aurora's way so strongly that the mayor eventually had no option but to release them.

On light cycle 4 since the arrest, the scheduled day of the first stage of "The Journey" as the people started calling it, Aurora was sitting in her kitchen, packing the last few things she wanted in a draw-string satchel, including her pad with Dr. Heinan's statement. She wondered if Dr. Heinan ever imagined that the repopulation of Upper World Earth would have happened this way. With such resistance from Egerton's leader, for one, and as the result of people deciding to leave on their own, rather than as a full community.

"Hey, Aura."

She didn't have to look up to know Merrick had entered.

"Hey, Merrick."

Curiously, he didn't come any further into the house. Neither did he say anything.

When she finally looked up, he handed her a pad.

"What's this?"

"Confirmation of the dissolution of our marriage."

Aurora's heart crumbled. While she knew it was a long shot, despite her budding feelings for Den, she'd secretly hoped Merrick would actually come around. "You sure you want to do this?"

"I'm sure."

"All the years we've been together."

To Merrick's credit he at least looked almost as devastated as she felt.

"Aura, you and I both know that we can't be married with you up there and me down here."

"Yes, but why don't you come with us?"

"I just can't, Aura. I belong here. Even if living on the surface would be better, I can't picture myself living anywhere else, and I don't want to live anywhere else."

Aurora took her pad from the counter, and Merrick sent the marriage dissolution to her.

"Really, I think it's better this way."

"You're probably right. I just wish it didn't have to be."

"Me, too. Goodbye, Aura."

"Goodbye, Merrick."

In the silence that followed, Aurora plopped down one to one of the chairs as tears slid down her cheeks. *Was it possible for a person to feel so conflicted?* To one moment want to stay with someone who clearly had other plans and desires for his life and the next to follow someone who shared her vision and was prepared to be a major part of that journey with her.

That night with Den on the surface when she blurted out her feelings, she really thought she'd put Merrick aside and out of the way. But maybe she'd just buried him for a bit and was drawn toward Den because of his enthusiasm for her effort and belief in her – though she still didn't entirely know why he believed in her.

She had expected Merrick to show the same kind of attitude and support her, but his reaction had been a complete surprise, though the topic had come up pretty suddenly and must have been a surprise to him. It wasn't as if she had planned it that way. The timeline of things as they had materialized had been overwhelming for her. While she understood Merrick's position on one logical hand, on the other, she was angry too that the same attitude would be trapping Caytor and her family here denying them the opportunity to experience the new life that Aurora had fought for.

At that thought, her tears dried up. She took several steadying breaths and stretched her back and shoulders.

"Ms. Cassle."

Aurora looked up, startled. *Uh oh.* One of the security officers that had taken her from the council room to the prison. Whatever the mayor's business for sending him to fetch her couldn't be good.

"Yes?"

"The mayor has sent me to fetch you. He requests your presence in his office."

"Oh? What for?"

"I don't know. I'm just a security officer. I just do what the mayor asks."

Aurora sighed and stood as she hefted the satchel onto her shoulder.

"But I'm supposed to meet--"

"He told me to assure you that it would only be a few minutes."

Aurora didn't believe that for a moment, but she didn't see a way to get out of going.

"All right, then."

Aurora followed the security officer to the mayor's office, her mind trying to come up with a solution to get her back to the journey. They were scheduled to leave in just under an hour. Den was expecting her, but her radio was in her satchel and she doubted she'd be able to relay a message that way with the security officer watching.

When she arrived in Mayor Goodwin's office, he was standing with his back to her, head straight. He appeared to be looking a portrait of one of Egerton's former mayors.

He didn't say anything for a few minutes, and Aurora wondered if he knew she was there.

"I'm here as you requested, sir."

"Yes, Ms. Cassle. You've caused me a lot of trouble, you know?"

"It may seem that way to you, but I just did what was right, sir. I gave the people of Egerton the choice that they rightfully deserved that the mayor's office has been denying them for generations."

Mayor Goodwin whirled around then, his face so contorted with emotions Aurora hardly recognized him as the mayor she'd always known. And, she knew her life was in danger. Her heart rate increased and her mind desperately tried to piece together a method of escape.

"Oh, no, Ms. Cassle. It's much more than that. You've successfully destroyed our way of life. You've successfully destroyed our civilization and you've successfully destroyed our city."

"Maybe I did. But it was necessary. We were never meant to be down here this long. Dr. Heinan said so herself. We belong on the surface. We can continue the culture and civilization on the surface."

"You know that's likely not going to happen."

"Why not?"

"Because you know as well as I do that once people are free they won't want to stay together."

"No, I don't know that. We're still family, sir. We've grown and lived together. Perhaps eventually people will venture out, but we've got so much work ahead of us to start our lives again. I imagine most of us will stay put."

Aurora approached the desk. "We need someone to lead us, to help us through this transition. Why don't you come with us?" Despite her recommendation to City Council that he be removed of his mayoral responsibilities, Aurora hoped that once he saw the surface and the potential there, he would be drawn away from the fear that had created this crisis in the first place. Maybe she could save him, too.

"And why do you think I would even want to do that?" Mayor Goodwin shook his head.

"Part of your mayor's pledge is to serve and lead our city. We will still need a ruling body on the surface."

"Oh, I will continue to lead, but there will be no city on the surface."

Aurora stepped back. "Why?"

The mayor rounded his desk so fast that Aurora didn't have time to

146

react before he pinned her against one of the stone walls with his hand over her mouth.

"Because there will be no 'journey'. You have been the voice of dissent for the people. Once you're silenced, everything will go back to normal."

Aurora's eyes widened as the mayor back handed her across the face. She landed in a heap on the floor, her last vision being that of the mayor standing over her with an expression she never wanted to see again.

"There you are, Den. What took you?"

Den jogged up to the head of the journey line in front of the door in the north catacomb. There were too many people in the city to go up at once, so they'd decided to journey in three smaller groups with Aurora and Den leading one, then Dom's group, then Barna's group. Aurora and Den's group would go first and report back to the rest of them when the next group could follow.

"Sorry, I'm late, Dom. I was waiting for Aurora. She was supposed to meet me twenty minutes ago. I stopped by her house, but she wasn't there although it appeared that most of her stuff was missing."

"Where do you think she could be?" Barna asked.

"I don't know. We can't really go without her." Den looked around. "I half expected the mayor to be here to try to convince us one last time to stay."

"I haven't seen him at all," Dom replied.

"What do we do, then, about Aurora?" Barna asked.

Den lowered his satchel from his shoulder. "Well, I guess I'll go look for her. I know she's not at home." He noticed Selleck in the group waiting to leave. "Maybe she went to say goodbye to her daughter. I'll go there. Be right back." With that, Den jogged off.

Minutes later he arrived at Caytor's house and found Merrick in the living area.

"Come to try to convince me to leave?" Merrick said when he saw Den in the doorway.

"No. I'm actually looking for Aurora."

"Really? Isn't the first group supposed to be leaving soon?"

Den was surprised that Merrick knew this, but then supposed there probably wasn't anyone in town who didn't know the schedule.

"Yes. Obviously we can't leave without her. When she didn't show, I thought perhaps she had come to say goodbye to Caytor and you."

Merrick shook his head. "No, Aurora and I said our goodbyes earlier."

"Earlier?"

Merrick stood. "Yes, I went over to our – her house to deliver a marriage dissolution certificate."

Den found that tidbit of information interesting, but decided not to comment. Finding Aurora was more important.

"So you went to her house. How long ago?"

"About thirty minutes ago. She was just finishing up packing. I'll probably move back, now, after she's gone."

Den decided to let that comment go as well. Thirty minutes ago. "You said she was finishing packing when you were there."

"Yes."

"Hmm. I waited about twenty minutes for her and she didn't show. So, I thought perhaps she'd forgotten our meeting time or had decided to go right to the journey line. But she's not at home and she's not with the first group."

"Curious."

"Yes."

"Well, I can't help you. As I said, I haven't seen her in about half an hour."

"All right."

Den left the dwelling. Something had happened to her and his gut said that whatever that something was wasn't good.

◆❖◆

Throbbing cheek. Burning eye. Bit of a headache. Something knobby digging into her back and the back of her legs. Head resting on something hard, cold, and every time she moved her arms or legs, they bumped into something equally hard and immovable.

Finally, Aurora got her eyes open. Yes, they were indeed open, but she still couldn't see. Her hands felt the hard thing behind her head and around her body. Cold -- no, icy, and lumpy, like stone. And adult size, although she wasn't able to stretch her legs out. In fact, she had to keep them bent almost to her chest like … like a baby in a womb. But this hole was adult sized. She felt the knobby things that were digging into her back. Even in the dark she could tell they were bones. Obviously, she was not the first to use this cell.

She craned then tried to rotate her neck only for her nose to meet the rock around her. *Not much space at all. And that meant not much oxygen.*

But then, why would there be? This catacomb was meant for a person who was already dead – or, considering how she'd arrived, whom the mayor wanted dead. Her hunch was that she was resting on the remains of someone else who had suggested returning to the surface.

Then she had the craziest thought, but in her heart, she knew it wasn't all that crazy. Barna had said her parents died younger than normal. Aurora let out a little cry as she reached up to cover her mouth. Barna had known the stakes of standing up to the mayor, because her parents had done so and paid the price. In essence, Barna was still paying the price and, yet, had agreed to face those same consequences to help her. Aurora wondered why Barna's parents hadn't been exiled like CMO Hillis and his family?

Aurora took long deep breaths to calm the panic rising up in her throat, then let her breathing go shallow. There wasn't much oxygen. She couldn't waste it. Then her left hand hit something smooth and cold and … metallic. It certainly wasn't like the rock on the other side of her. It had to be the door. Aurora pushed on it. Then risked the use of precious oxygen to bang on the door, near where she thought there'd be a latch, a couple of times, but it was sealed tight.

Aurora tried to keep the tears at bay, as she laid her hand against her stomach, wondering how long she had left.

Den's mind spun. *Where could Aurora be?* He'd looked everywhere even in the most unlikely places, places he hadn't seen since he was a child hunting for Egerton's lost door.

Without even realizing where he was going, he found himself in Center Hall, staring into Aurora's office, then his own.

"What're you doing here?"

Den was surprised that he hadn't heard the mayor's approach. "Nothing."

"You know you're no longer authorized to be here."

"I wasn't snooping. Just thinking."

"Thinking of staying?"

"Not at all."

The mayor harrumphed. "I thought you'd be with the first group on your way to the surface by now."

"We were supposed to be, but Aurora never showed and it wouldn't be right to go without her. After all, she made this possible."

"That she did."

Den narrowed his eyes at the mayor's tone. "What do you mean by that?"

"She's the one that had to go and make a fuss about the expansion project not being necessary, and corralled all you people to agree with her."

"She didn't corral or coerce us into anything. The evidence was right there in front of most of the people, they just needed someone with a little more courage to say what they already knew … that the city was dying." Den stepped closer to the mayor. "Little did they know that the mayor, the man they were supposed to be able to trust, was at the heart of it. If Mayor Warton had just done what was suggested so long ago …"

"Oh, you think it would have been so different, do you? Living on the surface." Mayor Goodwin walked around in a circle. "Do you really think it would have made all that much difference? You die up there, you die down here. What's the difference?"

"The difference is our children, grandchildren, parents and grandparents have a chance to lead a healthier life up there. The walls and lights that kept us alive are also what's killing us and bringing these medical conditions upon us that we have run out of medical resources to treat."

"You think there are going to be medical resources up there? Do you really think there's anything left up there? And if there is, do you really think anyone remembers that we're down here." The mayor walked away again. "We were locked down here and forgotten. No one remembers us. We were abandoned. The only thing that kept our civilization thriving and going was the belief that we were a family and working together kept us alive. That's all we have."

"We are still a family. But the head of that family started making choices that didn't actually solve anything and actually increased the possibility that our society would eventually die off. Your fear has brought us to this. Your fear of losing your power over the people."

The mayor laughed a hollow, evil sound that made Den's skin crawl. "You call it power, I call it leadership. Making sure that we all survive as long as possible. We've already been down here 400 annums. The physical changes may be progressing, but we were coping with it and still a vibrant community that worked together. There's not even a guarantee that life will be possible on the Upper World Earth. No one knows what kind of damage that war has done or even if it's ongoing. Who would trade a sure thing of life down here, for the uncertainty of life up there?"

"You mean a sure thing of death down here."

The mayor shrugged. "Depends on how you look at it, I guess."

"How I look at it?" Den raised his hands in surrender and pushed past the mayor. "No, I'm not even going to continue this discussion with you. I'm extremely disappointed in you, Marshall. I thought we'd become friends in the time we worked together. I never would have imagined you would choose power over the people's right to live."

"And their right to die right where they belong. We don't belong on the surface anymore. Anything that's up there is foreign to us. This is home."

"That may be, but most of Egerton is leaving whether you like it or not. If you want to die down here, without even having seen the sun – whatever that is – that's your choice. The First Ones were chosen to live and we want to do that, fulfill what Egerton was designed for and that is to bring life back to Upper World Earth again."

The mayor sighed and shoved his hands in his pockets as he met Den almost nose-to-nose.

"Well, I suppose I should wish you good luck, then."

Den didn't bother responding and turned his head away. "I'm going to find Aurora."

"Kind of odd that she didn't appear," the mayor said as Den turned his back. "I mean, this was her fight. I thought she'd be right at the front of the line, *dying* to get out." The mayor tossed a satchel on to the ground in front of him.

When the mayor didn't move to pick it up, Den stepped forward. As he looked at the contents he knew it was unmistakably Aurora's.

Den glared at the mayor. "What have you done to her, Marshall?"

The mayor answered with a smirk.

Den couldn't remember when he had been so angry with someone. He'd never hit anyone in his life and yet he was oh so close to hitting the man. Perhaps he should. But, if the mayor had done something Aurora, he needed to find her, which was going to prove difficult since Marshall wasn't volunteering any information.

"If I ever see you again, it will be too soon." Den slung Aurora's satchel over his shoulder and stormed out of Center Hall.

"You're a traitor, Den!" Mayor Goodwin shouted at his back.

Den turned back.

"You betrayed me and you turned against our city."

"No. You're the traitor and you're the one who turned against Egerton. You put your fear and wants above the needs of the people. And all your fear did was drive most of Egerton away. You can't keep people in the dark, Marshall. They belong in the light and that's where we're going. I hope you can live with your choice."

Den started to walk away.

"Will you be able to live with yours?!"

With one last glance over his shoulder, Den rounded Center Hall and headed for the north catacomb where the crowd looked expectantly at him and then curiously when they didn't see Aurora with him.

So much had happened in the week since he last stood here with Aurora, with her prodding him to approve this site for the expansion. *The expansion.* Den let his mind wander a bit as it pieced together fragments of his encounter with Mayor Goodwin.

Expansion project. Right to die where they belong. This was her fight. Dying to get out. The mayor had done something to Aurora that had to do with the expansion project and if he didn't find her soon, she would die right where the mayor believed she belonged.

CHAPTER EIGHTEEN

Everything in Egerton was pretty open and public. If the mayor had done something to Aurora, he wouldn't have been able to go to the north catacomb – the site they'd chosen – since the people were gathering there. And, with so many people congregating to send the Journeyers on their way, that left three other sites relatively empty, or where few would be around to notice what the mayor was doing.

He also likely wouldn't have gone that far and risk being spotted. Going to the west side of the city would have meant either crossing the Journey line, or going all the way around the city. So that left the west catacomb out. The south catacomb would have meant a long trek, though shorter than the one to the west catacomb. The easiest access for him would have been the industrial section in the east catacomb. Den remembered that Aurora had suggested that a site behind the industrial section be included in the expansion project location consideration, but City Council at the behest of the mayor had rejected it as a possibility.

Given the mayor's odd behavior, and anger over the decision to use the north catacomb, Den didn't think it was too odd to think that's there was something in the east the mayor didn't want discovered. And, since the mayor hadn't advocated for taking the north catacomb off the consideration list, Den wondered if whatever was in the east meant more to the mayor to keep hidden than the door. Den shuddered at the thought of what that could possibly be, and his blood ran cold to think that somehow Aurora was caught up in whatever the mayor was hiding.

Den wondered how many other citizens had died for this or another cause that posed a potential threat to the mayor, and how such actions could have found their way into the inner sanctum of the earth that was supposed to have kept them safe.

So far as he knew, in his lifetime anyway, no one else had ever disappeared without explanation, but that didn't mean it hadn't happened.

Aurora had already been unaccounted for nearly an hour. He didn't know exactly what the mayor had done to her, but he hoped they weren't too late.

"Did you find Aurora?" Barna asked as Den ran up.

Den waved Barna, Dom, Dara Killick, and the other councilmembers over out of the earshot of the people waiting.

"What's going on?" Dom asked.

"I think I know where she is."

"Well, where is she?" Barna persisted.

"I'm not sure exactly, but I think the mayor's done something to her in the east catacomb behind the industrial section." Barna looked poised to ask a question, but Den continued, "Don't ask me what or where precisely. I'm not sure." Den explained his theory.

Barna's expression fell. It was the first time Den had seen her somewhat crusty personality disappear.

"I know where she is. There are adult-sized burial catacombs built into the rock in behind the industrial section. I think they were originally meant for burials when the First Ones and later generations died, but we only ever used plasma gasification, as Dom can probably tell you."

Dom nodded.

"But not every death went through the CMO's office."

"What do you mean, Barna?" Dara asked.

"I was chosen as the Genetic Control Officer twenty-five years ago because my parents had died younger than anticipated and I had no siblings. They were unable to have any more children before they reached the age of twenty-one and asked the mayor for a little more time. Their request was denied and they were punished for questioning and challenging the law. They were buried alive."

"Your parents are buried there."

"Yes."

A stunned silence fell over the group.

"Why weren't they exiled like CMO Hillis and his family?" Den nearly choked on the question.

Barna shrugged. "Don't really know. There was no explanation given. I think the punishment is completely at the mayor's discretion."

"Barna, do you know how to get her out?" Den placed his hands on her shoulders and looked at her directly.

"To my knowledge, only the mayor has the keys."

"Why am I not surprised?" Dom said, exasperated.

"Excuse me, did I hear you needed a key."

The group turned to face a man even shorter than they were.

Den almost cheered. "Yes, Fransen! Absolutely! There isn't a lock in this city that you can't get into. Let's go. We might already be too late."

♦ ❖ ♦

Aurora couldn't keep her eyes open anymore. Her short breaths weren't by choice, but because there was very little air left. The coldness of catacomb had left her with no feeling in most parts of her body, particularly those in direct contact with the rock.

Her last thoughts were of Egertonians thriving on Upper World Earth. She knew she wouldn't be there to see the success of her work and efforts, but she was content in the thought that the city was now free. Free of the effects of living in the rock. Free to rediscover and live in the sun. Free to start life anew on the surface. And free of their maniacal mayor.

That last thought was cause for celebration enough. Who would have ever thought that the mayor was capable of actually taking life just because someone did something he didn't like. She wondered how many other people previous mayors had done this to. She could no longer feel the bones on which she lay.

Aurora's thoughts turned to what life would be like on the surface. She thought again of their trek to the surface the night before they were to stand before the council. That had been at night. There was so much more to experience. She wondered what the sun was and what it would feel like. How long would it take to reverse the effects of living underground for 400 annums.

In Dr. Heinan's history files, they'd learned about grass and trees and cities and even the area of North America where Egerton had been built. It had been really beautiful at one point – before the endless war that sent them into the underground into the inner sanctum of the earth. *What an ingenious concept Egerton was! To preserve the human race in a place where war couldn't go.* Who could have predicted, though, that the city's mayor would be the one to declare war on the people of Dr. Heinan had tried to save?

Dr. Heinan had said if people didn't know where they'd come from, they'd be doomed to make the same mistakes. She wished she would be the one to make sure the lessons of past Upper World Earth would not be forgotten. To ensure what happened in the centuries leading up to Egerton and the First Ones, and what happened in the 400 annums since would not be forgotten. She trusted that Barna and Den and others would create a better world than either Dr. Heinan or Mayor Goodwin could imagine.

She smiled as she imagined them settling into life on the surface with all the colors she'd seen in Dr. Heinan's files and the sounds and smells she'd experienced in their nighttime excursion. With one last longing recollection of the refreshing, cool night air, Aurora drifted into unconsciousness.

Den, Dara, Dom, Barna and Fransen walked to the very back of the industrial section which technically ended at the back wall of the gasification unit.

"Now where?" Dom asked Barna.

"I think I know," Den said, surprising everyone. "I was fascinated with finding Egerton's lost door, as I called it, when I was younger. I tried to go down here, but the head engineer caught me and sent me on my way." Den led them down a narrow corridor barely wide enough for a grown man to fit through and drilled at such an angle that it blended well with the surrounding wall, rendering it unnoticeable to those who didn't know it was already there. *How had the mayor managed to navigate it carrying Aurora?*

"I still can't believe someone would do such a thing," Dom said.

"I know," Den agreed. "I guess it was relatively simpler to deal with individual dissenters."

"I often wonder though, someone had to notice that people had disappeared," Dom continued.

"You mean like my parents?" Barna said. "So far as I know, my parents had mentioned their intentions to only a few very close friends. My parents were skeptical about how their suggestion would be accept by City Council and told us to keep quiet until they reported back. They left in the morning to appear before City Council, and I never saw them again. I didn't learn what had happened to them until security officers appeared at my house to explain where they'd been taken. I was old enough then to take on the responsibility of Genetic Control Officer."

Barna took a big breath. "Anyway, I was basically sworn to secrecy, then, because my job required me to be invisible. As for my parents' friends, I never saw them again since they were all above child bearing age anyway. But I imagine they were threatened with the same kind of death if they ever talked about it."

They kept walking until they'd gone deep enough that there were no lights and very little residual heat from the city's heating system.

Den shone a light at the wall revealing several rows of metal doors.

"So which one is it?"

"I don't know," Barna replied.

"Aurora!" Den's voice echoed through the cavern. "Aurora!"

The group headed deeper. The deeper they went, the colder it got.

Dara rubbed her arms. "It's freezing down here. I don't know if it's because it's colder or it's just creepy."

"Probably a little bit of both," Fransen said.

"How do we know which one she's in?" Den asked, again, unable to keep the frustration out of his voice. "Even if we open every single one it could take forever to find her."

"And time is one thing we don't have," Dom agreed.

"Aurora!"

"Let's start knocking on the doors. If she's here, maybe that will help her respond. Most of these would be fairly hollow, so we might be able to find her that way," Barna suggested.

"I guess it's the only idea we've got."

"Aurora!" *Bang. Bang. Bang.*

"Aurora!" *Bang. Bang. Bang.* That one was a little closer.

Aurora turned her head toward the sound. Someone was out there.

"Aurora!"

Den! Aurora tried opening her mouth to shout, but there was not enough air to even whisper.

Bang. Bang. Bang.

The metal door. Aurora slid her hand under her body, at least she assumed it was under her body, it was so hard to tell because she was so cold, and removed a bone. She didn't think she would have the strength to knock at all, let alone loud enough for den to hear.

"Aurora!" *Thunk. Thunk. Thunk.*

Den stopped. This door sounded different. *Thunk. Thunk. Thunk.*

Tap. Tap. Tap.

161

He hadn't made that sound. It was very quiet and he wasn't even sure he'd heard something.

Tap. Tap. Tap.

He definitely heard it that time.

"She's here! I found her!" Within seconds the other three joined him, Fransen jangling his set of tools. He selected two skinny metal pieces and stuck them into the latch.

"Aurora! Hang on. We're coming."

Tap. Tap. Tap.

The interval between each tap was getting longer.

Fransen grunted with the effort of trying to disengage the locking mechanism.

"What's taking so long?"

Fransen grunted again. "Sorry, Den. These little ones are tough."

Tap. Tap.

Only two taps. Den and Dom shared a knowing glance that that was not a good sign. With another grunt and a twist and the protest of metal, the door opened and Den stood there stunned for a few seconds before he and Dom lifted Aurora out. She was frozen and barely conscious, her arms dangling lifelessly beside her. Dom checked for a pulse, and then looked at her pupils.

"She's still with us, but we need to get her out of here and warmed up."

"Come on, Aurora. Stay with me." Den scooped her up and carried her out of the cavern, laid her down on the ground, then sat down next to her and cradled her upper body.

"The best place to take her is the medical bay," Dom said.

Den shook his head. "That may be, but we can't risk going there. What can you do for her here?"

"The best thing you can do is warm her with your body heat. Let her warm up gradually."

Den looked at Aurora's face and brushed a brown curly lock aside that graced the cheek he'd longed to touch the moment she'd re-entered his life. Normally, looking at her and being in this close contact with her would have made him smile. She had re-ignited a lot of feelings in him that he hadn't felt in a long time. Now, though, her face was almost lifeless, white and he realized just how close he came to losing her. He lifted her so that her chest was against his and buried his face in her shoulder.

CHAPTER NINETEEN

Barna appeared with some blankets – Den wasn't even aware that she had left – and wrapped them around Aurora's body and legs, then started massaging Aurora's feet.

"I should go update the people," Dara said. "They should know. Do you think we should reschedule the journey?"

Den looked from Barna to Dom and then back to Dara.

"No, I don't think we should reschedule. I don't think Aurora would want that." Den looked again at Dom for confirmation that Aurora would be all right.

"Let's give her an hour or two. But, we should still be able to go today."

"All right, "Dara said. "I'll see you guys a little later then."

"I'll come with you," Barna said. Fransen went with the women without a word.

"Do you really think she'll be all right in an hour or two?" Den asked Dom, once they were alone.

"Well, we've taken care of the suffocation possibility. She's got oxygen now. The only thing left is to help her conquer the cold. She wasn't in there long enough to have anything more than a mild case of hypothermia, but it's still going to take a while before she's completely warmed up."

Den scootched over so he could lean against a wall, being careful to keep Aurora shrouded in blankets. Then he drew Aurora's knees up so she was in a ball, and used his legs to help hold her that way.

"That's good," Dom said. "We've done about all we can do. Now, we just have to wait for her to wake up."

When Aurora started to shiver, Den let out a huge sigh.

As Dara, Barna and Fransen rounded the corner and neared the end of the north catacomb, they heard Mayor Goodwin's voice. The three looked at each other.

"Uh oh," Barna said.

They drew closer until they could hear the mayor's words clearly.

"Your leader hasn't even bothered to show up for your journey, today. She has decided to stay and live and die right where she rightfully belongs. Right where you rightfully belong. We have spent the last 400 annums as family. Let's not break up that family. Stay."

Mayor Goodwin's gaze roamed over the crowd until he saw Dara and Barna, then a cloud fell over his face.

Murmurs ran through the crowd, and several people turned and started to leave.

"No! Wait!" Selleck pushed the mayor out of the way. "Please! I don't know why my mother isn't here, but she wouldn't want you to change your mind. This is the right thing. Our society, human beings – perhaps the last on earth – belong on the surface. That's what Egerton was built to do. Save a portion of that civilization because the people of Upper

World Earth had forgotten what it was like to live in peace, without people dominating and dictating how other people should live and behave. The builders of this place didn't want us to die because of their past mistakes and did the only thing they could think of to help us survive and hide us away from the life their mistakes created.

"But I think they knew the day would come when that way of life would happen down here, just like they knew these medical conditions would eventually appear, and perhaps govern the new society on Upper World Earth when that time came." Selleck turned to the mayor. "That's what you are, Mr. Mayor. The side of social isolation that the creators of Egerton saw coming. Perhaps we were all too passive to demand things be different or notice things that were happening around us that we knew were wrong.

"We just followed blindly because we thought that's how life was supposed to be. Then my mother found information that that's not how life was supposed to be at all. That there was something else and that we were the last best hope for human beings to survive on UWE. Yes, death is inevitable, but we were meant to live.

"I beg of you all, please wait! My mother will be here!"

Dara jumped up beside Selleck. "We found her."

"You found her? Where?"

The mayor took several steps back.

Dara retold the story of the adult catacombs with Barna adding about her family. As they recounted, the crowd gathered closer together, the story seeming to galvanize the group.

"How can you accuse me of such things?" The mayor pleaded. "I've only wanted what was best for our whole family."

"I don't think anyone believes that now, Mr. Mayor," Barna said.

"You and your predecessors have been killing off people who dared challenge you and suggest that we could lead better, healthier lives on the surface – including Aurora Cassle."

Angrier murmurs rippled through the crowd.

"Aurora? Aurora. Can you hear me?"

"Huh?"

"Come on, Aurora. We need to get you moving so you can warm up more."

Den's face came into focus as Aurora's eyes opened and the haze from the cold and airless tomb cleared from her mind.

His was the most beautiful face she'd ever seen.

"Hi, there, beautiful." Den's mouth came down on top of hers. Whatever cold remained in her body seemed to disappear.

Aurora felt her cheeks warm, and she put her arms around Den's shoulders, and he wrapped his arms around her.

"You found me."

"Yes."

Aurora sat up completely then. Unfortunately, that meant that Den had to pull his arms away.

"I don't think I've ever been so cold my whole life." Aurora noticed Dom, then. "Both of you?"

"Dara and Barna helped as well."

"And we had a little help from Fransen," Dom added.

Aurora rubbed her legs and arms, and stood, though her legs were wobbly underneath her.

"Gotta give your legs and heart a chance to get used to you being upright," Dom said, as Den held Aurora's arm.

Aurora shook her legs to get the blood circulating again.

"Where are Dara and Barna?"

"They went to tell the people what happened to you and to tell them to wait for you," Dom responded.

"They haven't left, yet?"

"No. We didn't tell them that we thought something had happened to you, but no one wanted to leave without you," Den replied.

"How did you find me?"

"When you didn't show up at my place and you weren't at the journey site, I went looking for you. I had a chance encounter with the mayor who dropped little hints about what might have happened to you. Barna told me about what happened to her parents and I realized that I knew where this place was because I found it once as a kid. Fransen overheard us talking and volunteered. We called and knocked on the catacomb doors, hoping you would be able to respond and you did."

"I don't remember, but I guess I must have." Aurora took a few big breaths, and shook the pins and needles out of the ends of her fingers and toes. "Well, let's go."

"Are you sure? You don't want to wait a little longer?" Dom asked.

"Well, I'm not one hundred percent yet, that's for sure," Aurora leaned over, her hands on her knees for a moment, and then straightened, "but I'm ready to go." Aurora linked her fingers with Den's and knew he would never let go.

It took about fifteen minutes to get to the north catacomb since Aurora couldn't go as fast as usual. What they saw as they emerged from around Center Hall stunned them.

The group of Journeyers picked up the mayor. Fists shook in the air and angry voices ricocheted through the catacomb as Dara, Barna and Selleck tried to stop them.

Aurora had never seen such anger and she burst into a run.

"Aurora!"

Den's worried voice carried from somewhere behind her. She knew she shouldn't be running, but she had to stop them.

The group pinned Mayor Goodwin up against a wall as the group advanced.

"Wait! Stop!" Aurora's voice rang over the crowd, the catacomb amplifying. She ran up to the front of the group and forced herself between them and the mayor.

"Stop! You can't do this."

Angry bursts erupted from the crowd. "But he ..."

Aurora held up her hands, then turned so her gaze met Mayor Goodwin's. "I know what he's done. But this kind of thing is not what the builders of Egerton would have wanted. From what I learned about UWE before the First Ones were sent down here, wars were started from retaliation like this.

"I know he has done some terrible things. I know you want to punish him. I know he deserves to be punished for what he's done, for what all the mayors before him have done, but this isn't the way."

"He will get to live out his life down here, just like he always wanted. He's rejected the promise of the light on the surface, and the healthier life it could mean for him and the others who decide to stay behind. They will always be welcome, if they choose to join us. But, Mayor Goodwin, by his own choice will remain here and live out the life and death he wanted for everyone else."

Aurora turned to the crowd, Den and Dom arriving by her side by then Den handed Aurora her satchel. "As for us, let's go home."

Cheers rang from the Journeyers and from the other residents who'd gathered to watch.

Aurora gave the door a shove. There was a moment of awe as the people stared at the gaping hole and they realized the enormity of what they were about to do. Aurora stepped inside.

People gathered around to see the way to the surface. There were no lights, so it was difficult to see. Den pulled a night cycle lamp from his satchel and handed it to Aurora, who followed the cavern straight ahead for a bit before arriving at the base of a long set of stairs that curved upward into the darkness.

She looked back at Den, then back up the stairs. "Well, here we go." Up and up they went for what seemed like forever. Aurora stopped several times to let her lungs and body rest.

"You okay, Rori?"

Aurora sighed. "Yeah. It's a longer climb than I expected, and I don't think I'm quite recovered from being buried alive." She straightened with a big breath as journeyers bottlenecked behind her. "But, I'm ready to see the sun."

Several eternities passed before Aurora was stopped by the shield door. She stepped aside to let Den through with the key Fransen had made. The two of them pushed on the door, which gave way much easier than it had the night they'd ventured up. When it fell back against the ground, they were met with blinding sunlight. Even though they couldn't actually see the sun through the canopy of the trees, everyone had to cover their eyes with their arms and blink away as they looked toward the ground.

The receding glare revealed a wonderland of color and textures. They were surrounded by the tall, rough-skinned plants – which Aurora announced to everyone as trees – most of them with the needly kind of leaves and varying shapes and sizes of pinecones, similar to the one Aurora had shown City Council. The ground which she couldn't see when she, Den and Barna had come up during the night, was a deep brown and covered in a blanket of dry, crackling needles.

Smaller plants with diamond-shaped lighter green leaves and round things growing atop long green stems of varying shades of purple, pink, and white crowded their feet. Some Journeyers stooped to touch them, while others looked to the brilliant blue of the sky in awe as one by one and two by two, Egertonians stepped on to Upper World Earth.

Tiny, winged, buzzing things flitted to and fro, as did bigger, fluffier creatures above their heads. Those ones didn't buzz, but instead emitted cheerful musical tones.

Aurora placed folded hands at her chin as tears streamed down her face. She breathed in big gulping breaths of Upper World Earth air. She smelled the greenery, the earth beneath her feet, the intoxicating scent of the evergreens. Upper World Earth was simply breathtaking in a way that she hadn't been able to fully appreciate in the dark.

Den touched her shoulder as she turned this way and that trying to take it all in.

"Are you all right?"

"It's so beautiful, Den," she gasped, breathless as she tilted her head up once more. "More beautiful than I ever imagined. So many smells! So many colors! So many sounds!"

"I know. I think everyone is just as enthralled as you are."

Aurora looked from person to person and group to group.

This was all new territory and they had no idea what to expect. She dragged her mind from the wonder about her and focused on what the people needed at the moment and that was shelter before the light in the sky went out. It wouldn't do well for them to get stuck out here in the dark not knowing the lay of the land yet, or for someone to wander to the clearing she, Den and Barna had found.

"Well, I suppose we ought to round everybody up and try to find the city. That's the likely the best place to find shelter."

"Do you know which way to go?"

"Well, we went that way, last time." Aurora waved a hand to their right. "I don't think we want that to be their next vision of UWE, so let's go left. I believe Dr, Heinan left us a map although in the rush, I didn't have time to study it all."

Den reached into his satchel and pulled out his pad. As soon as it clicked to life, a new icon appeared "Acquiring Location."

"Better than that." He showed her the map that appeared on the screen with an arrow saying "You are Here" and a dotted path indicating how to reach the city limits. The journey would take them about an hour, although with 800 people, Aurora assumed it might take a bit longer.

"Well, let's get going then. It's about four hours after mid-light cycle. We should still have enough daylight to reach the city and then we can settle there for the night." Aurora turned to the gathered crowd. "Everyone stay as close to each other as possible. Do not stray into the forest. I will tell you all about what you're seeing along the way."

About thirty minutes later, the group emerged from the forest into a vast clearing which alternated between tall, skinny brown plants that swayed in the breeze and rocky, the structures of the city visible in the distance.

"There it is," Aurora said with a deep breath of satisfaction and anticipation.

A little farther along, the rocky and grassy plain gave way to a wide, hard-surfaced, black-topped path that led to and away from the city. Aurora had read that these were called roads and were usually used by motorized vehicles. But these roads weren't smooth like the ones in Dr. Heinan's pictures. They were cracked and uneven, as if the earth were taking back what humans had paved over. Aurora looked right and left and didn't see any cars, at least none that were moving. There were heaps of what looked like cars, but nothing moved. Some of the heaps were mid-road. Some were nose first into the rocks and grass on the side of the road.

She waited for Den to catch up to her. Her sense of excitement, anticipation and wonder, turned to fear as she imagined what lay before them in the city. She interlocked her fingers with his and squeezed.

"What? What is it?"

"Something doesn't feel right. These metal things, these cars should be moving and yet they're just sitting there. What could have happened to them?"

"I think they're just like the machines we found. What's this place called anyway?"

"Badgertown. Apparently, a badger is one of the creatures that usually live in the forest we just came through."

"They named their city after a forest animal?"

Aurora shrugged. "I guess so. Well, the sun is going down. We'd better keep moving." Aurora continued on, following the directions on the pad, though getting there was much simpler without all the rocks to navigate. Soon, they came to a string of single and sometimes two-storey structures down either side of the road. Aurora announced to the group that these were called houses and that people of Upper World Earth lived in them, though, like the cars, they were run-down and collapsing and abandoned.

She wouldn't let go of Den's hand. This was just too creepy walking where all these people had once lived and now served as their burial place. But, while there were circular and splattered black marks from what she assumed had been the bombs she'd heard in the recording, only a few of the houses appeared to have been affected by such a thing. Aside from the fact they were falling down, there was no other sign of structural damage. Hopefully, that meant some sort of building had survived and would be able to house the Journeyers.

By the third and fourth row of houses in, Aurora couldn't stand it anymore. She had to look in one of them.

She tugged Den in the direction of one, while telling the people to wait on the road.

"Aurora, you're not doing what I think you're doing, are you?"

"If you mean, looking inside of one of these structures, yes."

He stopped and stood in front of her so she had to look him in the eye, and lowered his voice. "You have no idea what could be in that place. You don't know if there's something that could kill us or not. If something could kill *you* or not."

"No. I don't. But I have to look. When you think about it,

everything up here is dangerous to us. Animals, the air. We know something happened here besides the armed conflict we saw in Dr. Heinan's message. This is a very dangerous place. But I have to see inside. I can't explain it."

"Well, why not just wait until we find Dr. Heinan's office?"

"Because I can't. I have to see for myself. Not just listen to her explanation or anyone else's."

"Look, it's not likely you're going to see anything."

"Then I have nothing to worry about, do I?" Aurora brushed past him.

"Aurora, I really don't think this is a good idea." He took her arm so she spun around to face him again. "You've already been through a lot today. You're exhausted. I'm exhausted. We're all exhausted. We need to rest and we need to get to the city before the sun goes down so we can find a safe place for us all to sleep for the night."

"I know. I won't stay long, I promise. And I know I might not see anything pleasant in there, but sooner or later we'll have to look. I have a feeling we have a lot of cleaning up to do. If you don't want to come with me that's fine." Aurora waited until Den released her arm, then headed up the smaller hard-surfaced road leading from the main road to the house. After several moments, Den's footsteps followed her.

This house was in slightly better shape than the rest they'd seen so far. It was at least still standing. *Probably not safe for living in anymore, but still standing.* The front yard Aurora assumed used to be covered in green grass, just like the pictures in the files. Now it was just brambles and brown spindly plants that swayed almost above their heads. It occurred to Aurora that there could be creatures living in there as well. She recalled the accounts of creatures called squirrels that climbed trees and gathered nuts, and cats and dogs that people used to have as companions, and raccoons that were black and white and had little masks on their faces. There was no telling how any of these creatures might react to their presence.

She slowed her pace as she neared the house, allowing Den to finally catch up with her. The hard-surfaced road actually finished in front of a smaller square structure separate from the house. Aurora walked up to this first and touched the metal door. It made a similar sound to the door of her tomb and she shivered. Her heart raced and her breaths came in great gasps as she felt like walls were closing in on her as she recalled her earlier ordeal.

"Aurora! Aurora!" Den's voice brought her back from the brink of panic. Then his hands were rubbing her back. "You're fine. You're fine."

"Yes, I'm fine." She managed between gasps.

"Let's look in this one," Den said as he led the way down a small paved path that ended at a small set of steps and a door. There was a big window beside the door, but it was too dirty to be able to see anything inside.

As they opened a flimsy wire door, Fransen Tines trotted up to them.

"Looks like this is my area of expertise," he said as he indicated the knob mechanism on the door with a wave of his hand.

"Looks like it is," Aurora agreed and stepped out of the way.

Fransen took a pouch of tools from his satchel and stuck two thin metal sticks into the lock. After wiggling the two pieces inside the lock for a second or two, the latch gave way and, with a turn of the knob, the door swung open.

The same sense of dread that was compelling Aurora to go back was also drawing her into the house. The first room, which was on the right, appeared to be a sitting area where there were some once-fluffy cushiony structures. But no critters, except the occasional spider and creepy crawlies that Aurora had read about. A hallway seemed to divide the house in two, and a little ways beyond the living area on the right was another small corridor leading farther into the house.

"Okay, Aurora. We've established that the house is empty. Can we please go now?"

Aurora was tempted to continue, but Den was right. Besides, everything was just far too creepy. She hadn't really been sure what they would find once they reached the surface, but she had at least assumed that there would still have been survivors of the war. She had never contemplated the possibility that everyone was dead. *What if they were the only survivors of Upper World Earth?* Yes, there were three other underground cities, but what if the people hadn't gone down in time? What if they had suffered the same fate as it appeared everyone in Badgertown had? Egertonians could very well be facing the possibility that they were the only human beings left – 2700 people left out of a world that used to hold several billion.

Aurora followed Den and Fransen outside and closed the door. She would have to do more investigating later. Right now, she needed to get everyone settled for the evening. When she reached the main road again, she waved a hand for everyone to follow.

CHAPTER TWENTY

As the road went on, more and more houses appeared, and smaller roads branched off from the main road into collections of houses – communities, Aurora recalled – though, like the earlier houses, they were mere skeletons of what they once had been. The occasional business-looking type building was mixed in with the houses. The signs were unreadable, so it was impossible to tell what the businesses had been for.

In the distance, taller skeletons could be seen. But a glance at the sun told Aurora they wouldn't be able to make it there before the night cycle. They had all walked a long way and it was time to rest. They came upon a large, single-storey oblong building that looked like it would accommodate a large crowd.

The Journeyers mingled in the large paved area while Aurora went ahead to inspect the building.

Thankfully, the double-doors opened without trouble and led into a smaller space, and then another set of doors leading to a large, flat space surrounded by a series of stone seats. It seemed people used to sit and watch whatever activity was going on in the flat space in the center – an arena. Well, the activity this time would be sleeping.

"What do you think?" Den asked from behind her.

"I think it's perfect. It's relatively clean. Let's bring everyone in. Assign one or two guys – perhaps Selleck and Fransen to do a bigger inspection of the building. There could be creatures hiding out in places that we can't see."

"What about food?"

"Everyone was told to bring several days' rations, but, yes, we'll have that to worry about, too. I seriously thought there'd be more here. But it looks like we're going to have to do everything ourselves. Dr. Heinan's files showed berries and fruit and which animals would be good for food, but there's no way to know if they still are okay to eat. We'll have to find some and test them. And it would take several months to grow anything."

"Well, it wouldn't take much to set up some growing shelters like we had in Egerton."

"That's an option. But according to the pad we're into what they would have considered the Fall or Autumn season. Things are going to start getting colder, cold enough that these clothes" – Aurora waved a hand at her body – "won't keep us warm enough."

Den held up his hands. "I know. There's a lot to worry about. Let's just get everyone settled. I'll get Selleck and Fransen investigating."

Moments later, Aurora could hear Den relaying instructions and directing people inside. Soon, happy chatter filled the center and seating area, while some choose to stay in entrance space.

She decided to do a little bit of searching for herself. A million thoughts flooded her mind as she considered the new life ahead of them, and she knew she couldn't completely hash things out with everyone milling about and talking. She needed a quiet secluded place.

She headed back out to the entrance area and noticed a hallway leading away from the arena. *Perhaps offices?* She wove her way through the crowd and discovered several open doors along the way.

The first door opened into what appeared to be an area used to prepare food. Assuming any of the cooking devices still worked, this room would come in very handy. The second door did indeed open into an office. An old desk and plastic chair sat in one corner. The place was dusty, but functional. Still, Aurora had a sense of the creeps as she entered, as if someone were running spindly cold fingers along her spine. Someone had died in this room. Four hundred annums had been enough for there to be nothing left of whoever had once occupied this office, but the spirit was here. She'd have to get used to it. There was going to be a lot of similar type feelings in the other buildings they would have to visit.

Aurora closed the door almost all the way, brought out a night cycle lamp from Den's satchel, turned it on and set it on the desk, then sat on a chair. That's something else she would need to worry about – electricity. The night cycle lamps would only work so long. Dr. Heinan's files had mentioned technology that was able to turn the sun's energy into electrical power for the city. She would have to see if those systems were still usable, or at the very least fixable.

As ideas, worries and problems fought each other for space in her mind, she laid her head against the back of the chair. *So many things to worry about. So many responsibilities, so many lives depending on her.* She really hadn't anticipated that Upper World Earth would be in such sad condition. She hadn't expected it to be pristine condition, but neither had she expected to have to repopulate it pretty much from scratch. She wondered how many of the 800 people that had come with her and Den had started worrying about the same things she had. How long would it be before they started grumbling to return to the relatively secure and familiar Egerton? And when they did, would she be able to convince them to stay, particularly if she were entertaining similar thoughts?

Coming to the surface stepping out of the darkness and into the light, had been a new hope for them. Now that they were in the light, and the challenges before seemed almost insurmountable, life in the darkness might be looking a whole lot more attractive to some.

It would be all too easy to turn around and go back. And, yet, she knew there would be no going back. They couldn't now. Not only would the mayor forbid it – she wondered for a brief second what kind of mind games he was playing on the rest of the Journeyers who were waiting for word from them as to when the next groups could come – but Aurora reminded herself that UWE was where they were supposed to be and that the First Ones had been chosen, set apart for the purpose of bringing life back to the lifeless planet when the time was right. Still, it seemed relatively small comfort given the odds facing them at the moment – power, food, shelter, clean up, rules and guidelines to keep everyone safe and the new civilization flourishing.

"You're not having second thoughts are you?" Den stepped into the room, flooding it with light, although the light likely would have been brighter if during midday rather than the end of the day.

He leaned his back against the wall and Aurora went to him and wrapped her arms around his waist and laid her head on his chest. She sighed as his arms wrapped around her.

"I had them for a brief moment," she admitted, as his heart kathumped beneath her ear. "But I know there's no going back. I just never imagined there'd be so much to do. I mean, there's barely shelter up here suitable for all of us. There's just so much for us to learn to even begin to live up here. In Egerton, everything was really provided for us. Here, we have nothing."

"You really think we have nothing. I think we have what we need. It's around us. We just need to discover what this world has to offer and learn how to use it. Carry on a civilization of helping each other and looking out for each other. That was something that the later citizens of Upper World Earth lacked."

"Yes. I'm determined to not repeat those mistakes, but it would be so much easier if I didn't have to worry about children starving to death."

Aurora listened to his heartbeat for a moment. "I just had to get away from them. They can't see that I have even an inkling of doubt or discouragement. They trusted me that this was the right decision and they're looking to me to make this happen.

"I have no way of knowing what doubts or expectations any of them had about coming up here, whether Upper World Earth meets their expectations or terrifies them."

"Well, from the chatter I've heard as people have been moving in, some are frightened. Obviously, this is a huge step, and things are very uncertain. But they also understand that it could take some time to really get Badgertown up and thriving again. If that's what we're going to call it."

"Well, I guess they have more faith in me than I do, right now. And, what do you mean 'if that's what we're going to call it'?"

"Just something I've been mulling over. If we're going to make a new civilization, why keep the old names?"

Good point. "Great. So not only do I have to come up with food, long-term shelter and electricity, I also have to come up with a new city name?"

"Who says you have to do all that?" Den tilted her chin up so her gaze met his. "You're not alone, Aurora. I know you feel like this is all on your shoulders, but I will help. Selleck and Fransen and a few others will likely step forward as the need arises. Once the other groups start coming up, you'll have Dara and Barna and the other city councillors as well."

"When the other groups get here?" Aurora slumped against his body. "That makes me feel loads better. Instead of 800 people, I have to worry about 2500 people."

"*We* have to worry about 2500 people."

Aurora sighed. "Okay. *We.*"

182

"Aurora?"

"Mm?" Aurora looked up him

As Aurora tilted her head up to look at him, Den slanted his mouth over hers in the deepest, most passionate kiss she'd ever experienced. If it weren't for the sounds coming from down the hall, she was sure they wouldn't stop. The sounds of a new civilization faded out until all she knew was his body against hers, the scent of him, the memory of his face and his arms around her when she awoke from being in that burial chamber.

When the kiss stopped, Aurora rested her forehead against his, her chest heaving. She laid a hand on Den's chest, as he too wrestled with his impulses nibbling just below her ear along her neck. She was a free woman Merrick had made sure of that. And, surprisingly, it wasn't the memory of him that had stopped her. It would be so easy to give in and surrender to the heat in her body right now. As Den nuzzled the spot where her neck and shoulder joined, his breath sent her nerves spiralling. It would be so easy. But, although her body was ready, her soul wasn't yet and she needed to be sure it was before joining with him.

"Not yet," she said, her voice barely audible as he brought his mouth back up to hers and nodded.

"Not yet," he agreed. "I've waited 20 years to do that."

His quick, heavy breaths left no doubt in her mind what his body wanted to do. She kissed his lips lingeringly before pulling away.

"I know. Me, too. But it's not the right time yet."

"I know." He almost growled it.

"I'll take one more, though, before we go make sure everyone's comfortable."

◆❖◆

Aurora rested her head against the brick building as she looked up into the sky. It was a shade of blue she never even knew existed. Strange that she hadn't noticed it that night they'd come up. Perhaps it was because of the trees overhead when they'd emerged. But, it was such a change from looking up at a constant, never-changing hue of gray-ish brown rock and laser lights.

Many of the residents had already settled down to sleep. Given the ordeal of her day, Aurora knew she should be asleep too, but her mind spun with the possibilities of tomorrow and the incredible expanse of sky above her. Next to the vision of the forest and sunlight as she came up out of Egerton, the night sky with its smattering of sparkling twinklers had to be the most beautiful thing she'd ever seen.

"Hey, mom."

Aurora ripped her gaze away from the stars overhead and hugged her son.

"Hey, honey. They're beautiful aren't they?"

Selleck looked up, as she had been doing just a moment ago. "Yeah. What are they?"

"They're called stars. Apparently, they're balls of super-hot gas and they're far away from here. The sun is a star, too, but it's much closer than those ones. According to the files, people from Upper World Earth used to travel to the stars. They'd made it to the moon – that object over there." Aurora pointed out a c-shaped object. "They'd sent probes and automated explorer robots to other planets, and there had been plans to try to build colonies on the moon, and a planet called Mars. Don't know if that actually happened or not."

"So much to learn."

"I know." Aurora turned her attention fully on her son. "How are you and Sinnie doing, and Morgan and Mayley?"

"We're fine. I think we're all sufficiently tired that it didn't take much convincing to get them to go to sleep. Sinnie's asleep now, too. I just wanted to see you and tell you how glad I am that you're all right and that Den and the others found you."

Aurora hugged him and kissed his forehead. She covered her mouth with her hand when she realized what she had done.

"I'm sorry. I don't know why I did that. It's not like you're a child."

Selleck laughed. "Don't ever be sorry, mom. Like I won't ever be sorry that I followed you here."

"Not even a little? We've got a lot to do. And what about Caytor and your father--"

Selleck raised his hands. "They made their choice. And I'm sure Caytor will follow when she feels the time is right. But we made ours and we're behind you, mom."

"Thank you."

"Well, I'm going to get to sleep."

"Good night, then."

"Good night, mom."

Aurora sat on the ground, her back and head against the wall, and closed her eyes. She didn't just want to see this whole new world, she wanted to hear it. There were so many sounds and she really had no idea what any of them were. She'd have to review Dr. Heinan's history files again. The loudest sound was a high-pitched chirp, actually a series of high-pitched chirps, probably from several of the same creature that never seemed to stop. She remembered reading about small, black, flying creatures that jumped that rubbed their wings together to make noise and wondered if they were making that sound now.

The crunch and shuffle of footsteps coming toward her dispelled her enchanted mood.

"You going to come in and get some sleep?"

Den sat beside her and took her hand and even with her eyes closed, Aurora could feel him looking at her.

"Yeah," Aurora replied, dreamily. "The night sights and sounds are so different than the daytime ones. Almost makes me forget all the work ahead of us."

"Yes. They are."

"I wonder if we'll ever get them all figured out which sound belongs to which creature when we hear it but likely won't see them."

"I don't know. What I do know, though, is that you need sleep. I don't know about you, but this has been one of the longest cycles in my life."

"I think they're called days, here, Den."

"Days, huh? Even though the sun has gone down?"

"Yep. They called a full twenty-four hour period, light and dark, a day."

"Come on, Aurora," Den said with a sigh as he stood and held out his hand. She looked up at him. "You're beyond exhausted. I've cleaned out that little office as our space."

Aurora smiled and took his hand. "Our space. I like the sound of that."

186

CHAPTER TWENTY-ONE

Bright sunlight streamed through the windows of the entrance hall, at least those parts of the windows which weren't completely caked with grime. But it was just enough light to wake the new residents of Badgertown, and just enough to wake Den and Aurora.

Aurora sighed as she felt Den's arms around her and his body spooned against hers. She rolled over and completely buried herself under the blanket and around his body.

"I could handle waking up every morning to this," she murmured.

"Me too." She sensed his smile as he kissed her forehead. She raised her mouth to his, and desire spiraled through her, as his hands found their way under her shirt, and then down around her bottom and pulled her closer.

"Mmm. I could definitely handle this." She kissed him again as she traced the outline of his chest. It was dark when they'd entered the night before and this was really the first time she'd seen him without a shirt on. His chest was smooth except for a mass of curly, black hair just around his collarbone, and well-defined. His stomach was smooth down to the waist band of his boxers that barely contained what he was feeling. She lowered her mouth to tease a nipple eliciting a moan from him.

"You're so beautiful, Den." She felt her cheeks flush with heat and she raised a hand to her mouth as he chuckled. "Ah, I mean … ."

He tipped her mouth up to meet his. "Thank you. Don't you ever be shy around me. I think I can handle it."

Aurora smiled. "Okay."

"Besides ..."

"What?"

"You're the most beautiful thing I've ever seen."

Aurora pulled herself away and abruptly stood and walked away.

Den flopped back against the hard floor and groaned. "You sure know how to kill a mood, you know."

"What about Melle?"

"What?"

Aurora turned back to him her arms crossed. "What about Melle? You had to have thought she was beautiful at one point."

Den sighed, then stood and pulled his pants on before approaching her and rubbing her arms with his hands.

"So that's what's got you so serious all of a sudden. Yes, she was beautiful to me. Still is. And, I assume Merrick is still to you."

Aurora shrugged and nodded.

"They will both be a part of our lives. I know for me, I'll never regret my relationship with Melle. I regret, in some ways, not asking you to marry me when we were younger ..."

"You what?"

Den looked at the floor. "There it is; I guess my little secret is out. Yes, I was about to ask you when Melle came into my life, which was about the same time Merrick came into yours."

Aurora nodded again. "What was it about Melle that made you not ask me?" She didn't know why she felt bashful with him. She'd never really battled with her self-image before, but there was a certain bit of competition. If he'd been so close to asking her how could he have been distracted by Melle's entrance into his love life?

Den shook his head and drifted toward his shirt laid out on the desk. "I really don't know. Why did you go with Merrick if you'd wanted me?"

This time Aurora shook her head. "I don't know, either."

Den pulled the knit sweater over his head, then drew close again and pulled her against his body.

"You're not competing with Melle in my heart, Aurora. You and she are two totally different women, and you're both beautiful. And it just so happens, you're the one I'm with now, so you're the only one that matters. You don't love Merrick the same way as you love me, do you?"

Aurora shook her head again. "Absolutely not."

"Well, then I hope I've made my point. So, I will say it again, you're the most beautiful woman I've ever seen." He kissed the tip of her nose. "And I can't wait until I can have all of you."

"But, before that, we have a civilization to build."

Den groaned good-naturedly. "Ah. There you go again, killing a perfectly good mood."

Aurora slipped on her clothes, then touched a hand to his cheek and kissed him. "That's okay. I'm pretty sure you'll have more of them."

As she took her pad from the top of the desk and tapped it on, she realized he was completely right. She loved him in a totally different way than she had loved Merrick. *Had loved?* Didn't she still after being together so long? As she thought about it, she knew she hadn't felt this kind of emotion coursing through her right now when she was with Merrick. Den had touched her in ways Merrick hadn't been able to. And she really couldn't explain why or how. There was no competition in her heart either.

"So, what are we doing next?" Den's breath on her cheek startled her and she jumped. "I'm sorry. Was I interrupting a deep thought?"

Aurora's cheeks flushed again and she tried to counter his effect on her by focusing on the day's chores.

"I made a list, last night, of a lot of the things we have to do. I'm sure more will come to me over the course of the light cycle—er day. They're in no particular order. I just wanted to get them on a list with the hope that it would help me figure out what to do next."

"Well, perhaps we should send word to Egerton to send the next group."

"But, where would we put them?"

"I suggest leaving our group here. We only got this far because we left so late in the light cycle. While we're waiting for them to come, you and me, and perhaps a few others, can continue on ahead, deeper into the city. There's got to be another building like this one, or something else that could host the next group. We obviously can't live in these places forever, but it'll give us a couple of days to explore the city more."

"I did have this thought of settling each journey group in a different area of the city, but I think splitting us up like that might prove too difficult for some and too sudden for others, given all we have to do and learn before we can really thrive up here."

"Perhaps it's just enough to have us in this general area to start, just a couple of streets apart, and then we can split up."

"Okay. Who should we send back, then?"

"I would say, send Selleck. Leave Fransen here to establish waste facilities, and to let the others rest."

"I'm not sure we can leave every one cooped up in here that long. I'm sure there will be others who would like to explore this world as much as I do and we have to maintain some kind of guideline so that people don't get too curious and we start losing people."

"Why don't we start by assigning clean up duties to every family or a few families at a time around this building? Not only would the cleared out area give the children room to play, it will give everyone some sense of purpose while we figure out what to do next. We can assign a few others to venture into the surrounding houses to see what can be salvaged and reused. Maybe some of them are suitable for people to live in them. We can report back here at the end of the light cycle."

"I think it's called 'sundown'."

Den smiled. "Sundown."

"Speaking of sun, let's get out of here."

Once everyone had eaten and been assigned different tasks and community related responsibilities, Den and Aurora set out along the main road toward the business center of the city. According to the map in Den's pad, it would take a good portion of the light cycle to reach it.

Den didn't say much as they walked, but then again, neither did she. She was too engrossed in her own thoughts not only about the indomitable tasks ahead of them, but also about the reaction of the remaining Egertonians when Selleck reached them and told them to come and what was up here. *Would they still come? Had Mayor Goodwin wheedled his way of thinking to those that waited?* She had no way of knowing what happened after they left or what the others who had observed the altercation with the mayor had told everyone else?

As they passed street after street and row after row of houses and businesses and other buildings, Aurora's mind turned to the world in front of her and her heart ached for the lives of so many who had been lost. Dr. Heinan's files had shown the world population in the Upper World Earth year 2150 at 9.6 billion. If indeed there was no one left alive on UWE, what could have wiped out that many people, and what could have done it so quickly that people died in their seats? There appeared to be no fuzzy creatures either that people used to keep as companions, and aside from the feathery flying things in the forest, she hadn't seen any animals at all. That frightened Aurora just as much as all the people being gone.

Being the last 2500 human beings on earth out of a population of 9.6 billion was a staggering realization. So much so, Aurora wandered over to a discarded automobile and leaned against it and just stared at the ground. It gave a whole new depth to the level of her responsibility now to get this civilization not only surviving, but thriving. Her chest felt like it was collapsing in on itself. Aurora struggled to breathe.

"Rori, what's wrong?"

The terror in Den's eyes just added to her pain. He, too, was counting on her.

She reached out with one hand and rested it on his shoulder, hoping somehow to just absorb some of his strength so she could at least stand up straight again.

"I-I can't – breathe."

Den dropped to his knees in front of her, peered at her face, and gave her a basic physical examination.

"Well, you look fine. But your heart is racing." He glanced down at the atmosphere readings on the pad. "The air is clear and safe, although a little high on the allergen scale. This looks like the same thing you experienced when you knocked on that metal door, yester-light cycle."

Aurora nodded. "Though not ... this bad."

He looked back at her. "Do you know what triggered it this time?"

"It just hit me again," Aurora gasped as she tried to gulp in air, "the importance of making this work, Den. We're the only ones left. That means it's entirely up to us to save the human race. And it's entirely up to me to make sure that happens."

Den placed both his hands on her shoulders. "As I said, last night, it's not entirely up to you. It's up to all of us working together. I don't know if anybody else thought it would be an easy transition, but we all want this to work. No matter what the challenges up here, I don't think anyone wants to go back to the darkness of Egerton. Besides, you don't know what's happened to the other colonies. They might have survived."

"I know." Aurora stood up straight as the pain in her chest subsided. It still took several more gulps of air before she was able to get her feet moving again. "But until we find out for sure, we're still the last 2500 people on earth out of almost 10 billion. That's a pretty humbling number."

Den sighed. "Yes, it is. But the only way we're going to get things settled and established is to find Dr. Heinan's office and any information she might have left behind after her statement. Hopefully, she'll have something that will help. She was a brilliant woman. I don't think she would have left us down there with the intention of us coming back up to continue the species without having left something that would help us do that."

Aurora nodded. Her steps were coming easier now.

"Come on, we're almost there."

"Do you think Selleck and the others will be up by the time we get back?"

Den craned his neck at the sky. "I think so. I haven't really seen anything down this road that would be suitable for a large group. We'll have to venture into some of the surrounding housing areas for larger group buildings."

"Well, we can't continue to live in an arena either. I should have told Selleck to bring up more waste processing units. We probably won't be able to use the ones up here for a while. The history files showed smaller home buildings like the ones we saw, bigger home buildings in other cities, and tall buildings with hundreds of people living in them at once. They called them apartment buildings or condominiums I think. Those might be more along the lines of what we're already used to in community living. Perhaps one of their education buildings might work as well. Multiple rooms designed to hold a group of people."

"Keep everyone together as long as possible before we split up."

Aurora nodded.

It was another hour before they reached the building indicated on Den's map or at least it used to be a building. It was strange seeing this giant skeleton up close instead of from a distance. The picture on the pad showed rows and rows of shiny windows towering way above any of the buildings below. The building in front of them had no windows at all and the remaining structures stood about the same height as everything else.

"Well, what do you think?" Aurora asked.

"The map is still telling us to go inside. But her office was on the tenth floor."

"Doesn't look like there is a tenth floor anymore."

"Nope. Certainly doesn't. But my gut says, let's keep following the map.

"All right then."

Aurora followed Den through the broken glass doors and into the building, their feet crunching on the debris. The bright blue sky above her would have been beautiful if seeing it through the floor above her didn't remind her of why they were seeing the sky through the ceiling of the ground floor.

Den had doubled back and taken her hand. "Come on."

The map led them to the end of a long hallway to a door with a picture of stairs on it. An arrow on the map pointed down. Den pushed the door open and they followed the steps down. The map stopped them at the third door down, which opened into what looked like an archive, but not just with pads, but with flimsier boxes, too, with even flimsier sheets with printing on them.

The arrow on the map urged them further into the dungeon, dim lights coming on automatically over their heads. Perhaps the map would also lead them to the source of this electrical power.

They wove through rows and columns of shelved crates until the arrow on the map changed to a stop sign and announced, "You are here!"

"Well, it says, we're here, but I don't see anything but a wall," Den said.

"Me neither. But the room just ends here. We can't go left or right. There must be something here."

Aurora placed a hand on the brick immediately in front of her, and in an instant the brick pushed inward and, with a *CLUNK* a portion of the wall slid away, similar to the door to Barna's office. Inside, was a single room with a desk and chair and ancient Upper World Earth electronics.

"Why did the map lead us here?" Aurora wondered aloud.

At the sound of her voice, a glowing body of a man appeared in front of her out of a small disc on the floor. She recognized him immediately.

"Shallon Hillis."

"Hello."

"How can you … ?"

"This is not the real me. I created this hologram of myself to tell my story to whoever followed. It was set to activate at the sound of a human voice, just like the brick was programmed to trigger at the touch of a human's hand."

Aurora walked around the figure. She could see Den right through the man's shimmering body.

When she returned to stand in front of it, the hologram continued talking.

"I tried my best to anticipate what questions you would have for me when you arrived, but I'm afraid I might not be able to answer everything. I'll have to leave Dr. Heinan herself to do that, which is whom you were likely expecting to see, not me.

"I was exiled, along with my family, to Upper World Earth in the earth year 2350, or in the 210th annum in Egerton years. And actually, that was quite all right with us. At the time we left, my wife and I were nearing our 40th year of life. My wife passed from this life in her 60th year, and as of this recording, I'm 65. I assume you've come in search of a longer, healthier life in the light, and you can be assured that you've found it." Hillis smiled and Aurora couldn't help but smile back.

"I have no way of knowing how far into the future this is recording is being watched or what has happened to the people of Egerton, how far the situation has progressed, but I'm glad you've come just the same. That means there's hope for Egerton and Upper World Earth will live again.

"When I and my family arrived on Upper World Earth, we found it probably pretty much the way you did – barren, empty and devoid of life. It was clear to me that nothing human or animal, except for a few species that are relatively harmless, had lived here for a long time. Long enough that any effects of past conflicts on the environment and atmosphere had cleared away."

Hillis raised his arms at the elbows with a wave of his hands.

"When we first came to the surface, my pad led me to this building and the only surviving part was these archives. This was actually the site of Dr. Heinan's office, but not her laboratory. It took me several months to find that. It's on the outskirts of the city. I knew anyone who followed me would be led here first, so that's why I put this holographic projector here kind of as a first step, if you will. When this recording is done, the map will show you how to get to Dr. Heinan's laboratory, which is a journey for another day, but one you must make for the sake of your survival.

"I chose to leave what I found there because I hoped one day someone would follow and would need the information to help re-establish Upper World Earth, something that the four of us could not do on our own and it seemed a shame to waste it. You'll learn, perhaps you have already learned, that there is a time and a place for everything.

"I chose to speak the truth to Mayor Warton, and he decided to disregard it and come up with his own rules to deal with the problem in the way he thought best for the civilization. Or at least, I think that's what he seriously believed. At the time, I wasn't able to convince anyone to come with me. The exile happened so quick, I don't even think many people knew about it. I don't really know why, in the grand scheme of things I was sent to the surface first, but I like to think it was to help whoever followed find what they needed to make Upper World Earth thrive again."

"What about the other underground cities?" Aurora asked.

Hillis smiled again. "I never made contact with any of them. Again, I didn't think it would be worth making contact since it was only myself and my family. We accepted that our role would be to simply point the way for those who came behind. I never received any communications from the other cities either, so I have no idea if they've even survived this long. I suppose, you'll be the ones to find out, but only Dr. Heinan can help you do that."

"Then why not just let us go to Dr. Heinan's lab first instead of coming here," Den asked.

"Because you need to see what's down here. What you see before you is an entire history of Upper World Earth including the period after the First Ones went into Egerton. You may have already learned some of this history, but you wouldn't know what happened after the First Ones. I spent many hours reading the files, both paper and pad, here. It's a very sad history. One filled with jealousy, people killing other people over petty things like money, which you'll discover is how business was conducted on Upper World Earth for many hundreds of years. Humans seemed to invent new ways of killing themselves and each other, and new reasons for justifying killing and maiming and destroying the earth around them.

"There are a few bright spots of people who tried to make a difference, in some cases a worldwide difference. A few voices seemed to last forever, at least until the time of the last war. That's when any signs or desire for peace disappeared and I suppose what killed them in the end was better than living without any hope for peace."

No hope for peace. That explained Dr. Heinan's expression and tone of voice in her message – totally defeated, nothing left to live for.

"So they didn't all die because of the war?" Aurora posited.

"No, it wasn't because of the war, though the war destroyed a lot of surrounding areas and creatures."

"Then what killed them?" Den asked.

Hillis looked down at his feet. "I knew you were going to ask that, and even though I do know the answer, I think it's best that you find out for yourself. It's something that I don't think you'd ever imagine given the way the world was going at the time and the technology that was available. They never saw it coming either."

Never saw it coming? Aurora's heart leapt into her throat.

"If they never saw it coming, what if that something comes for us?"

"The only thing I'll say is that what killed them is long gone. Most things can't survive if they don't have anything to eat. Let's just say that it simply ran out of things to eat and has long since died off itself."

"But, what if it comes back?"

"It's highly unlikely that the exact same event will occur again. You may experience different challenges. There's no way to know how your bodies will react to being on the surface and to what's in surface air. I'm afraid I can't be of any more help than that."

Aurora sighed. There wasn't much more Hillis' hologram could tell them. Anything from here on they would just have to experience and figure out how to handle for themselves.

"Thank you, Shallon Hillis."

"You're welcome. And welcome to the *New* World Earth. It's yours now and I promise you, you've done the right thing."

With that, the light image of Shallon Hillis disappeared.

CHAPTER TWENTY-TWO

Aurora turned to look at the shelves of files in the room they'd come through. *How would they ever learn so much?* She supposed most of what was in those files was already included in the file she downloaded from Dr. Heinan's pad message, but she felt it was important that these all be read for the sake of clarity and thoroughness. If these files would add understanding as to how to help keep their civilization from growing into a bickering, warfaring one like before, it would be worth reading. But first, they needed to find Dr. Heinan's laboratory.

She started back through the stacks, mentally adding "more reading" to her society establishing to-do list.

"He's right. Here it is, look," Den said, once they were back outside, and shoved the pad under her nose. The map showed a new path leading through the rest of the industrial center and then away from the city.

"Do we follow it? Or go back to the arena and set out another day?"

"It's about the same distance from here to the laboratory as it is from here to the arena. We could make it there in one day, but we wouldn't be able to make it back to the arena. If we left here now, we'd make it there before sundown."

"But then that means leaving everyone on their own with Selleck bringing up Dara's group, and the other groups will follow tomorrow. I'm not sure I'm ready to do that yet. It's not that I don't trust Selleck and Fransen. But I think we need to get everyone up and somewhat comfortably housed, first. Then we can return for this."

"All right. Let's head back. We still have to look for any type of building that might be sufficient to house a large group of people." Den craned his neck to look at the buildings around them. "Since most of the taller buildings aren't tall anymore, the condominiums and apartment buildings we've read about are probably not an option."

"There were a couple of small bunches of business areas on the way down, and wandering into some of the more residential areas might bring up something, too."

"Well," Den said as he glanced at the pad, "we'd better get going if we want to make it back before night fall."

"Hey, look at these." Aurora jogged over to a metal contraption with two wheels, one at each end of a long bent-up pole, and one foot rest on either side between the two wheels. They weren't in as bad a shape as the automobiles. "Perhaps we can figure out a way to fix these?"

"Looks relatively simple to me. They're not that heavy either." Den hoisted two of them onto his shoulder.

"Good thing because we have to carry them a long way. But hopefully when they're working again it won't take us so long to get around."

It took several days for the rest of the migration from Egerton, and to get everyone settled in their various buildings under the direction of their own leaders, since Aurora wouldn't be able to manage everybody being in different locations. They'd been able to find one suitable business building and one educational building. Those would do until they explored the city further.

With everyone up, it was time to set to cleaning up the city. Houses and buildings needed to be cleaned and searched and if too dangerous, completely taken down. The overgrowth of plant life also needed to be cleared away, as well as all the broken down cars. Also, the days and nights had grown colder and that meant they would have to find warmer clothing and blankets and shelter.

Every day, several of the teen boys would go out and look for more two-wheeled metal contraptions – which they learned were called bicycles – and they and several of the men worked on straightening the wheels and cleaning and greasing the chains and getting them ready to use.

With all the families divided into their community-care groups and assigned their various responsibilities, Aurora waited for Den at the end of the road leading out from the arena. Everything had gone much better than she thought it would. No grumbling over their assignments. Everybody had delved into their work readily and eagerly; though it wasn't like they weren't used to working. The scenery had changed, but they all still had a purpose and a way to contribute to their society. The mood had stayed positive and everyone looked forward to seeing the human race flourish again on New World Earth. Aurora hoped that whatever she and Den uncovered today wouldn't affect that zeal.

This would be her and Den's first night apart from the group. It would take a good portion of the day to reach the laboratory, so they planned to stay at the laboratory, investigate all they could, and then return on the third light cycle. Den walked up wheeling two bicycles on either side of him.

"What's this?"

"Bicycles."

"I can see that."

"Joyner and Kersey have been working on them with a little bit of help from Dr. Heinan's files." Den handed her one, which she looked at curiously.

"They're beautiful!" What was once rusty metal was now a much more pleasant shade of blue. There was no rust, the spokes in the wheels had been straightened, and Joyner and Kersey had somehow managed to get air in the tires. She touched the two levers on each side of the handle bars.

"Apparently those are brakes. Pull on those to make the bike stop."

"Bike?"

Den shrugged. "That's what it said on the file."

"Oh."

He swung a leg over the middle part until he was perched on the seat. Aurora did the same.

"Now, you're supposed to balance on the two wheels and push on these foot rests to make the wheels go around."

Den demonstrated. He steered around in a rather unsteady circle and managed to stop the contraption just short of where Aurora was watching.

"Well, here goes." She pushed off. It took a few wobbly moments before she settled into a rhythm around the arena. She pulled up beside Den and stopped. "You sure this is a good idea?"

"In terms of getting there faster, yes."

"Okay, well, let's go." Aurora pushed off harder this time and was up on the road before Den had a chance to react.

"Hey, no fair. Wait for me!"

The world raced by a lot faster than had their first trek into the city, though they stopped a couple of times to give their legs a break and to drink the water wicked from the dew on the leaves that morning or eat some of the small blue berries that, according to Dr. Heinan's records, were safe to eat. They reached the laboratory about mid-afternoon, passing through many more housing developments on the other side of the industrial center, of which they discussed also investigating for resettling. The laboratory itself was an hour outside city limits. It was actually a small development of single-story buildings surrounded by a wire fence that had withered with time and Aurora and Den were able to ride through a hole in the fence. The map on the pad led them to the center building, the door to which was already open, likely from Shallon Hillis' visit. They leaned their bicycles against the wall and entered.

Inside, the building was very much like everything else – empty, dusty, and littered with broken pieces of a past civilization. Just inside the door was a main meeting area with a central desk and several hallways leading away from it. The map told them to take the hallway to the left, so they did, curiously casting glances in the half-open doors of the other rooms they passed. At the end of the hallway was a set of double-doors that stood slightly open like all the other doors they'd seen.

"This is it," Aurora said as she glanced around at the tables and desks all askew and disintegrating. "I can feel it."

"Feel what?"

"Not what. Dr. Heinan. She was here." Aurora took tentative steps as she followed she knew not what to a sheltered alcove in one corner of the room.

"How did you know that?" Den showed her the map on the pad which had stopped right where she stood.

Aurora shrugged. "I don't know. Maybe I just have a strong sense of people." She turned a chair right side up and sat in front of Dr. Heinan's desk. She imagined that the desk had once been covered in scientific stuff and electronics. It was clear now, except for several generational layers of dust.

Drawn by the same mysterious instinct, Aurora opened the drawer to her right and took out the only thing inside.

"It's a key," Den said.

"To what, though?"

"I don't know. What does that sense of yours say?"

Aurora shrugged again. She turned the key over and over in her hand waiting to see if an idea would come to mind.

"Hey. Look at this." Den motioned her over to see the map.

"What?"

"The second you touched that key, the map changed. Guess you don't have to follow any instinct this time."

The map led them out a set of doors at the back of the lab and far into the grassy area behind. But when the map stopped, there didn't appear to be a door. There was no building of any sort – just barren wasteland.

CHAPTER TWENTY-THREE

"What now?" Den asked.

"Well, something must be here." Aurora paced back and forth as she thought. "There's a purpose for this key. I can't imagine the map leading us here for no reason." Her foot landed on something harder than the dirt around her. She stomped on the area and was rewarded by the sound of vibrating metal. She shook crippling live-burial memories from her mind as she looked at Den for a split second before he joined her on his knees and started hand-digging and brushing the soil away. Eventually, a door emerged.

"I believe they used to call this a bunker," Den said. "I read that they used to build these just in case they needed to take shelter from the war going on."

A little more hand sweeping revealed a lock.

Aurora held up the key. "Well, here it goes." She put the key in and with a little effort the lock turned. Den pulled on the slide latch and then up on the door, which swung open with a loud metallic protest.

"What do you suppose is down there?" Aurora asked as they both looked down into the darkness of the bunker.

"Only one way to know."

"I suppose so." Aurora followed a shallow set of steps downwards into a hollowed out cavern. Den landed beside her moments later. He took a night cycle lamp from his satchel and turned it on. The cavern angled downward and appeared to be going back toward the main laboratory building.

"Why does everything have to be underground?" Aurora asked.

"I guess when things get too dangerous above, there's only one place to go."

"I guess so."

Eventually, the dirt floor, walls and ceiling changed to concrete and they came to another set of double-doors, in better condition than the ones on the surface. They pushed through into another large laboratory-like room. Unlike the first laboratory they were in, this one was relatively undisturbed aside from several layers of dust and cobwebs.

Aurora shivered as she took in their surroundings. "It's just as creepy down here as it was walking through the dead city above us."

"I agree with you." Den stepped in beyond the doors, dust spiralling away from his footfalls. "You seem to have a sixth sense about these kinds of things. What next?"

Aurora shook her head. "I really have no idea." She stepped into the middle of the room and turned to visually examine the entire room. Three desks stood in one corner of the room, creating a kind of office alcove, looking out onto the main laboratory floor. It had been entirely unlikely for her to have found a key in Dr. Heinan's laboratory on the surface; surely, it was just as unlikely for her to find another key, here. But, she walked over to the desks and started opening and closing drawers. Finding nothing, she turned back to Den.

"I can't imagine her using this place to select the First Ones. Why would she hide that away? No, this seems to be about something else. Perhaps this is where she came as a last resort, at the very end of the war or to wait out whatever killed them."

"We need to find that message that Hillis said was waiting for us. Too bad he didn't say where it was hidden."

The pad in Den's hand chimed.

"A file has been uploaded."

Aurora peered over his arm. On the screen was Dr. Heinan – a significantly older-looking Dr. Heinan.

"I think we should sit down for this," Aurora said and brought over two chairs onto which they sat, then Den touched "Play".

"Hello ..." Her voice sounded scratchier than the archive recording. Given the doctor's rugged and sallow appearance, Aurora knew she was watching Dr. Heinan's last days.

"My name is Dr. Imogen Heinan, the geneticist who screened and selected the first citizens of Egerton." Imogen smiled, though the smile didn't quite reach her eyes and it seemed to take great effort. "But, then again, I imagine you already know this. You couldn't possibly have triggered this message if you hadn't already heard about me somehow.

"That you are watching this message at all means that Egerton was a success, although I have no way of knowing how long after my death you are watching this. As of this recording, twenty years have passed since the first citizens were sent down into Egerton. The idea was to bring you all back up after fifty years to assess some of the biological impacts people might have experienced because of living underground."

The smile ran away from Dr. Heinan's face and the fatigue Aurora saw in the archive recording returned.

"Unfortunately, that will not happen. We created Egerton because we feared the war would wipe out or virtually wipe out any possible chance of life on the surface." Imogen shook her head, wearily. "We had no idea that it wouldn't be the war that killed us."

Aurora reached for Den's hand. *Here it comes.*

"This bunker," Imogen continued as she looked around her, "was created for the express purpose of being a safe place to hide out from the war when the outcome was obvious. But it had another purpose. While we were screening and choosing the people of Egerton, we were also compiling a collection of DNA from all of earth's creatures, most of which the war was also destroying. Depending on the extent of things by your time, you may not need to use all of the samples to repopulate every species. For example, those creatures that live in the ocean, or that live in what's left of earth's jungles or deserts, but we've included them anyway.

"We've also included a complete study of ecosystems and habitats and food chains and webs so you understand when and why certain creatures should or should not live together and what behaviors you can expect. Read these through carefully before re-establishing any of the species. We've also included instructions on how to thaw out the DNA samples, screen them for any abnormalities that might have occurred, however unlikely, because of the cryogenic process, and clone these creatures properly since this science will be new to you. All this should have been uploaded with this file.

"As of this recording, the three other underground civilizations have been sealed off, and, to my knowledge, their designers and builders and genetic engineers have created a similar creature DNA database. It is highly recommended that you try to contact these other civilizations to determine if they, too, have survived and if their DNA database remains intact. You can do this through the shortwave radio system. All the cities have a shortwave radio system tuned to the same frequency. All one of you has to do is turn the system on and it will send a signal to the other cities assuming, of course, they've also come to the surface."

Dr. Heinan stopped talking and sucked in air noisily. Aurora had never heard anyone breathe like that before. Imogen looked as though she was going to die right in front of them. Aurora could barely stand watching this woman struggle for life who had worked so hard to preserve it.

"Y-you m-must know," Imogen managed, her voice barely audible, "the war didn't kill us. Twenty-four hours ago a supervirus appeared in a city in South America. It went airborne and within eight hours, everyone in the city was dead. Within twelve hours, everyone in Brazil was dead. In eighteen hours, everyone in South America was dead. As of now," Imogen sucked in another noisy breath, "it's already spread across North America, Europe, and Asia-Pacific regions. We can't do anything ..." another noisy breath, this one longer "... to ... stop ... it ... . I can only hope ... *wheeze* that your civilization *wheeze* ..." Imogen's cheeks and chest collapsed in on themselves with every breath "... will do better ... *wheeze* ... than us. Good luck."

The screen went black.

"No! Wait! Where is it?!"

As Aurora's questions rang off the vacant walls, a door slid open at the end of the room just beside the desks, and revealed a large steel door, probably triggered by a similar mechanism that uploaded Dr. Heinan's dying words to Den's pad.

Aurora yanked the handle down then pulled back on the door. A blast of frigidly cold air sent her reeling back. When the cloud cleared, she ventured inside, Den behind her.

In front of them were rows and columns of metal compartments, each labelled with the name of a different creature, which seemed to be sorted by species. One of the rows was labelled "Felines" and the compartments that followed each bore the name of, Aurora assumed, a type of feline.

Suddenly, the feeling of anxiety that had swarmed over her earlier came back, as the enormity of the world situation hit her. Not only was she, basically, in charge of establishing human civilization on the earth, but she would also be responsible for re-establishing animal life as well, as if she were some form of superior being and master creator, which was a role she knew she couldn't fulfill.

Her chest cramped and she gasped for air as her head swam and the world around her spun. She was about to drop to her knees when Den pulled her out of the freezer and thrust her into the chairs they'd just vacated.

Aurora shook her head. "I ... n-need ... t-to ... get out ... of here."

"All right."

Den ran back to close the freezer door, then carried her back out the corridor and out into the light again. He sat her down on a rock, as Aurora worked to take bigger breaths.

"I-I'm sorry, Den."

"No need to be sorry. You just gotta stop giving me a heart attack like that. What happened down there?"

Her mind was starting to clear. "I think ... it was just ... all the information and the responsibility ... this information means at once. Did you ever imagine ... that your simple question about whether the population of Egerton was really growing or not would lead to completely repopulating Upper World – I mean, New World Earth?"

"No. I had no idea." Den sat down beside her and took her hand. "But I'm not sorry I asked."

She turned to look at him. "Neither am I. Really, I'm not. But just when I think we're making progress, I'm shown just how much more there is to do. I'm sure it will all lay itself out into a plan, but right now it's all just overwhelming." Aurora looked at the main laboratory building ahead of her and rubbed her hands on her thighs.

"Well, I don't think we have to worry about the actual science of what's down there?"

"What do you mean?"

"Well, that's going to be Dolan Markus' job, right?"

Aurora nodded. "Yes, you're right."

Den looked off into the now-setting sun. "The whole key to this resettling is going to be having the right people handle the right things. Like Dara, Carter, Phoenix and Rella doing most of the city administration kind of things. Dom doing the medical and scientific stuff, and I'm sure he'd have a good idea of others in our groups who would be suitable to help him." Den raised his eyebrows. "Granted this is a much bigger scenario than we've worked with before, and we are really rebuilding from the ground up, but the duties needed to run such a city haven't changed. And I'm sure the historical files will help us figure out some of these things, too."

Den turned toward Aurora and took her hands so she was forced to turn and look at him, then smiled.

"I keep telling you, you're not alone in this. You're not doing this by yourself. It's impossible to do it by yourself and we wouldn't let you anyway. What kind of friends would we be if we did that?"

Aurora returned his smile. "I know that. But I feel like it's my responsibility, ultimately, and no one else's. I think everyone is looking to me to make it work and if it doesn't, any small part that goes wrong or becomes a challenge, I'm afraid they're going to blame me for." Fear and uncertainty drained the smile from her face and she looked down at the ground. "I'm waiting for some of them to start whining to go back to Egerton. I promised them life on the surface. What if one of them dies while we're still settling because we don't have the right resources to help them?"

Den conceded with a nod. "That may indeed still happen. But from what I've seen so far, everyone is behind this move. They believe it was the right choice. Yes, there will be hardships, but the results of their hard work will be worth it in the end. In the last few weeks, I haven't heard anyone complain or grumble or wish they were back underground.

"Try and think of it this way. This is an amazing opportunity for us. Not just to live here, but to see, not only this city, but the whole planet reborn and resettled. And not just see it, but have a hand in recreating it and, hopefully, avoid the mistakes that saw it destroyed in the first place."

"That is an amazing thought," Aurora agreed with a sigh. She laid her back against Den's chest and he wrapped his arms around her, as she looked back and forth at the emptiness around them. "I can't imagine what it must have been like for Dr. Heinan and everyone else to look at the world crumbling down around them and then to be hit by that supervirus and know there was no way anyone was going to survive."

"I guess it was kind of the same thing as us realizing that staying in Egerton no one was going to survive, only on a much bigger scale in this sense. Egerton was only 2500 people. Upper World Earth was billions."

"And we, at least, had a place to go that brought the promise of life – they didn't."

"But they left us with the building blocks we needed, the basics we needed to re-establish life on New World Earth. We know how to heat our homes, we know how to make clean water, and we know how to grow food. Seems to me these are the best building blocks for a new civilization … the basics. Keeping things simple."

Aurora shivered. The sun had completely disappeared behind the rocks around them.

"We'll have to find a way of creating warmer clothes, though," Aurora said as she stood. "Let's walk back and get our stuff."

CHAPTER TWENTY-FOUR

"It's weird," Aurora said as she gazed up at the glowing blanket tented above their heads.

"What's weird?" Den rolled over and looked at her, but Aurora didn't meet his gaze. She just let her mind wander freely under the gentle light from their night cycle lamps.

They'd swept away the dust around Dr. Heinan's desk cubicle and had draped a couple of blankets over the desk and some chairs to create a kind of tent. Two night cycle lanterns sat outside the blankets, lighting up that portion of the room, while one more lit up the inside. It was quite cozy, particularly at the end of a very exhausting day, and Aurora almost fell asleep before she replied.

"Lying here without everybody around us. It's really the first time I've been alone ..."

Den glared at her.

"... okay, not alone, apart from everyone else. I've never known what it would be like to be separated from the community like this. I wonder what they're doing?"

Den turned onto his back. "Probably the same thing we're doing?"

"Wondering how we're going to run an entire planet or which animal we should resurrect first."

Aurora sensed Den's smile even though she didn't look at him.

"No. I mean, lying there talking with their families. Talking about their day, what they did, what they'll do tomorrow, and how great it feels to be building a new life."

"Mmm. Do you think they miss us?"

The fabric of Den's shirt rustled as he shrugged. "Don't know. Probably in some way."

"I feel like a mother that's left her babies behind." Aurora paused as her heart ached for the baby she did leave behind. "I wonder what the others are doing?"

"You mean, the others who stayed behind in Egerton?"

Aurora nodded, and she couldn't stop the tears that started to fall.

"Hard to know. It's pretty hard to run a city when so many of our civilization came up here."

Aurora swept some tears aside. "Do you suppose some of them will change their minds or will they … just die faster…now that the structure of Egerton is pretty much gone?"

Den rolled to his side again, crooked his elbow and rested his head on his hand. He brushed a couple of tears from her cheeks with his other hand.

"I don't know, Rori." Aurora smiled at his use of his nickname for her. "Maybe they will decide to join us out of loneliness. I can imagine it being very difficult to get used to so many people being gone. Whether or not Caytor agrees with her father, I know she misses you and Selleck. You're her family too."

Aurora almost sobbed. "Selleck talked to her when he went down.

She said she felt it was her duty to stay with Merrick until he died and then she would come up. That could be another fifteen years."

Den sighed and rested a hand on her stomach. "I often think of Peggie and wonder if she'll eventually come up, too."

This time, Aurora turned onto her side, which brought her almost nose to nose with Den.

"I'm sorry, Den." She reached out with a hand to touch his shoulder then pulled it away.

Den looked at her and took her hand. "Thank you. And I'm sorry you had to leave half your family behind. But we have a chance to start over here, both you and me. We have a whole new life ahead of us. And I can't imagine ever spending my life apart from you."

Aurora smiled. "Me neither."

"Well, I guess we don't have a mayor or even a family control officer anymore to declare us official." Den removed a little circular piece of metal from his pocket.

"What's that?"

"It's a little tradition they used to have on Upper World Earth. I was reading about it and thought it was worth bringing back, besides," he paused and kissed her deeply, "I want everyone to know you're mine." He slid the object onto her finger. "It's called a ring. Men and women used to exchange them during Upper World Earth joining ceremonies."

"It's beautiful." Funny how a little bit of metal could have such significance. Under normal circumstances, it would have little to no value at all, just a piece probably off one of the bicycles they rode here or perhaps a fence. But it was a gift of love, a symbol of love and that made it the most beautiful thing on New World Earth. Her eyes filled with tears again, this time of joy.

"I-I don't have anything for you. I didn't prepare anything."

Den shook his head and placed a finger on her mouth. "You don't have to right now. Just you accepting it is enough for me."

Aurora could barely speak and nodded first. "Yes, I accept it." She kissed him, then, with a passion she'd never known and the ferocity of his response told her he felt the same thing. His hands tenderly caressed her torso, her nerves tingling with every touch. Her fingers followed the contours of his body as he nuzzled the base of her neck.

Within a few moments Den had lifted her shirt over her head, and she did the same with his and was overcome by all that had happened in such a short period of time – all the emotions, all the battles, all the challenges.

"How do I deserve you?" She whispered against his mouth as tears fell, and he pulled her close so that all she felt was his skin against hers.

"Funny. I was just thinking the same thing about you." He leaned back a bit and met her gaze. "I'll say it again, you're the most beautiful woman on New World Earth. And I can't wait to make you mine." He growled as blazed a trail of tingles from her neck down to the waistband of her pants, a feral sound that ignited her senses and just about drove her insane. With practiced hands, Den swept her pants off and then his, then laid her down beneath him. Their climax was the most amazing thing Aurora'd ever experienced, their bodies were so in tune with each other, and she was glad that this place had been their mating place rather than that office with people potentially milling about.

When Den collapsed on top of her, breathless, both their bodies covered in a sheen of sweat, Aurora drank in the scent of him, and let her hands lightly trail down his body.

"Mmm. Better not keep that up," he murmured as she twirled her fingers in the patch of hair at his collarbone, and nibbled on his earlobe.

Aurora grinned. "Why not?" She nipped his ear then tugged on it.

Den hoisted himself up on his hands and looked down at her.

"Because I've barely just caught my breath."

"Gee, that's too bad," Aurora said as she reached up with a hand and pulled his mouth down to hers.

Aurora awoke with a shiver and for one panicky moment forgot where she was.

She sat up with a start. The blanket that had served as their tent had partially blown away, thanks to the breeze sweeping in through the war-shattered windows. Plus it didn't help that she was naked. Just a thought of the passion she and Den had shared throughout the night warmed her. She turned and reached beside her to find him gone.

Her heart plummeted. She had so looked forward to some more lovemaking or at least a little bit of afterglow in his arms before they started their day. Since there was no one but them around Aurora didn't bother putting her clothes back on. She just wrapped a blanket around herself and stepped out onto the floor of the laboratory.

"Den?"

He wasn't in the room. Perhaps he'd gone outside. Aurora padded across the cold floor to the back door. She pushed it open and headed out until she reached the end of the concrete path.

"Den?"

"Coming!" Den's voice came from far away and a little above her. Then his silhouette appeared on the rocks just above and beyond the entrance to the underground laboratory.

Moments later, he arrived beside her and took her in his arms, as she wrapped the blanket around him, and kissed her.

"I don't know what's more beautiful, the sunrise, or you standing there naked in front of me." His voice deepened as he stroked her neck with his tongue.

"You know, we were supposed to be working, today?" she managed while just barely keep her legs from collapsing under her as his breath brushed her body.

"I know."

"Why didn't you wake me?"

"I didn't have the heart to. I wanted to see the sun come up this morning, on this the first day of the rest of our lives together. It really is quite beautiful. It's quite a good view from atop those rocks."

"Mmm. Perhaps tomorrow I'll come with you then." His hands pulled her hips against him, and his lips continued their assault on her neck and shoulder, rendering her nearly speechless. "But, first, perhaps you ought to come back with me now."

He smiled as he brought his mouth down on hers. "Perhaps," he said against her lips.

The sun was higher in the sky when they emerged the second time, their bodies sated for the time being and their hands intertwined. They carried pads in their free hands.

Down inside the underground laboratory, they went straight to the freezer to take an inventory of the DNA samples and followed Dr. Heinan's instructions on how to test if the samples had survived and could be used. The whole process took several hours. Even though Aurora was sure that Dom would want to conduct his own tests, she needed to know what was here so that Dom could easily and, hopefully relatively quickly, start the thawing process of the creatures they needed for food. It would still take time to make sure the thawing out process worked and then for the creatures to do what creatures do, but it was a place to start.

Several times through the afternoon, Aurora felt the weight of the burden placed on her. She remembered reading about the belief systems of Upper World Earth and about how a great number of people had believed in a supreme being, God, who had created everything. Here she was, essentially, playing God, and she wasn't entirely sure she was ready for such a responsibility. Perhaps that was part of the issue with the previous citizens of Upper World Earth. Perhaps they, too, had tried to play God and took control of things they couldn't and shouldn't have tried to control in the first place.

She didn't like that she was picking and choosing which creatures would be repopulated and which ones wouldn't be. Each possibility of creature reawakening brought with it the concern about how reintroducing these creatures would affect the plant and water resources that humans also needed. Some creatures ate massive amounts of plant life and needed vast open areas to live. Others would eat humans or their chickens and cows and other animals that would be needed for food.

From what Aurora gathered, much of the earth's biological history had an ebb and flow to it. Creatures lived for a while, thrived and then, eventually as climate and other earth circumstances changed, died off or adapted.

But it was just a weighty decision holding life and death essentially in the palm of her hand, whether certain creatures would be brought back to life and which ones wouldn't. There was a value in each creature's life and she didn't think it fair that she would be picking and choosing. There was the possibility that some of these creatures would never live again because they posed too much of a threat or the environment wasn't quite right for them. She hoped eventually they'd be able to find a place for all the creatures, but this whole reawakening had to be done so carefully.

She wondered what Imogen would have done faced with the same decision. Perhaps she had encountered the same dilemma deciding whether or not to include certain creatures or not in her DNA collection.

At that moment, Aurora knew what the new city would be called – Imogen. The mother, basically, of them all and an appropriate name, she thought, for a city that would birth a whole new civilization on New World Earth.

CHAPTER TWENTY-FIVE

"Hey."

Den's voice in her ear startled her.

"Where were you?"

Aurora shook her musings from her mind.

"Just thinking about all these creatures, deciding which ones get to come back and which ones don't. It's really a big decision."

"Yes, it is."

"Do you believe in this God we've read about?"

Den looked at her with a raised eyebrow. "Where did this question come from?"

"I don't know." Aurora shrugged and set her pad on her lap. "Many of Upper World Earth's cultures had a story or legend about a supreme being, a creator of all things. Looking at all those creatures in there, deciding which creatures to revive and where they should all go so they can live the way they were made to ... that doesn't seem like a human decision. When you consider how each creature has a certain purpose and a certain way of dealing with its natural environment, it's kind of difficult to accept that there wasn't some form of plan behind these creatures and the habitats they need and the value and role they play in our survival as well. Like these things don't just happen without a reason. Everything works together because it's designed that way. We're designed that way. When we all use our gifts and abilities together, it's like we're all part of one body and that we all have a purpose.

"Dom said something a while ago that if one part of the body isn't working, then it affects all the other parts of the body too, the other bodily structures and organs become overworked from trying to compensate. I think that's because these systems were designed to work together. I first felt something like this when I held Caytor and Selleck in my arms when they were born."

Den smiled. "I did, too, when I held Peggie for the first time. How could all these little systems have just happened? It's like they were knit together. How could we have so many people in Egerton that were all so unique and each have a personality or certain characteristics that made them good at what they did and able to contribute to society? It's almost like we were designed to work together. And I don't just mean being chosen by Dr. Heinan either. This goes beyond her."

"I was thinking the same thing." Aurora nodded. "I suppose doing what we're doing was bound to bring up such heavy thinking. I was also thinking that Imogen would be an ideal new name for the city. There is also an ancient Upper World Earth story about a garden where the first humans and first creatures were placed. I think we should call this building complex Eden."

"Eden and Imogen. Sounds good to me."

With their inventory and scanning work completed, Den and Aurora sat atop of the rocks, fingers intertwined, watching the sun set, brilliant orange and purple tinting the sky.

"It's got to be the most beautiful thing I've ever seen," Aurora whispered.

"You haven't seen the sunrise from here," Den whispered back.

"Next time, you'll have to bring me with you." Aurora looked up expectantly and was rewarded with a deep kiss that sent her stomach spiralling. Den turned so their bodies pressed together and cupped her buttocks so that she was pressed up against his arousal.

"I don't know what we're going to do when we go back to the others."

"What do you mean?" Aurora sighed.

"I just can't get enough of you and the arena is so … public." He freed the tie of her pants, then slid his hands inside her shirt. She moaned in response. "Exactly." He smiled. "We can't do all we want to do when every sound carries."

Aurora sucked in air as he suckled on a nipple.

"I guess we'll have to find a place of our own, then."

"Sounds like a good idea." He brought her hands to his waistband where she deftly undid his pants and slid them down. She pushed him onto his back, kicked off her own bottoms, then sat astride him yielding from him a femoral moan. "See what I mean?"

She leaned down and kissed him. "Definitely."

The sun had long-since set when Aurora and Den returned to the laboratory.

"So, where do you think we could live?" Aurora asked as they lay drowsily in their makeshift tent.

Den sighed. "I don't know. Everything is so rundown. I would be tempted for us to stay here."

"It's a little far away."

"I know, but we have to oversee the process here."

"We still need to monitor the people, too, and get them established in some form of community living."

Aurora found Den's hand under the blankets, then turned and snuggled her head against his chest, the thumping of his heart filling her ears and relaxing her.

"Let's worry about that tomorrow." Her last conscious thought was of Den wrapping his arms around her. It was a feeling she never wanted to be without again.

Aurora stood on top of the rocks after having watched the sun rise with Den and looked down at the laboratory complex.

She didn't want to leave. This place had been such a special time with Den and the discovery of a new life for them, for the creatures they found, and for the citizens of Egerton. But what could she do? Before she even came here she was worried what the people would do without her and Den for three days. Were they really ready to do things on their own, yet? How had the tidy-up efforts and other community activities gone with her and Den so far away? She would know the answer to those questions in a few hours.

They could move everybody here, but that would mean uprooting everyone. They would have to be uprooted anyway, since there was no way they could all continue living at the arena. She also wondered what the other sections had been doing and how much overall progress had been made to establish housing for all the families.

She really felt it would be best if they were all in the same general area with easy access to each other. Perhaps it would be worth building shelters out of recovered materials from the other buildings, here, on the property surrounding the laboratories, and as time went on perhaps they could completely clear away the old city of Badgertown and replace it with Imogen. They really did need a central location from which to run everything, and the laboratory complex seemed to be the most stable building they'd found yet. This could be the center hall, since this would also be the center of research and life.

She didn't realize Den was standing beside her until he took her hand.

"You ready to go back?"

Aurora shook her head and looked at the ground. "Not at all." Then she turned to face him. "Being here with you for the last three days has been more special than I could ever have imagined. Just the thought of going back … ." *How could she make him understand?* "It's like getting a taste of freedom and then realizing you have to go back to the way you were. Like not having any desire to go back to Egerton after coming out into the sun. How can we ever go back?" She wrapped her arms around his waist and his arms fell over her shoulders and down her back.

"I know completely what you mean." After a few moments, he tilted her head up so her lips met his, the kiss tender and gentle. Still, her knees sank beneath her and if Den weren't holding her, she would have fallen.

"We need to come back here."

"You mean, bring the others?"

Aurora nodded.

"It won't be the same."

"I know." Aurora sighed. "But it's the only way I can think of trying to run the city. We need a central place. The arena has served that purpose so far, but we really can't use any of the other buildings as they are, and this is the biggest plot of land around. Seems the perfect place to start a new city while we work at breaking down the old one and bringing the animals back." Aurora shrugged. "And building a city around where, essentially, our society was chosen and put together."

Den let her go, and she wandered along the edge of the rocks.

"Well, we'll need to get going if we're going to make it by sundown."

"I know." Aurora started down a path leading down to the buildings. "There's just one more thing I need to do before we leave."

Inside, Aurora walked through the laboratory they'd stayed in and started searching all the rooms in all the hallways and the other laboratories.

"What are you looking for?" Den asked as she entered the umpteenth empty room.

"The radio room." Finally, she entered a room with a chair and a rectangular contraption sitting on a table.

Aurora sat in front of the radio and dusted it off. Other than the dust, it seemed intact. She tugged on a segmented piece of metal stuck on the top until it had reached its full length. *Would it even work? Did it have a self-sustaining battery like their pads?* She was about flip the black on switch when she stopped.

"What are you waiting for?"

"The importance of flipping this switch is as significant as reviving the animals. It's almost terrifying. What if we're the only ones that survived?

What if the other civilizations haven't come to the surface yet? What if they don't want to be contacted?"

"You're never going to know until you turn it on."

"We've just learned in the last few weeks that our world is far bigger than we thought. It was big enough when we just discovered Upper World Earth, then we discovered animals and three other civilizations. What if those other civilizations are not ready for contact from us?" Aurora cast him a sideways glance with a raised eyebrow. "What if we're not ready?"

"I guess we can't assume everyone is as ready as we are."

"That's just it. I'm not sure if I'm ready."

"Then why did you come looking for it? Why are you sitting there? Why was it so important to you to find it before we left?"

Aurora rubbed her thighs with her hands and let out a big breath. "I guess you have a point. I don't really know what was driving me to find it. Don't get me wrong. I want to see if the other civilizations are out there. There is the possibility that they may have answers to questions we may not have found yet. But it does make our already big world seem even bigger."

"Maybe, but maybe they're thinking the same way as us. We're the only people we've known in 400 annums. We need to know who else is out there."

He was right, of course. She knew that.

She sighed again and looked up at his face once before turning back to the radio.

"Okay, here we go."

Aurora flipped the switch and numbers appeared on the digital display, similar to the genetic scanner she used for Finals. The radio seemed to be working, surprisingly. The battery indicated a full charge. Dr. Heinan had said the signal would be activated once the radio was turned on, but Aurora couldn't hear anything. Despite her fears, she had hoped to hear a signal from one of the other colonies.

She sat back in the chair and let out a deep breath. She sensed Den's disappointment, too.

"Well, that's that, I guess." Den picked the radio up. "It does seem to be working, though. Why don't we take it back with us? Perhaps whoever's on the other side isn't sitting right next to it. It might take a bit for them to realize the signal is coming in."

Aurora nodded and stood. "All right. Let's go."

Chapter Twenty-Six

The sun was just starting to dip below the horizon when the arena came into view. Moments later, Selleck appeared on the road ahead on a bicycle.

"Something must be wrong," Aurora said.

"Maybe he's just happy to see you," Den countered.

"Maybe." She wasn't convinced, and the feeling of dread that had flooded her heart almost threw her off the bicycle.

"We were wondering when you were getting back!"

Selleck was pedalling full tilt, his face was beaming. The cloud around heart vanished.

"What? What is it?"

They stopped cycling as Selleck pulled up alongside.

"I have something to show you! Come on!"

They pedalled after him. Where there had been broken down old houses now sat several vacant lots. As they neared the arena, piles of sorted materials appeared and people buzzed around carting newly gathered boards and solar panels and other things that could be reused in rebuilding the city. They'd even managed to build a number of rolling carts, making it easier to truck more and heavier items back to the arena site.

"Wow!" Aurora pulled up beside Den and Selleck, who had

practically screeched to a halt.

"I know!"

"This is amazing, Selleck! So much gathered already."

Aurora stared at it all. *How could they have accomplished so much in three days?* Although with 800 people working together, perhaps this kind of progress wasn't all that surprising.

Selleck toured her and Den around describing each of the sorted material piles. When he'd shown them everything, Aurora sighed as her heart ached. Seeing all the work that had been done lifted a lot of the burden and wonder and worry about whether or not the civilization would survive. She leaned against the back wall of the building, her hands teepeed in front of her mouth, as tears threatened.

"What?" Den asked his brow crinkled in concern.

"What is it, mom?"

"N-nothing. It's just seeing all this" – she waved a hand – "and seeing everyone working together to make this happen … we came up here with nothing. And now … we have what we need to take care of ourselves." Aurora's voice faltered. "This is just what I needed." She couldn't say anything for several moments as she gathered her emotions. "I need to talk to the people," she said, finally.

Selleck's brows knit together, all happiness and excitement gone. "Why?"

"You'll know later. For now, just spread the word that everyone is to gather inside the arena just after evening meal. I have a lot to tell them."

Selleck looked like he was going to ask more questions, but to Aurora's relief, he said, "Okay, mom," and cycled away.

"This might actually work," she said once Selleck was out of earshot.

"Relocating?"

"Mmm." Aurora nodded as she looked at what the people had done while they were gone. "I really didn't think they'd make this much progress in such a short period of time."

"It is quite amazing."

"This is really the first time since we came up from Egerton that I've felt like we're going to make it."

"Of course, we're going to make it. A change like this doesn't happen in one night cycle."

Aurora shook the tension out of her shoulders.

"Come on; let's go get unpacked before I have to stand in front of everybody."

An hour later, Aurora stood in the outer area, looking down upon the community gathered in the heart of the arena, her palms sweaty and her entire body on the verge of another panic attack. She hadn't felt this nervous since the day she had to stand in front of City Council to suggest that they return to the surface. They were in this place because she'd taken that stand. She hoped they'd be more receptive to her proposed relocation than City Council had been.

Den's hands massaged her shoulders.

"Okay," Aurora said with a deep breath, "here we go."

The room fell into an awkward silence when she entered, as if people had been talking about her and didn't want to get caught doing it. She took that as a sign that people knew that this was a serious meeting. It didn't make her nerves flutter any less.

Aurora wove her way through the crowd to a small spot in the very center, the acoustics carrying her voice to the outer ring of the people.

"Good evening, everyone."

Hundreds of muttered "good evenings" echoed back.

"I know you are all anxious to hear about our trip and what we found and I'm anxious to tell you about it, but before I do, I wanted to thank you all for the effort you have put in while Den and I were away. You have really come together as a community and that was wonderful to see. So give yourselves a round of applause."

"Now," Aurora continued, once the applause had died down, "down to the business that we're gathered here for."

Aurora described the laboratories, the location, what they'd been used for, and Dr. Heinan's final message. Then she talked about the animal DNA, her ideas for renaming Badgertown, and finally her proposal that they take all they had salvaged and move everyone to the complex. When she'd said all she needed to say, Aurora took another deep breath and paused.

"I know this is a lot to take in," she said after a few minutes. "Believe me, my mind has been reeling with everything that I have learned in the last three days and what it means for us trying to re-establish life on New World Earth."

Murmurs trickled through the crowd. Aurora wasn't sure if they were positive or negative.

"Any questions?"

"What about the other groups?" Someone shouted.

"Den and I have already presented this same idea to the other groups on our way back, today, and they're onboard with it. We did think it right, however, for our group to go first since we have been here the longest and really need to get out of these tight quarters."

There was more murmuring, this time mixed with chuckles.

"The other groups will follow approximately one week at a time. There's enough room in the complex to house this group until we get other shelters built. Once we have everyone in the same area, building of other shelters can begin, and Dolan Markus will be able to begin the cloning process with the animal DNA. Many of the duties you have been doing already and you will continue doing at the relocation site because they are things you're already skilled at, but it's going to take everyone's effort to get us settled before it gets any colder and from the files I have read about Upper World Earth, this part can get very cold. Any other questions?"

"What about the other underground cities?" Someone else asked.

"We found a shortwave radio, which we turned on before we left the complex and brought with us. So far, we haven't had a reply, but that doesn't mean we won't get one. It's impossible to know what has happened to the other people that were sent underground, but there's still hope that some have survived and that someone will answer."

A hush fell over the crowd.

"Any other questions? No? Okay. Now, we need a vote on my proposed name change. All in favor of renaming the city Badgertown to Imogen signify by raising their hands and saying, 'aye'."

An ocean of 'ayes' rose up.

Sounded like everyone, but they still had to follow some form of protocol.

"Those opposed signify by raising their hand and saying, 'nay'." No one. People started chattering enthusiastically when everyone realized they were in agreement. "All right! We have our new name!" The gathering broke into applause.

"The relocation will start tomorrow," Aurora said when the clapping had subsided. "Those teams that are responsible for materials collection will focus on moving the materials that have already been gathered. Everyone else, we will leave just before high sun. Thank you, everyone, for your attention!"

Aurora wove her way to where Den was standing at the back, as the people chatted behind her. Her entire body bristled with pent up tension to the point she couldn't speak, and simply waved at Den to follow her into the outer area and down the hall to their room. Once there, she collapsed against the wall and took big heaving breaths.

"You're not going panicky on me again, are you?"

Aurora shook her head as she tilted it back. "N-no."

"I thought that went pretty well. Could have been much worse."

Aurora nodded. "I know. I think they were all getting tired of living in such a tight space and relieved that there was an actual place to rebuild."

Den surprised her by taking hold of her hands, pressing his body against her and bringing his mouth down on hers. Her lips bruised with the force and a moan escaped, but was stifled in the kiss.

"Where did this come from?" Aurora asked, breathlessly, as he laid a line of kisses down her neck.

"I don't really know," he chuckled. "I just couldn't help myself. You know the day I knew I was completely in love with you?"

Aurora shook her head.

"That day in front of City Council. Then again when you intervened to stop the crowd from killing the mayor, and then again, just now, as you stood in front of all those people giving them hope for this entire thing." He kissed her again. "You just never cease to amaze me. I don't think the people really see the toll it takes on you to do such things, and yet you do them anyway.

"You keep doubting yourself as a leader, doubting your recommendation and everyone's decision to follow you up here. And I couldn't be any more proud to have you as my wife." He kissed the ring on her finger.

"You know I couldn't do half the things I do," Aurora began, as she looked him in the eye and brought a hand to his cheek, "without you behind me. It makes being strong for everyone else so much easier. And, I have a feeling the next few weeks is not going to be easy."

She sought his mouth and lost all sense of what was going on outside the room.

Aurora looked over the group as the last few stragglers wandered up. She had really doubted whether or not everyone could be gathered and ready to leave before high-sun, but here everyone stood.

Maybe this would work.

It was going to be tight getting everyone there by sundown, which was coming sooner and sooner with each passing day. Aurora knew the much colder weather was coming, and they had no time to lose to get everyone moved. Some of the smaller children and older citizens would ride on carts pulled by a couple bicycles. That would at least make the trek easier for them.

Aurora knew it would be virtually impossible to keep the group from becoming separated as they walked. But with the larger group divided into smaller, more manageable ones, and Den, Selleck, and Fransen each assigned to one of the smaller groups, she figured they wouldn't lose anyone.

With strict instructions for people to keep together and not to venture into the city or any of the buildings as they passed through, Aurora led them onto the main road toward the center of town.

After a couple of hours, they stopped to rest and drink. As the second group caught up with the first, Den dashed up to her followed closely by a panicked mother.

"What's wrong?"

"Palia jumped off the wagon ran off before I could catch her. She's so fast. In a split second she was gone. I called and called for her, but she wouldn't come."

"I said, it was better to let you know what happened first and then go back and look for her," Den interjected.

"It's okay, Joylyn. We'll find her. We can't afford to get stuck here, though. We'll never make it before sundown if we do." At that moment Selleck arrived with the third group. "Selleck, I need you to take over these two groups as well, so we can go back and look for Palia. If we're not back in thirty minutes, then keep going. We'll catch up."

"Yes, mom."

Aurora followed Joylyn and Den back about five city blocks.

"She ran that way." Joylyn pointed toward a small, single-lane street in between two buildings that ran the entire length of the block, with multiple buildings on either side.

"She could be anywhere." Many of the buildings looked unstable and the overgrown plant life only added to the endless possibilities of where a little girl could be hiding. Would they be able to find Palia at all, or, at the very least, alive? She and Den shared a glance and Aurora knew he had the same doubts. They proceeded down the alley calling Palia's name. About halfway down, a little face looked out of the second floor window of a brick building.

"There she is," Den said as he pointed.

"How'd she get up there?" Aurora asked.

"Must have gone inside somehow. She's little. Little ones are resourceful and find ways we can't imagine."

"You speaking from experience?"

Den shrugged and gave her a hint of a smile. "Yeah, I guess I am."

Aurora trotted closer to the building and saw the opening the girl must have crawled through, which was way too small for any of them.

"How are we going to get her down? It's too high for her to jump."

Palia started to wail when she saw her mother.

"It's okay, Palia. Just wait there. We're going to get you down."

"How about that?" Den pointed to a ladder going up the side of the building that passed right beside the window.

"I don't know, Den. It doesn't look very safe."

The ladder ended just above Den's outstretched arms. With a little hop, he grabbed hold of the bottom rung and gave a tug.

"Seems sturdy enough." Den grunted as he pulled again.

"So, how are we going to get her down?" Aurora asked as Den let go.

"Well, I guess the only way is for me to climb up there, bring her down and hand her down to you."

"Den, are you sure about this?" Aurora couldn't hide the terror from her voice at the thought of something happening to him. "Maybe we can find a doorway in the front or something …"

Den shook his head. "Ordinarily, probably not a bad idea, but we have no way of knowing if there's any other access to where she is. Besides, something could happen to her while we're searching for a way to get to her. This is the quickest way." Den jumped up and grabbed the rung again. "Just be ready to grab her when I come down."

CHAPTER TWENTY-SEVEN

Den hoisted himself up onto the ledge, dust wafting down at the effort.

Aurora held her breath as Den waited for the ladder to stabilize, then continued slowly up to the window, repeatedly assuring the little girl that he was coming to help and to wait for him. When he reached the window, he held out his arms to her.

"Come on, Palia. I'll take you down to mommy."

"It's okay, Palia! He's there to help!" Joylyn called up.

The girl hesitantly lifted her arms up and Den picked her up out of the window, the ladder shifting slightly from the movement and added weight. More dust rained down on Aurora and the girl's mother below.

Aurora thought for sure she was going to choke on her heart as it seemed to clog her throat.

With each step Den took down toward them, the ladder rocked and rattled more. At one point Den stopped and looked at Aurora, then he set Palia down on the step in front of him. There was still one more turn before the landing that led to the final rung.

Den leaned down and whispered something in the child's ear and she looked down at her mother.

"It's okay, Palia. Come to mommy. I'm right here." Joylyn settled at the bottom of the ladder. Step by tiny, timid step, Palia inched downwards and then across the landing to the edge. "You'll have to jump, sweetheart." The child wailed. "I will catch you." Joylyn held out her arms.

The pull of child to mother won out and after a few moments, Palia bent her knees and launched herself toward her mother, who caught her in a bear hug and carried her away.

The force of the jump, though, caused more dust to fall. Den took tentative steps downward, the ladder now rocking completely beneath him. Aurora watched in horror as the ladder finally came loose from the building and the brick wall crumbled and fell forward. The ladder landed with a metal-grinding crunch and then Den disappeared beneath the broken bricks.

"No!" She ran to the pile of rubble and started flinging them aside. "Den!"

"Stand back, mom!" Selleck grabbed her by her shoulders as Fransen and a few other men ran up. "We'll get him."

"What are you doing here? I told you to keep going."

"Sorry, mom. Something told me to follow you."

It took a few more moments before they uncovered Den's body. The metal ladder was surprisingly intact, even if it was mangled. Except Den's legs were mangled in it. Aurora knelt down and touched his face, which was scratched and bruised. The fact that he didn't move at her touch terrified her and she hung her head as tears fell to the ground.

"Even if we can get him out of here, we can't carry him the rest of the way. We'll need Dolan Markus, too," Selleck said.

Aurora shook her head. "Dom is over an hour away."

"Go find Lander and send someone with a bike to get Dom," Selleck instructed one of the men behind him, who turned and ran off.

"Lander was one of Dom's medical assistants. I don't even want to try to extricate him until Lander gets here," he explained as he stood.

Aurora stayed on her knees, but nodded. She leaned down as close as she could to Den's ear. "I love you, Den. I'm right here. I'm not going to leave you."

"Mom?"

Aurora looked up to see Selleck jerk his head to the side and walked out of Den's ear shot.

"I know you don't want to hear this, but he doesn't look good, mom. I don't think we've ever seen such injuries, let alone know how to treat them."

Aurora hung her head. "I know."

Selleck turned the ring around her finger. "What's this?"

Aurora managed a smile and felt heat rush to her cheeks. "We committed to each other while we were away. I'm sorry. I guess I should have told you."

Selleck smiled. "No, you're quite free to do what you want. It was kind of obvious what was happening between you two, especially with you and he sharing a room the first night."

Aurora nodded and smiled somewhat sheepishly. "Yeah, I guess we didn't hide it very well."

"You shouldn't have to hide it, mom."

Aurora raised her eyebrows. "You're not angry?"

Selleck placed his hands on her arms and smiled, again. "Not at all. I haven't seen you this happy in a long time."

"Don't get me wrong, I loved your father very much and he loved me. It was he who told me that he wouldn't be continuing with the marriage with me planning to return to the surface. We shared twenty years together and a part of me will always love him." Aurora looked over at Den's still form. "Den's always been a friend. I have to admit I never would have thought we would be together, but he's different than your father and was precisely what I needed when I needed it. Heck, we wouldn't even be here if it weren't for him." Aurora's smile turned to tears as she recalled the three days and nights they'd spent together and she gripped Selleck's arm. "We've only been together a short time and I can't imagine what I would do if … if he were … ."

"Mom, again, I know you're not going to like what I'm going to say, but I really think your place is leading the people to the complex."

Aurora shook her head vigorously. "No. I'm not leaving him."

"You said yourself they'll never make it before sundown if they don't leave now. We can't have eight hundred people milling about the city. We could end up with another Palia situation as people get restless. They need you, mom. You need to let him go."

She almost doubled over from the pain that hit her heart at the sound of Selleck's last statement and the thought of having to leave Den behind. She sucked in a breath that sounded like Imogen's last breaths, as though her lungs couldn't expand. Den was always the one who brought her out of her panic mode.

She looked at Den, and then looked at Joylyn and Palia watching and waiting. She hadn't realized they'd stayed. Selleck was right. The people were her responsibility. She imagined Den telling her to go. It was what he would want.

Lander ran up at that moment and immediately took charge of the situation.

"Go, mom. We'll take care of him."

Aurora glanced down at Den and then back at Selleck.

"All right," she acquiesced with a sigh. With one last squeeze of Selleck's arm for strength she turned toward Joylyn and Palia.

"I'm so sorry," Joylyn said.

"Thank you." Aurora ruffled the little girl's hair. "I'm just glad we found you and that you're safe. Let's get back to the others and get going. We've still got a long walk."

As Aurora walked away, she felt like she was leaving a piece of herself behind.

God, please don't let him die.

They reached the complex just as the sun disappeared behind the rocks, beyond exhausted. There was very little chatter as Aurora divided the group among the various rooms and laboratories.

She looked in on all the groups to make sure everyone was settled before heading out the back door and up onto the rocks where she and Den had watched the sunrise just a day earlier. She sat where they had, burying her face and sobs in her bent knees. She had no idea how long she sat there before she heard her name being called from a distance.

"Aurora!"

Den?

Aurora leapt up and turned around and saw a figure standing in the back door of the laboratory.

It wasn't Den.

"Aurora!"

Aurora waved and the figure moved toward her. In a few moments, he had joined her.

"Dom!"

She disintegrated into more sobs as he held her.

"You came," she said, once she'd caught her breath.

"Of course, I came. Lander is with him now. I thought I'd come and find you. Selleck told me everything."

"Everything?"

He looked at her dead in the eye. "Everything."

"Then you know we're committed."

"As I said, I know everything."

Aurora managed a smile. "Well, not everything." She was glad Dom couldn't see her blushing cheeks in the dark light.

"No. Some things are best kept to yourself," he jibed.

Leave it to Dom and his sense of humor. She swiped the tears from her cheeks and took another heaving breath to rein in her emotions. She sat on a bolder and rubbed deep pressure into her thighs.

"H-how is he?"

Dom sat beside her. "Alive and very lucky to be. The metal framing actually saved him. It could have been a lot worse."

Aurora let out a breath.

"It could have been worse, but it's not over, Aurora. He still suffered severe head and spine and leg and muscle injuries a lot of those I'm not even sure how to treat."

"What about historical records?"

"I've read many of them and will be reading more tonight, but we simply don't have the technology that they did. I did bring a portable life support system, but we've never faced anything like this."

"Can you save him?"

"Aurora ..."

"Just tell me, Dom."

They exchanged a glance and even though they couldn't actually see each other in the darkness, Aurora knew Dom was fighting between telling her the truth and trying to ease her pain. She didn't look away.

"Tell me."

Dom looked down at his lap, then back at her. "Look, I don't know what you think I ..."

"Just tell me the truth, Dom."

His hand touched her elbow. "I'm certainly going to do my best. My gut says he will survive this, but I really don't know how or how long it will take before he even regains consciousness and, if he does, if he's going to be anywhere near what he was before this happened."

"Thank you. I can live with that."

"Will you be able to live with the possibility that despite my best efforts, he may still ... ?"

Aurora swept a hand in the air. "Don't say it."

"Aurora …"

"Don't say it! I have to believe he's going to make it."

"Aurora …"

"Dom …"

"… no, let me say this. I know you don't feel it, but you're stronger than you think."

"No, I'm not."

Dom gripped her shoulders. "Yes, you are. You had to be to follow your instincts about the expansion project and all the little things leading up to bringing everyone out of Egerton."

Aurora straightened her shoulders and took a breath of cooling night air, her exhale coming out as a puff.

"Only cause I had you guys backing me."

"No. Even if we hadn't backed you, would you still have continued your search for the truth?"

Aurora nodded. "I probably would have."

"Cass, whatever happens to Den, never doubt yourself, your decision to find a way out of Egerton, and to lead the people out. Never regret it. You have saved us all."

"Not 'all'."

"The rest decided for themselves. I'm tempted to call them fools, but some are just too stuck with the way things are to try something like this. If they're content with the way things are, there's nothing you can do about that. You gave them a choice, a choice they would never have had …"

"If Den hadn't asked about the actual population and …"

"… if you hadn't counted births and pregnancies and visited the archives and found Dr. Heinan's message, and stood in front of City Council … . Don't you see, Cass? That was all you."

Dom stood and walked away from her.

"Den is a lucky man."

The emotion inherent in the tone of his last statement surprised her. She stood and walked up behind him.

"Dom?"

He turned back and grabbed her shoulders. "Den's the luckiest man on New World Earth."

"Why didn't you ever tell me?"

Dom shrugged. "Just was never the right time. You and he seemed pretty tight through the whole City Council thing … it was really obvious, by the way. You reached for his hand, not mine when you stood in front of the council."

"I'm sorry."

"Don't be. Please. You're happy. Den's a great guy. You both deserve each other. That's enough for me." He wrapped her in a bear hug that she returned. "I will do my best to save him, Cass. I promise."

She pulled away. "Thank you." His smile told her that he knew she meant thank you for far more than saving the life of her husband.

"Come," he said as he took her hand. "You probably want to see him. Lander's probably got him all settled by now."

Aurora didn't move at the tug of Dom's hand. He looked back.

"Don't you want to see him?"

"I do, but I'm terrified of what I'm going to see."

"He's a little banged up. But really, aside from the stuff going on inside his body, he just looks like he's sleeping."

Aurora took a tentative step forward.

"Come on."

CHAPTER TWENTY-EIGHT

Dom led her down the cliff, back into the laboratory which had been divided into sections for each family sharing the space, and to the third room down the hall on the left.

Joylyn was just coming out with Palia in her arms.

"Oh, Aurora, I'm so sorry. Palia and I wanted to make sure he was all right." Joylyn touched Aurora's hand.

Aurora managed a smile, which was easy when she looked at the little girl drooped over her mother's shoulder sound asleep.

"Thank you for coming. I'm glad Palia is safe."

"Thank you for bringing us home. New World Earth is beautiful, Aurora."

Aurora watched her go and let her words soak in. It was the first time someone had directly said, "Thank you." Even though the circumstances weren't ideal and Aurora feared for their ultimate survival, someone was thankful.

"She's not the only one who thinks that, either," Dom said as he put his hand on her shoulder and opened the door with the other.

"Really?"

"Really."

Aurora stepped in. Den was laid out on a table in the middle of the room. Lander was hovering about with a medical scanning device while an oxygen mask covered half of Den's face. He was shirt- and pantless which allowed Aurora to see the extent of the injuries. He was quite literally black and blue all over, and gashes and cuts had been neatly cauterized.

"It was actually easier to extricate him than we thought. We managed to minimize any spinal and other injuries he might have sustained as a result of the fall. The metal steps actually saved him. It if weren't for them, there wouldn't have been any barrier at all between the brick wall and the ground. He would have been crushed."

Aurora raised two hands to her mouth. She stood barely inside the doorway, some form of fear kept her from moving closer.

"Amazingly, there were no broken bones. But there was significant ligament and muscle damage, particularly in his back and legs. We're still assessing the precise extent of that and what it might mean in terms of recovery and function. We are also trying to figure out how much of a head injury he suffered because he took a significant blow to the head, but there was no skull fracture.

"We've got him mildly sedated, right now, with some of the stuff I brought up with me and we are managing the pain, but I also have to ration the supplies. I'm pretty sure with the rebuilding that's about to happen there'll be more injuries."

Aurora's chest felt like it was collapsing in on itself. She could barely breathe. All she could manage for a response was a nod.

"We'll also have to make a more suitable bed for him. He obviously can't lie on this hard, cold surface while he's recovering."

She finally pushed away from the door and neared the table. She looked down on his beautiful face, the strong brow and cheek bones that she had touched and the wide, full mouth that had once kissed her. She traced the outline of his face with her fingers.

"Can he hear me?"

"Probably. Even if you don't say anything, I'm sure he knows you're there."

Aurora lowered her mouth to Den's ear. "Stay with me." She kissed his cheek and forehead, then gently laid her head over his chest above his heart, which thumped beneath. Aurora closed her eyes as tears fell.

"Aurora?"

Her eyes snapped open.

"Aurora?"

"Hmm?" She raised her head.

"You fell asleep." Dom's cheerful face came into focus.

"Oh, did I?"

"Yes, you did. You should really get some rest. We'll be running a few more tests through the night to assess the overall damage."

Aurora stood. Apparently, Dom had rolled a chair under her while she was sleeping.

"All right." She touched Dom's arm. "Thank you both. You will tell me if anything changes?"

"Of course."

With one last look at Den, Aurora slipped out into the hall. She turned toward the sleeping room she'd come through earlier. She knew she was exhausted, but didn't really want to be with people. Heck, she didn't even know where she'd sleep. Every corner was probably full and there wouldn't be much privacy for a while until they got other shelters built.

Aurora sighed and looked around at the people settling down in family groups. She was about to descend into a bit of a pity party, to which she figured she was kind of entitled, given that her new husband was so severely injured, but she took a deep breath, shook the tension from her shoulders, and forced the pity from her mind. She needed to focus on the coordinating the jobs at hand and getting the people established while Dom did his job. Palia and her mother were counting on her and there was a lot to do before the winter set in.

According to historical records, this area that was once a part of Canada experienced particularly cold winters and often several meters of snow. By old earth calendars, they only had about thirty more days before snow would start to fall and stay. They really needed to start building shelters right away. The group would need to take at least a day to sort through what they'd been able to salvage and decide what they still needed to make adequate shelters. She knew the building crews Selleck and Fransen had established were working on plans and having a place for them to build would certainly be a big help.

"Hey, mom."

Aurora turned at Selleck's voice seconds before his arms appeared around her shoulders with a hug.

"Hey."

"How are you doing? How is Den?"

Aurora coaxed a smile as a further attempt to stave off feeling sorry for herself and keep her focused on the coming days.

"I'm doing all right. He's going to have a long recovery. But I have a lot to do here. We don't have much time to get shelters built and the other colonies moved down here."

"You know, mom, I've been thinking, why can't we just leave the other pockets of Egerton where they are? Why move them here at all? They could just salvage what they can and demolish the rest and rebuild right there."

"It would seem simpler wouldn't it? And if we had more time, I probably would agree with you. But things have changed so much for everyone, I really think it's better for us to build a community here, continue to dismantle the old city piece by piece and then gradually rebuild from here. Obviously, we all won't be able to live here forever."

Aurora stifled a yawn. Selleck did the same. They both laughed.

"Miss Aurora?"

It was Mr. Poly. Aurora knew from her Family Control Officer responsibilities where she needed to track the older population to anticipate needing to perform their EOLs that Mr. Poly would likely not live much longer since he was close to fifty.

"Yes, Mr. Poly."

"How's Mr. Den?"

"He's going to be a long while healing, but Dr. Markus says he will heal, thank you for asking."

Mr. Poly patted her hand solemnly before saying, "We all know he saved that girl."

"Yes, he did."

"Everything will be all right, you'll see. You can't live as long as I have and not come to understand that everything will turn out all right in the end."

Aurora teared up at Mr. Poly's gentleness. "Thank you, Mr. Poly. I'm sure it will."

"Of course it will. Now, follow me." He turned and headed off into the relative darkness where only a few night cycle lamps were lit to allow the adults to move around a bit while the kids slept.

Aurora turned to Selleck. "I guess I'd better follow him. Good night, honey." She kissed his cheek.

"Good night, mom."

She looked after Mr. Poly who seemed to have disappeared.

"Mr. Poly?"

He dashed out of the shadows, took her hand and tugged her along behind. How he was able to move so quickly at his age amazed her. He led her to the desk and the little alcove.

"I reserved this spot for you because I figured when Mr. Den is all better you both will need your own space."

Aurora couldn't stop the tears from falling this time.

"Mr. Poly, I-I don't know what to say."

"Now, don't think another thing of it. It was my pleasure. You have saved us all, Miss Aurora."

"But ..."

"I know, I'm an old man," he said with a dismissive wave, "and probably won't live long enough to start seeing all the changes of the sun like you've talked about, but it was worth it to know that my children and grandchildren will live longer, healthier lives. And having even just seen the beauty of the sunrises and the sunsets, well, that's just made my lifetime."

Aurora knew, even though she could barely see his face in the darkness, he was beaming. "You have saved us all, Miss Aurora. There's a couple of blankets in the corner." With one last pat on her hand, Mr. Poly scuttled off.

Aurora laid out a couple of blankets to take the chilly edge off the floor and settled with another bundle of blankets at her head. Her mind buffeted back and forth between worry over Den and excitement and anticipation for the days to come.

CHAPTER TWENTY-NINE

Aurora awoke to bright sun filling the room and many of the people, already up and having tidied their sleeping areas, likely out exploring. She felt a little guilty for having slept so long. There was so much to do. As a leader, it was her responsibility to be up and working with her people, not sleeping. Though, she probably had good reason to have slept late, and no one had come to wake her.

Aurora stood and stretched, just as Selleck poked his head around the corner.

"Oh good. You're up."

Aurora yawned. "Yes. I'm sorry to have slept so long."

"Don't worry about it, mom. I've got our builders working on plans for the new residences and most everyone is exploring what's here."

"Oh, that reminds me, there's a bunker about 30 meters out that way." Aurora waved a hand toward the rocks out back. "It's full of frozen DNA of the creatures that used to live on Upper World Earth. I don't know if it's better to leave it unmarked and hidden or to mark it and just restrict access. My fear of leaving it hidden is someone's going to find it accidentally and do something unfortunate."

Selleck nodded. "With so many people, it's bound to be discovered even if we restrict access to the rear of the building."

"Probably better to let people know it's there and that it's off-limits

259

except to authorized people to protect the life that is down there. We're not even sure how the technology all works yet."

"Probably a good idea. We should mention it at the next gathering."

Aurora yawned again. "Well, I suppose I should go see what the builders are planning."

"Well, I thought you might like this, first." Selleck held up a satchel.

"Oh, gosh. I never even realized I didn't have it." Aurora took it from him and looked inside. "I was so focused on Palia and Den, I didn't even think about it."

"I know. Someone picked it up for you."

Aurora took the radio out and set it on the desk and eagerly turned it on.

"What is it?"

"It's a radio, a shortwave radio. It can pick up signals from around the world, specifically, from the three other colonies. One moment I'm excited about possibly making contact, the next I'm frightened of it. We have no idea what the people in the other colonies are like. Did they survive? Are they still underground or have they been on New World Earth for a while? Do they have our same values, sense of working together for the social good, or are they more ... evil, for lack of a better word?"

"Guess we won't know until someone responds. How will we know when someone responds?"

Aurora shrugged. "I don't know. At this point, I don't even know if there's anybody on the other side to answer. It's supposed to be sending out a signal the moment it's turned on. Then I suppose we're supposed to talk into it."

Aurora leaned over the device and examined the display. There was a red button with the world TALK printed on it. Aurora tentatively pressed the button.

"Hello? Hello. Can anyone hear me? This is Aurora Cassle of the underground city of Egerton in what was once known as North America. Are there any other colonies out there? Again, this is Aurora Cassle from the North American underground colony of Egerton. We've just come to the surface a couple months ago. Hoping someone from the other three colonies might be listening."

She released the button and waited … and waited … and waited. Her shoulders slumped.

"Guess it was too much to hope that someone would be right there waiting."

"Maybe," Selleck said, who leaned over to examine it. Looks like there's an internal memory. So if someone isn't sitting right there, it'll hold the message as long as it's turned on."

"Well," Aurora said, "let's get a move on. We've got nearly 2700 people to get settled in here before the snow comes."

"Winter and cold, huh?" They left the laboratory room and headed down the hall toward the room where Den was recovering. "They couldn't have built Egerton below some place warm?"

Aurora laughed. "That would have been nice. I suppose it was the most structurally sound spot for our civilization. Plus, we really had no way of knowing what kind of season it was up here when we decided to return to the surface. I think we should just count ourselves lucky we didn't come up in the middle of it."

"That's true."

Aurora stopped outside Den's recovery room, knocked then turned the knob.

Inside, Dom was working intently, almost frantically, and moving from pumping on Den's chest to breathing in his mouth. The reality of what was happening in front of her hit her as though she'd walked into a brick wall. She watched Dom and Lander work. They were so intent in their efforts that they didn't see her and Selleck slip in and close the door.

After several more moments of breathing and pumping, Den took a deep breath and then a few more. Dom and Lander both sighed in relief and Dom swiped the back of his hand across his forehead.

Dom turned and startled when he saw her standing there. The haggard, weary expression on his face confirmed the severity of what had just happened.

"Aurora. I didn't hear you come in." Dom rubbed his face with his hands, then looked down at the floor and back up at her. "He seemed to be doing all right, considering. I'd just completed an assessment scan which reported no change, and then he just stopped breathing. We almost lost him."

The room swirled around her and she leaned back against the door.

"Well, you said, it wouldn't be an easy battle for him, didn't you?"

Dom nodded, clearly exhausted from this overnight vigil and the stress of trying to bring Den back.

"I think he'll be all right for a few moments. He seems to have stabilized. I'll leave you alone with him."

"Thank you."

Dom, Lander, and Selleck all stepped out of the room.

Alone, Aurora suddenly didn't know what to say. She watched Den's chest rise and fall rhythmically as her mind and heart warred between collapsing in a chair next to Den's bed and not caring about anything else or anyone else but him, and staying strong and keeping going at all the things that needed to be done before the first snows. She knew she couldn't do the former, although it was awfully tempting. But, as Dom had reminded her, they were on New World Earth because of her, not anything Den had done, and that she was stronger than she believed herself to be. She took a deep breath as she recalled that conversation. She smiled as she thought of Mr. Poly's and Joylyn's words – and the sight of little Palia sleeping on her mother's shoulder, and Aurora knew she had to go on.

She pulled up a chair beside Den's head, laid her hand over his resting on his chest, then leaned over and laid her head on his chest and just listened to his heartbeat, as she had done the night before. After a moment, she raised her head and looked at his face, her hand tracing a caress along his brow, the other still holding his hand.

"I believe you can hear me, Den. I have a job to do. *We* have a job to do. I know you believe I can do this – you probably have more faith in me than I have in myself. But I have to trust that and keep working to get Imogen built. You need to get better and heal up because New World Earth would be empty without you. You can't leave me, Den. There's too much to do. But, I can't sit here, either, wallowing over you. The first snows are due any day now. So, I will go and do what I believe you would want me to do if you could talk to me right now."

Aurora stood, then leaned over and planted a kiss on his lips.

She straightened and chuckled. "Kinda reminds me of the Old Earth fairy tales I was reading about with the handsome prince kissing the sleeping princess and bringing her back to life. Don't suppose it works the other way around?

"Anyway … I must get out there and let you rest because there'll be a whole new world waiting for you when you wake up. I love you, Den. I'll see you later. No more of this almost dying stuff, you hear me?"

Aurora found Dom, Lander, and Selleck milling about aimlessly in the hall.

"Let's get to work. It's time to get this civilization working. First thing, let's gather everyone outside. I know the various work teams already have an idea of what needs to be done and the time frame we have to do it in, but this is a new location and we need to make sure everyone knows what's expected of them and where help is most needed.

"Dom and Lander, you guys stay here for now, but you need to have a medical team and find out what other devices they used in Old Earth that might help you take care of Den, and help you get started on the reviving some of the creatures we need. I also anticipate that Den won't be the only injury or situation to deal with, so we will also need to have more than one room as a med bay."

"Finding people shouldn't be difficult," Dom responded. "I know of a few already who were part of the team in Egerton."

"All right. Well, decide who you want and what kind of rotation you want. But you and Lander both need rest, and soon."

"I'll attend the meeting," Lander said, "and bring people back so we can get them oriented with what needs to be done so we can spell each other off. At least until the other groups get here."

Aurora nodded. *Of course, the other groups.* She kept forgetting about the other groups. She was so focused on trying to run a community with this many people that she forgot that the other groups would be able to contribute too. *But, one group at a time.* Her heart raced in momentary panic as she thought of trying to accommodate almost 2700 people in this relatively small area, and all within the next few weeks, if not less. While it was overwhelming, it was also tempting to call for those other groups to come now to help with the rebuild.

She knew from her and Den's visits with the other colonies on their way back from the compound that they had also been collecting materials that could be reused. So it wasn't as if the materials they had now would have to stretch to accommodate the new groups. They would just incorporate the new materials with the ones her group had brought.

But, first things first. Time to get this smaller community built.

"We'll meet you outside in about half-an-hour, then, Lander."

Aurora turned with a wave and she and Selleck headed toward the main doors. On their way through the main entrance hall, Selleck called a couple young men over to him and told them to spread the word about the meeting.

"What's next?"

"I need to talk to whoever you chose to head up the recovery and rebuilding. I need to know how they're planning to house everyone and how quickly this can be done and how much protection from the cold weather these shelters will provide."

"That would be Tripp Hendle."

Aurora cast Selleck a sideways glance. "That's the same guy who worked on the concept drawing for the planned expansion. That's a relief. I keep forgetting we have people with all these skills. Somehow I keep thinking that we're all doing this from scratch and have no idea what we're doing, and yet we really seem to have everything we need." Aurora shrugged. "Although we may have to work for it."

"Yeah, kinda neat how that worked out."

"Well, when you think about it, that's what Egerton was designed

265

for. That's why Dr. Heinan went to so much trouble to select the people she did and why Egerton has always maintained a cycle of working people. Older citizens teaching the younger ones to carry on certain trades and roles within the city, to keep the civilization alive. When we came up, we split up that knowledge and experience amongst the other groups so that everyone had a little bit of that knowledge."

As they approached the chosen building site, Aurora noticed that the area had been roped off into numerous sections each of them large enough to hold a single family, similar to the catacombs in Egerton. She followed Selleck in between two of these stringed rows until eventually they found Tripp supervising the stringing of more sections beyond. Selleck waved as they approached.

"Good morning!" The greeting was accompanied by a broad smile and a firm handshake. "Come to see what we're up to, eh?"

"I seem to remember seeing this layout before somewhere."

Tripp laughed heartily. "Why mess with a good thing? At least, it's the fastest solution I could come up with."

"Well, it certainly makes sense. We have a lot of people to get into this limited space," Aurora said.

"It'll do the job for now, at least get us through the cold months and then we can figure out how to rebuild the city. I've been studying the files from Old World Earth about how they built their cities. I don't know that we'll be able to build things as tall as they did, at least not initially. We don't have the machinery they did, but the basics of building wood structures and bricks and concrete we should be able to do to on a smaller scale, at least enough to do what we need to do."

The three of them started roaming along the lined-out lots.

"What about heating? Shelter is one thing. From what I read of winters in this region, shelter won't be enough."

"We've managed to salvage a lot of the piping involved in the ground source heat pumps as well as a lot of the other systems that are surprisingly in good shape, or at least not so damaged or broken down that the engineers on my team can't get them working. There is the slight problem of what do we cover the windows and doors with, otherwise the wind will just blow right in. Most of the glass windows we've seen no longer have any glass and we don't have the technology right now to make our own, at least not in time for them to be useful this winter."

As they approached the end of the lot, several men could be seen starting to dig in preparation for laying out the heating and cooling coils of the ground source heat pump systems that they would use.

Aurora looked back over from where they'd come and then at the sky which was gray with clouds. She shivered as a cold wind blew across the area. *Would they be able to get things built in time?*

"Would it be worth asking the other groups to come and help with the digging and building?" Aurora paced a bit, the men watching her. "Not that I don't have faith in your crew, I know they'll work hard, but there's just so much to do and am I right in assuming that you and your crews will have to work virtually night and day to get everything ready?"

"Yes, that would be helpful and, yes, we will be working around the cycle to get things built in time."

"It would also be easier for them to move now before the cold weather comes than when there's snow on the ground. Their shelters are pretty make-shift as well," Selleck continued.

"The only thing is, where would we put them? There's hardly room for our group in there." Aurora waved a hand toward the compound.

"Perhaps it's just enough to get those who can help with the building of the residential places, and the families could come later," Tripp answered.

"Perhaps. But again we can't ask families to travel in the bad weather either. We still don't have clothing that's suited for the colder weather." Aurora paused. "I guess that's something else we need to work on, too. Making warmer clothes."

The three were silent for a few moments as Aurora's mind whirled with all that needed to be done in such a short period of time, and how best to organize the people to accomplish it all.

"Okay," Aurora said, finally. "Carry on as you have been doing. We're holding a community meeting in a few minutes that I have to get back for. I will send someone back later to update you on what's going to happen. At this point, I don't think we can afford to pull any one of your team members to attend the meeting, but if you want to select one person to attend and report back to you, kind of a spokesperson or liaison so the rest of you can keep working that's fine."

"I'll come with you," Tripp replied. "Everyone's pretty much set in their jobs right now I can get away for a bit. Let me just radio them." Tripp stepped out of earshot as he unclasped his radio from his belt.

"You really think we can make this?" Selleck asked.

Aurora started walking back toward the compound. "I know. Time's pretty tight. But we really don't have much choice. If we don't, we won't survive or at least not all of us. And I have a feeling this keeping warm won't be the only challenge. Food will also be an issue. Our compostable and human waste conversion systems will work for now, but it would be nice to reintroduce some of the foods that used to grow on earth. We've come up so late in the year we can't hope to grow anything."

"Perhaps, I can help with that as well," Tripp said as he jogged up.

"What do you mean?" Aurora asked.

"I mean, I can zone out a portion of the lot around the compound, whichever side or sides you would like, and we can have growing houses, similar to what we had in Egerton. Perhaps you can start with some of the edible plants?"

"Well, we could certainly get the super sweet potatoes and such going. The only one qualified to get involved in the thawing out of the samples in the underground bunker is Dom."

Aurora's heart felt as though a hand had gripped it and squeezed it, sending air gushing from her lungs and her muscles spasming in pain. She stopped walking and grasped Selleck's arm until the feeling abated. She'd been fighting all morning to stay focused on getting housing and heat and food and now clothing set for everyone to keep from thinking about Den, but her concern for him bubbled underneath the surface. Nothing really completely removed him from her mind.

"I know," Aurora managed when she finally regained her breath. "And he's busy." Aurora paused again, then continued with a sigh, "I guess we really do need everybody here, don't we?"

"It would certainly ease the work burden," Selleck agreed.

"Well, then, what I would suggest," Tripp started, "is that the first set of buildings we make be a 'bunk house.'"

"A what?" Aurora asked.

"A bunk house. All the workers on the site could stay there. It would free up space in the compound for the other families and keep the guys here for quick access and easy turnover of schedules."

Aurora nodded. "Sounds like a good arrangement, though I will still need some of the people with medical experience to spell off Dom and

Lander and help with food processing and other challenges that may come up."

"I'll be happy with however many people you can get me, Aurora. We have to all work together to get Imogen built."

"Thank you."

Aurora led the way through the crowd that had gathered around the compound. As she passed, several people stopped her to thank her. Aurora hardly knew what to say. *Would they be as supportive when the weather got colder?* Her heart told her, no, though it appeared people were willing to stand by her decision. Still, there was always the possibility that someone or several someones didn't feel the same way. But, her mission right now was to get people mobilized and working.

She reached the makeshift steps that had been made out of a couple of desks and chairs so that everyone could see and hear her. She scanned the people's faces, most of whom looked up at her expectantly while the children played in an area off to the side. The sounds of their laughter and squeals at the simple freedom of running and playing brought a smile. Her gaze caught when she found Dom's face among the crowd. She thought he'd be sleeping. He smiled, and she smiled back, and she knew he had come deliberately to encourage her where Den could not. With one last visual pan of the crowd, Aurora took a deep breath.

"Good morning, everyone."

"Good morning!" The crowd responded. The strength of the response surprised her. They hadn't muttered the greeting. They were happy to be there.

She smiled as she continued, "As you've probably guessed, I've called you all here, this morning, because I need your help to get the town of Imogen thriving. Let me tell you some of the challenges we're facing, and then I'll talk about how you all can help."

Murmurs and nodding heads bobbed through the crowd.

"First of all, we have the impending cold, as you have probably figured out by the chill in the air, this morning."

The crowd chuckled.

"Our first challenge is heating the compound; second, getting bigger family shelters built; third, making warmer clothing; fourth, getting some food growing; and fifth, moving the other colonies and families here before it gets too cold for them to travel.

"So, here's what we need to do. The first priority is to get holes dug for the ground heating pumps that need to go under the new residences, get those systems repaired as needed and installed, and then to get the new residences built. For that, we will need people with engineering and mechanical abilities, as well as those who are able to handle the physical labour of digging. To get these things done within the short time frame that we have, work crews would be working in shifts around the cycle. I would ask those of you with those skills and abilities meet with Tripp after the meeting so he can get a schedule set.

"I will need at least one set of engineers and other qualified people to get the ground source heating pump under the main compound working."

Tripp gave a curt nod.

"Next thing, despite our cramped living quarters at the moment, we really feel we need the help of the other colonies, so we will be sending messengers to those colonies today. We need the manpower to do everything we need to do before the weather gets too cold."

A few hands shot up into the air.

Aurora raised her hand. "Please, let me finish, and then I will answer any questions you might have. You might find I answer your questions anyway. To deal with the influx of people, we will be asking everyone to kind of bundle together a bit more. In the meantime, Tripp's crews will focus on constructing one building which the work crews would use to sleep in while they're working on the residences and heating systems, and so on. While it means we will be a bit crowded, eventually that will ease when those people working on construction move into that residence. I know, for some that means being separated from your families, but it will make for easier transition in the work schedule and help get the residences built as quickly as possible, and then you will be back together again.

"Third thing, clothing. I know we have a lot of weavers and cloth makers in our group and at the moment, while the construction crews are building, everyone else will be making clothes. The ones we have won't be near warm enough. Again, once the other colonies get here, that will mean extra hands to get this work done, and hopefully it won't actually take that long with all of us working together.

"Fourth thing, food. Upper World Earth did have more to eat than our human compostable products. Those of you who were part of the growing house workers in Egerton, we will need you to do that again. Because it's too cold to actually plant a real Upper World Earth garden, Tripp has suggested that we zone a couple of places around the compound as greenhouse areas for the purpose of starting to grow the food that we had in Egerton, which will help us through the winter, and allow us to reintroduce some of the Upper World Earth plants as Dom gets them thawed out.

"We will also need those with medical and science experience and knowledge to work with Dom and Lander in reintroducing some of these food sources.

"I've already talked about bringing the other colonies here to help get everything established and building and growing and living. It's really going to take everyone's effort to keep us warm and safe and our tummies full, but I know we can do it."

To Aurora's surprise, the crowd murmured positively. All those who had raised their hands with questions earlier, had lowered them.

"Any questions? Anything I haven't addressed that you think needs to be?"

"What about a government?" Someone shouted.

Aurora nodded. "Good question. I hadn't really decided what form of government we would use. A few of Egerton's councillors as you know came up with us. It would be useful to have their experience in running a city, but I like the concept of you, the people, choosing whom you would like to lead the city. In the past, that decision has always been made for us. I think along with the freedom to decide to come to the surface, we should exercise that freedom of choice as well in selecting our new leaders."

"Aurora for mayor!" Someone shouted, and a lot the people chanted her name.

After several moments, Aurora silenced the crowd with a few waves.

"Thank you for your vote of confidence. You will have your chance to choose a little later when everyone else gets here because everyone deserves the right to be considered and to choose. For now, let's get divided into our work groups. Fransen, I want you to be my messenger to the other groups. Weaving, clothing people over here." Aurora waved a hand. "Construction people with Tripp. Medical, science people with Dolan Markus."

CHAPTER THIRTY

Seven day cycles later, Aurora looked over the compound and the surrounding grounds, from her favourite spot on the rocks behind, in what could only be described as amazement. She'd known if everyone pulled together and worked hard that they'd be able to get a lot done, but she never imagined how much.

The ground surface heat systems had all been installed, and the one in the compound repaired and working. All those who weren't working on construction, or with Dolan Markus in medical and science, spent a good portion of the first couple of days harvesting plant life found in the surrounding wetlands that, according to Upper World Earth files, were good for food, insulation, clothing, and potentially other uses, though some of them would have to wait until spring.

While the gathering of these materials was going on, another group worked on making warmer footwear by tying together older shirts and lining them with the cattail cotton the gatherers collected. Once the harvested plants started coming in, those skilled in weaving started immediately processing the fibers and had already made window coverings for the new residences, blankets and coverings for the children.

The first residential structure had also been completed using a combination of hemp plant fibres, which had grown untamed since the end of life on Upper World Earth, and naturally occurring lime that laced the ground in the area and had been harvested from the unusable bricks and rubble, which would also provide an insulated living area for the families once the buildings were ready. But this first one was large enough that most of the construction workers had already moved out there, leaving room in the compound for the next colony.

This particular morning, Aurora awaited the arrival of Barna's group. In another seven day cycles, Dara Killick's group would come, and then they'd all be together.

In the seven days since the construction and organization work started, the weather had grown even colder and snow had already started drifting down, not heavy enough to build up on the ground, but enough to remind Aurora, and everyone else, that winter was not far off and they had no option but to move the other groups in now. By the time the third group arrived, it was highly likely that the snow would be upon them, the gathering of clothing materials would have to stop, and the construction of the residences might have to be stopped or at least slowed down which also likely meant the possibility of many of the people still living in the compound over the winter and no one relished that. It would be great to have the other members of the other colonies help in those efforts as long as possible.

There were still adult clothes to make, particularly for the construction crews who were going to continue working no matter the cold.

It was almost high sun and the suspense of waiting to see the second group had made it hard for Aurora to concentrate on anything else. As her mind mulled over everything that had happened in the past seven days and what lay ahead, she collapsed onto a rock under the weight of it all. Without any conscious thought, her heart reached out to the only person she knew would hear her. She couldn't exactly say how she knew. It was really a matter of instinct. The same logic that told her that no one else in the compound could help her battled with the logic that the existence of a Higher Being, a Creator, with whom she was free to communicate, was impossible. But as she had told Den seemingly eons ago, she'd known there had to have been a Creator the moment she looked into her baby's eyes, and that belief had been confirmed by records of old Upper World Earth religions.

The fact that all the people they needed to make the civilization survive had been ultimately chosen and contained in Egerton, that over the centuries they still maintained the skills and abilities needed to make life on Upper World Earth possible again, and the rhythm with which everything seemed to be flowing told her that there was an ultimate plan at work. She certainly couldn't have orchestrated everything like this, or even organized everyone to work together as they had, if they hadn't already been chosen and learned after centuries of tradition and teaching started, ultimately, by the First Ones.

One of the things she was still curious about was how she had ever ended up being the leader for these people. She certainly never intended to seek any kind of leadership role. Her initial intent was simply to save their lives and, as Imogen Heinan's files revealed, fulfill the original intent for the city's people.

Her mind was drawn to an ancient Upper World Earth story that she'd read over the last seven days. With Den still fighting to recover from his injuries, she'd found herself inexplicably drawn to these stories about God and the Israelites. The story her mind focused on was that of Moses who led the Hebrew people out of Egypt in the book of Exodus. The similarities between the story of Egerton and that of that ancient earth exodus were so striking that it pretty much solidified her belief that Someone's plan was at work here. These weren't just random events happening by accident. And these things were happening at this specific time for a reason. It might be as simple as it just being time to re-establish life on Upper World Earth, or there could also be reasons intended for each person who had accompanied her and each person who had stayed behind.

Of course, she wondered why this appeared to be the appointed time of Egerton's exodus with winter bearing down on them. It would have been so much easier if they'd come up even a month earlier. Although, as she thought about it, they would have come up in the heat of summer and perhaps would have been harder to adjust to given the controlled climate of Egerton that they were used to.

She worked through all these thoughts until all that was left was her clear heart and mind. The previous ache of her heart that led her to collapse on the rock under the weight of everything expected of her, lifted. It was almost as if a hand had reached down from the Heavens, scooped out that burden and lifted it out, leaving a peace she couldn't explain – particularly in the light of everything that was still left to do – that it was all going to work out. It didn't mean there weren't going to be challenges. The Israelites in the ancient earth story encountered hunger, discouraged spirits and bickering amongst the population, and the disappointment of not seeing the land that was promised to them because they seemed to have difficulty following simple instructions from the God who had protected them from Pharaoh's army and led them across the Red Sea.

The constant in that story was no matter what the Israelites did or bickered about, and even though they didn't follow God's directions, God still provided for them. Aurora took great comfort in that, and the fact that obviously they were up here for a reason and had been brought up for a reason, that they were meant to survive. The ancient earth story also recounted how God provided food when the Israelites complained of being hungry, of providing shoes that never wore out during their 40 years in the wilderness.

Aurora thought again of all the resources surrounding them for heating, food, building materials, for clothing and even shoes and knew that their being here was no accident and that everything they needed had been provided and would be provided in the future. One question she mulled over now was why would a Creator go to so much trouble for a bickering group of people who hadn't followed His seemingly simple instructions? The Hebrews' disobedience had led them to slavery in Egypt for 400 years.

When they cried out to God to save them, He did, but they still bickered and didn't trust.

The more recent history of Upper World Earth seemed to follow the same track as the ancient story. As people continued to disobey and not follow the rules that would lead them to peace between each other, eventually war and disease consumed the planet, even though God had provided everything people needed to survive. Why would a Creator with control over everything, continue giving people chance after chance after chance even though it seemed the only thing people knew how to do was disobey His instructions or make up their own rules? It seemed insane really.

Aurora thought of her children when they were little. How many times did she ask them to pick up their things, or clean their teeth or wash themselves, or be home for the late-cycle meal on time, and yet they didn't always obey. Sure, there were certain consequences in going to bed with empty tummies or losing the privilege of having their things for a little while. And, yet, she kept giving them chance after chance. Why? Because she loved them and want to see them succeed and knew that they needed opportunities to try and fail because that was the only way they were going to learn that their decisions and actions had consequences and not always happy ones, which hopefully would help them make right decisions next time. The discipline of consequences was necessary to teach them what they needed to make a life of their own when they left her home and made their own families.

As she thought about it, why else would anyone do anything like that over and over, second chance after second chance, with the hope that people would finally start making the right choices. The construction of Egerton was the result of people having continually made wrong choices and were on the verge of destroying one another. And yet Egerton had been another second chance. A chance for them to come back into the light and get things right.

Although, she supposed, not everyone had got things right, and the unfortunate consequence of their decision would mean that those who chose to stay behind would die down in the dark without ever having seen or experienced the life that they were meant to have by the very fact that they had been chosen to live in the first place. They would never know the light. Perhaps that was another way of ensuring the survival of the new civilization of Imogen. Those who would have passed negative thinking through and been the source of bickering and dissension among the people had been wheedled out. If they had come up, Aurora could just imagine them calling for everyone to return to Egerton with the impending weather upon them and the challenge that presented. Once out of Egypt and faced with a little bit of trouble, the Hebrew people had bickered about wanting to go back to slavery rather than live free and trust that there was a plan at play and trust in the God who was working out the plan and, therefore, would take care of them.

Aurora had been afraid that such negative thinking would have come up with everyone working so hard to prepare for the cold weather, but none of that had happened. Not that there wasn't the possibility of negative thinking in the future. Their battle and struggle wasn't over yet. But it seemed that everyone was thankful for and looking forward to this second chance of living in the light and, despite the challenges, no one had even raised the idea of returning to Egerton.

Aurora stood from the rock and looked down over the compound again with people buzzing like bees back and forth. Buzzing like bees ... an old earth phrase. She'd actually seen a couple of the fuzzy, yellow-and-black-striped creatures working until the very last second to find food. A pretty accurate description of what her people were doing.

One of the things she was most proud of was the greenhouse. If she had had any doubts at all about what they were doing and what they would accomplish in such a short period of time, getting the greenhouse up would have been the biggest of them. The appropriate materials for a greenhouse had been pretty hard to find as most if not all of the glass that would normally have been used was broken and they didn't have time to learn how to make it. And even if they could find alternate materials, how could they replicate the effect of the sun to make them effective given the short day cycles in the winter? The solution actually solved two problems.

Two of Tripp's teams were assigned to seek out the town's plasma gasification generator, repair it and the connection between it and the compound as needed. This meant that they could use some of the UV lamps they'd brought up from Egerton in the greenhouse and use whatever housing material they had on hand, and that they now had electric lights in the new residences and in the compound. There wasn't enough power yet to light up the whole town, but there was enough for the compound, and as they continued to recycle what materials were left in the town, the things that couldn't be reused would be incinerated to generate the power they needed.

Now instead of a burden of worry and concern, Aurora's heart surged with gratefulness and wonder at how all this had come to be, far beyond all she ever could have imagined when Den first expressed his thoughts on the expansion project to her. Never in a million years, would she have even contemplated all this.

Now, she stood overlooking a bustling, thriving, happy civilization waiting for another part of their family to join them.

The brief thought of Dom doused her joy a little bit, knowing he'd been splitting his time looking after Den and overseeing the thawing efforts of some of the plants and animals that would most help them survive. Last report was that the plant regeneration could start in the greenhouses and that the creatures would best be done in the spring when they would be able to build bigger and more animal-friendly structures. Since they couldn't know how their bodies would react to having these kinds of foods added back into their diet after 400 years, Dom had suggested that they reintroduce these new nutrient sources a little bit at a time so that he could monitor people's reactions and sensitivities.

Den's condition had improved and there hadn't been any other resuscitation incidents. But Den still hadn't woken up or shown much movement even though Dom's scans continued to show that Den was healing. With a couple of medical science teams available, Dom had started scheduling muscular rehabilitation activities for Den. These involved stretching and gently moving his legs and arms, pretty much his entire body to keep his muscles from atrophying. The movement also kept lymphatic fluid flowing which flushed toxins out of his body and encouraged healing. All their efforts appeared to be working according to the scans, but there was really very little they could do about any potential of brain damage that they couldn't measure. The longer he slept, the more concerned they all got that there was far more brain damage than they'd originally thought.

Her heart ached again at her loneliness for him, but it wasn't as crippling this time as it had been earlier in the week. Perhaps she'd just gotten used to working and doing things on her own, that she never dreamed she'd be doing on her own, let alone succeeding at it. But the built structures below her and the thriving community told her that she was succeeding at it – they all were.

The crunching of footsteps on the gravel below the crag alerted her. Moments later, Dom's head appeared above the ledge and then he was standing beside her.

"Thought I'd find you up here."

"You keep saying the same thing every time you find me."

Dom smiled, a warm friendly smile that made Aurora instinctively smile back.

"Yeah, I couldn't stay inside any longer."

"They're not going to come any faster if you're watching for them.

In fact, it'll seem like they're not coming at all."

Aurora shrugged and looked at the ground. "I know. I'm not just watching for them, I'm also looking down at all we've accomplished. I hardly know what to say." She shook her head. "It's not at all what I ever imagined our new civilization would look like. From the very beginning I felt like I was just making this up as I went along and now as I look back on everything I realize it might have seemed that way to me because I can't see what's ahead of us, but there's a time and purpose for all this – a plan, that we can't see and everything is working together for that plan."

"Interesting thought. You've been reading those ancient Earth stories again."

Aurora chuckled. "Yeah, you caught me."

"Can't say I disagree with you, though. I know as a doctor and scientist I should only believe in the things I can prove, but some things are just a gut instinct and you can't prove or disprove that, but that doesn't mean it's not real. I think it's because I'm a doctor I can appreciate how our bodies are knit together and how the body works best when all its systems are functioning together. If one of those systems is just slightly out of sync, it affects all the other systems. They're so intimately intertwined; the systems and the relationship between those systems just can't be by accident. They were designed to work that way."

"Kinda like the people themselves. When they're all working together with their various skills and abilities, the civilization works well together. So far, none of those systems have encountered something we haven't been able to resolve, and people are happy and working together."

"There's always a chance that something will happen."

Aurora looked down at her feet and kicked a stone that tumbled – clackety-clack – over the edge of the rock and down the side.

"I know. It already has."

Dom took her hand. "I wasn't talking about Den."

"I know you weren't. But you have to admit that's one part of the system that has definitely affected other parts."

"You really think so?"

Aurora met Dom's gaze. "Why, you don't think so?"

"Well, it's certainly had an impact on your life, I know that. But sometimes these kinds of things happen because we need to learn to do certain things on our own, or at the very least learn that we can actually do things on our own. True, Den probably could have helped out in a lot of areas, but the people aren't suffering without him, not as much as you are."

"I guess so."

"You guess so? You guess what?"

"I guess I see what you mean about needing to do this without him, even though I never imagined me doing this without him, and realizing that I could do it on my own."

"You're so much stronger than you give yourself credit for. I've said this to you before and I think it's what Den was trying to show, and probably why I – er – he fell in love with you."

Aurora looked at him again, and noticed Dom's cheeks flush a bright pink.

"Thank you."

He glanced back at her with an upward twitch of his mouth. "You're welcome."

"Guess I can't live without you, either."

His mouth broadened into a wide grin. "Good thing cause I'm not going anywhere."

"Even though I'm a married woman."

Dom nodded, a little sadder. "Even though."

Aurora let go of Dom's hand and folded her arms across her chest. "I just wish he was awake to see this. To see everyone coming home. To see everything we've done. He's believed in this from the beginning even though even I had my doubts. He never had any. He deserves to see it."

"I'm doing the best I can …" Dom turned away.

"Oh, no, no. That's not what I meant, Dom." She rested a hand on his shoulder. "I know you are and I don't blame you at all. We've all been wishing that he'd wake up, and it would mean the world to me if he could be standing beside me to see it, but I know that's not going to happen. But I'd just be happy if he woke up." Aurora moved to stand in front of him and kissed his cheek and hugged him. "Please don't think I believe this is your fault. You're awesome with him and I couldn't think of anyone else I would have chosen to care for him."

Dom looked at her as the sadness lifted from his eyes and his face lightened in a mischievous smile.

Aurora stood back. "What?"

"Well, you've just reminded me of the reason I came out here in the first place."

"I thought you just came out to cheer me up."

"I did." Dom's smile grew broader.

"You mean … he's awake?!"

Dom laughed. "He is. Just a few moments ago."

Aurora squealed and took off down the side of the rock. "Why didn't you tell me?!"

Dom waited until they reached the ground again. "Because you needed to believe in yourself. That you're more amazing than you give yourself credit for. I wanted to make sure of that, because I know Den thinks the same thing and I wanted that to be first thing he sees when he sees you."

Aurora stopped her charge back to the compound because her eyes had filled with tears.

"If I'm amazing then what does that make you?" She asked once Dom caught up to her. "That's got to be one of the most amazing things you could have done for the both of us."

"So, you're not angry with me for keeping the secret?"

"Not at all. I really don't know what I'd do without you. Not only because of how you care for me, but you saved him, Dom."

"Just doing my job." Despite Dom's easy-going demeanor, he actually seemed bashful.

"No. It's more than that and you know it."

Dom looked at her. "I was just doing my job, but I knew anything I could do for him, I'd be doing it for you. That's what love does."

Tears fell down Aurora's cheeks as she reached up and tenderly kissed his mouth.

"I know."

"Well," Dom said after a few moments, "let's go see him."

CHAPTER THIRTY-ONE

When Aurora burst into the room, Den initially had his eyes closed as he rested his head on pile of cushions behind, but immediately awoke at the sound of the door.

Aurora lost her remaining composure and burst into tears as she rushed to the bed and fell across Den's chest. At his sharp intake of breath, she snapped straight up again.

"Oh, Den, I'm so sorry! I forgot, you're still healing."

"Yeah, and I think I'll have to do a bunch of it over again." Den rubbed a hand over his ribs.

Aurora laughed. Den did too even though it hurt to do so. Their hands instinctively reached for each other and Den raised one of hers to his lips. When she leaned over, their mouths connected, the intensity releasing all the pent up worry, fear and relief that had built up since the accident. When they stopped, Den gave in to the support of the cushions behind him, exhausted.

"I'm sorry, I didn't mean to wear you out."

"Nah, that's all right. Can't think of a better way to wear me out … well, actually I can," he amended with a quirky grin, "but that'll have to come later."

Aurora laughed and blushed.

"So, tell me what's been going on."

Aurora told him everything, his eyes growing drowsier as she continued, but he nodded in certain places.

"See, I told you you could do it," he said when she was done.

"I think you had more faith in me than I did," Aurora said, glancing sheepishly at the hands clasped in her lap. "I still don't really feel like I know what I'm doing, but so far things are working out much better than I ever thought they would."

"When's Barna's group supposed to get here?"

"I've been watching for them virtually all morning, until Dom pulled me down here to see you, but we're expecting them before the late afternoon meal."

"Well, then, I guess I better rest up so I can be there to see them."

Aurora smiled and took his hand which he grasped with more strength than she thought he had.

"I guess you'd better."

She leaned over and kissed him again, almost not wanting to let go. At the end of the kiss, Den drifted off to sleep. Aurora watched him for a few moments. Her heart ached, this time in joy and thankfulness that Den was back in her life. She gently lay across his chest, hoping not to disturb his rest, and just cried. Cried out the fear that he would never recover, cried out all her worry, and then her joy and relief and the most amazing gift she could have received with their community being reunited and her being reunited with Den. As she cried, Den's hand rubbed up and down her back until her tears were spent and she just lay there in the quiet listening to Den's heartbeat. His hand stopped rubbing and she knew it was time to go.

A knock on the door alerted her.

"Yes?"

Dom stuck his head in the door. "Um, there's something you need to see."

"Okay, coming."

Dom shut the door and Aurora straightened herself and her clothing, and swiped the remaining tears from her face. She wasn't going to be able to hide her swollen eyes from the others, but Dom sounded urgent.

"What is it?" She said when she emerged.

Dom looked her over quickly, but didn't comment. "Mr. Poly will show you. I need to get back to my patient."

Mr. Poly stood a little ways off appearing like he feared he was intruding, but also nearly bristling with excitement.

"What is it, Mr. Poly?" Aurora asked, as Dom and his team, disappeared back into Den's room.

"Oh, I just had to come find you right away, Miss Aurora. I know you're waiting for the others to come, but I just thought this couldn't wait."

Aurora gently touched his arm, and he started dragging her into the sleeping area. Aurora couldn't help but notice his arm felt thinner than the last time he did this, and he didn't move quite as quickly as he had when they first arrived and he had shown her to the little alcove reserved for her. She knew he wouldn't be with them much longer and that whatever he was trying to tell her might be one of the last exciting moments of his life.

"That's all right. Thank you for finding me. Now, tell me what's got you so excited."

"Oh, it's just so wonderful! I just can't tell you! I have to show you. I know having Mr. Den awake and healing is wonderful, and having the others coming home, today, but this … ." Mr. Poly stopped tugging on her for a moment and lifted his eyes to the ceiling. "I just can't describe it."

As they neared her little alcove, a group of the people who'd been working inside on the clothing had gathered around it.

"They've contacted us, Miss Aurora. They've contacted us!"

Aurora clapped her hands to her mouth. "They? You mean one of the other colonies?"

"Yes!"

Aurora pushed through the crowd to the squawking radio. Golan Inson, another one of the older men, waved her over.

"Just a minute," he said into the microphone. "She's here." Then he stood and ushered Aurora into the chair.

Aurora glanced from one piece of the apparatus to the other, wondering what she would say, and supremely aware of the audience around her.

She tentatively raised her hand to the TALK button and pressed it.

"Hello. This is Aurora Cassle. We are from the North American underground colony of Egerton."

"Hello. So nice to hear another human voice. We'd about given up hope that you had survived. I'm Solek Tar from the former Asia-Pacific colony Altona2 located in what used to be Australia. Where are you?"

"We're in what used to be Canada, Province of Ontario, in the northern part of the province as we understand it. It's getting cold here."

"Ah, down here it's getting hot. I guess our weather systems are in reverse, cold up there, hot down here."

Aurora smiled. "I guess so. What do you mean you'd given up hope that we had survived?"

"Well, we haven't heard from the Equatorial city that was in Brazil and they were first to be hit with the virus so we're assuming they didn't get down in time, or perhaps they came up for debriefing and were wiped out before they went back under."

"They may just be late risers?"

Solek laughed. "They could be. I suppose we'll never know for sure until we send a team down there to look. The European city," he continued, "Nelson, came up just after we did, but only about half of that city survived."

Aurora thought about the people still living in Egerton. Their survival rate was better than Nelson's, but she still grieved for those she couldn't save.

"Well, we have about ninety percent of our people out."

"What? What happened?"

"The other ten percent decided to stay. Our population had actually started to decrease because of birth defects and experienced skeletal deformities and other medical effects of having been underground for so long. When I suggested that we all return to the surface, some resisted and refused."

"That's too bad." The sorrow in Solek's voice came through very clearly. "We had about ninety percent survival, too. Same as you, not everyone wanted to come back up. We experienced the same kind of physiological changes that you did."

"Hmm. That's interesting. How long have you been up?"

"About 100 years actually."

"One hundred years?!" Aurora sat back in the chair with a hand to her mouth.

"Yes, that's another reason why we'd given up hope that anyone in Egerton had survived."

"So you probably don't remember living in the city then?"

"No, my grandparents did. My parents were born on the surface."

"So, you're much further along in your New World Earth resettlement, then?"

"Yes. By the way, that's what we call it, too – New World Earth."

Aurora smiled. Despite their being half-a-world apart, there were similarities.

"Well, I know I could sit here and talk for hours, but winter's coming and I have to keep everyone on their toes so we can get things finished. Another group of our citizens are joining us today from where they were living in another part of Imogen – that's what we've decided to call our new city – until we could get our compound area ready for them. The third and last group will arrive in another seven days or perhaps sooner," Aurora amended as she glanced outside at the snow drifting downwards. "Not sure the weather will hold off long enough for us to wait that long to move the other group."

"Well, it was wonderful talking to you. Everyone will be thrilled. I will report to the Europeans as well. They actually stopped monitoring the radio. We – they and us – communicate electronically now with a lot of the systems that were left over from Upper World Earth."

"It's probably something we can work on over the winter."

"Do you have pads?"

"Yes."

"Then I'll send you instructions on how to repair the system and how to contact us. We've also started using air travel, and will send you instructions on that, too. I know you're not quite there technology-wise, yet, but it'll give your scientists something to work on."

"Thank you. We'll check in with you later."

Once Solek signed off, Aurora sat back in her chair again, vaguely aware of the murmuring of the people around her, and some of them dashing off to tell the others.

One hundred years! She couldn't get over that number. The physiological changes they discovered in Egertonians had certainly been happening long enough to have been noticed a hundred years ago. The advantage was that Solek's people were further along in the resettling process than her people were and would be able to help even if it was from a distance.

While having everyone working together certainly gave them all a purpose, and a drive to succeed and contribute and achieve, she hoped that it wouldn't always be this hard to provide food and shelter and she looked forward to the time when animals and other edible and versatile plants were cultivated and ready for them to eat. It was important to balance this easier lifestyle with a working schedule, though, similar to what they had now. To take that feeling of purpose away by making life too easy would also take away this feeling of community that they'd known all their lives and people would become too focused on doing things for themselves rather than for each other. They'd forget where they came from and how survival took contribution from everyone. They'd forget to be thankful for what they have and only long for those things they didn't have yet.

From what she'd read of life on Upper World Earth, this kind of greed was all that had led to the last war. It would be a mistake if they ignored what happened to UWE. The next stage of human survival depended upon them not making the same mistakes the civilizations of UWE did.

This was a chance for them all to come back home and make up for those past mistakes and do things right so that their civilization could prosper. She thought about the Israelites again and how many times they disobeyed God's instructions and how many hardships their disobedience led to. As she had studied what had happened to UWE, she realized that the more and more people turned from following God's instructions, the more civilization fell away from those guiding principles, leading ultimately to the wars she read about.

She thought it curious that, out of all the ancient earth stories, this one would strike a chord. There were many ancient civilizations. Perhaps it was similarities between that ancient earth story about Noah's ark and the Exodus and Egerton and, at least in the Noah's ark story, the way society seemed to be heading when the floods and rains came. It was just too difficult for her to dismiss these similarities and for her to deny that the ancient earth accounts weren't real.

After all, here they were basically in the wilderness, as in the Exodus story, but they had what they needed – shelter, clothing, food. It was provided for.

Her mind turned back to her talk with Solek and what he had said about the Nelson colony. *Why hadn't everyone survived? And what happened to the Equatorial city?*

Aurora guessed she may never really know the answer to either question, although the thought did cross her mind to find the Equatorial city and find out, perhaps with the air travel technology that Solek was going to send her.

But, first things first, and that was to make sure Imogen would make it through the winter.

She stood from the desk and emerged from the alcove, the earlier eavesdropping crowd having dispersed long ago. A quick glance out the window at the sun starting to disappear behind the crags behind told her that the other colony would arrive shortly.

Her heart leaped in excitement. It had been such an amazing day. She hadn't enjoyed a day so much since she and Den spent three days alone here. With so many people around and him still recovering, it was probably going to be a long time before they were able to spend some alone again. In the meantime, she looked forward to everyone finally being together.

CHAPTER THIRTY-TWO

"There they are!" Someone shouted.

The crowd erupted into cheers and applause.

Aurora touched Den's shoulder. Den had insisted on coming out with her, and sat next to her in a wheelchair built by some of the bicycle repair guys. He reached up and covered her hand with his.

A mass of bodies appeared on the horizon less than kilometer away from their vantage point. It was another ten minutes before the group was close enough for Aurora to see Barna out front. Aurora squealed and ran and Barna did the same.

Aurora hugged Barna, tears streaming down her face.

"It's so good to see you. It feels like eons since we saw each other."

"I know."

Aurora pulled away and saw tears on Barna's face, too. But they weren't just tears of joy.

"What's wrong? What's happened?"

A face appeared behind Barna.

"Caytor?"

"Mom!" Another round of tears and hugs. It was a while before

Aurora found her voice.

"Wha What are you doing here?" *If Caytor was here, maybe others had come with her. What about Den's daughter Peggie?* Aurora expected her to erupt from the crowd when she saw her father. Perhaps it was a shock for Peggie to see her dad in a wheelchair.

"What about Den's … ?"

"There's a lot we have to tell you."

Aurora was taken aback by Barna's interruption. "What do you mean?"

"Let's not do it now. Let's just celebrate being together and getting everyone to their places and seeing what you've got going on here," Barna suggested, "then we can talk about that."

"You're right. Come on." Aurora waved a hand forward, her other hand clasped with her daughter's. "We've been working overtime to get everything ready. We'll be hosting most of the residential work crews at the construction site. Everyone else will be in the compound. It'll be tight quarters obviously until the dwellings are completed, which is why crews need to be close to the site.

"We have a greenhouse that will need gardeners. Dom will likely love to have some more health and science team members. Everyone else will be involved in weaving and making winter clothes and shoes."

"Wow. You've been busy."

Aurora nodded.

"And you've done this all by yourself."

Again, Aurora nodded and tears threatened to fall again as she thought about the circumstances that led to her managing the establishment

296

of Imogen by herself.

"Although Dom and Tripp have really been great supports."

"What about Den?"

By this time, they'd reached the waiting crowd and Barna caught sight of Den in the wheelchair.

"Believe me, it's a miracle he's sitting there," Aurora responded to Barna's sideways glance. "We'll swap stories later."

The two groups merged in conversation and reunification as the sun descended farther beyond the horizon. Aurora knew there was limited time to get the groups inside and assigned sleeping spaces. The little ones were tired, her group had worked a long and hard, and Barna's group had journeyed a long way. They all needed rest.

Aurora led them to the front of the compound and, standing on a similar impromptu dais to the one she'd used a week before, instructed the new arrivals on where they'd be sleeping and working. When those groups branched off, the amount of people left would just manage to fit in the compound. Citizens filed into the building and divided into the available rooms and spaces.

Den was growing weary again from all the exertion, so once everyone had been sorted, Aurora wheeled him back to his room, and settled him against his pillows with a lingering kiss. It didn't take long for him to fall asleep, so she left him and went in search of Caytor and Barna.

She found Barna laying out her bed space in one room, and Caytor in the other, after having settled her children. Aurora looked down at their slumbering faces.

"I can't believe they're here. I can't believe you're here." Aurora hugged her daughter again.

"I know, mom. Come on. Webber will be on the medical team and doesn't have to report until tomorrow. He'll watch over them." Caytor waved to her husband and Aurora let herself be ushered out in to the hall.

"I don't know about you, but it's feeling kind of claustrophobic in here. Can we go outside?" Barna asked.

Aurora laughed. "Claustrophobic? Do you realize what you just said? How ironic is it that we've spent all our lives in an underground city and in all this openness we feel claustrophobic."

Barna laughed, too. "I know, eh? Guess I kinda got used to the open space and now I'm part of a community again."

"It gets chilly at night now, but we've made a shelter out back just because it is a lot of people to house in one spot and the children need a play area."

Aurora led the way down the hall toward her group's room. As they passed Den's room, Aurora stopped and poked her head in the door. She exchanged glances with Lander, who was taking the night shift.

"He's okay," Lander mouthed.

Aurora nodded and closed the door.

"Aurora, what happened to him?"

"Mom … ?"

Aurora held up her hand to keep them from asking any more questions, until they'd passed through the last sleeping room and headed out the back door into the sheltered area.

There was a grouping of boulders off in one corner and the three of them each chose a rock to sit on. Aurora recounted their journey to the compound, how Palia had run off, and how Den had rescued her but was injured in the process. She recounted the time Dom had had to resuscitate him. She told them about the decisions that needed to be made regarding housing as winter neared, and all the resources they'd been able to find and use in their rebuilding efforts. She finished off with a recap of her conversation with Solek Tar.

When she'd finished, Barna just shook her head.

"Wow." There was dead silence for a few minutes. "What you've done here with all the challenges you've faced is truly amazing."

"I'm so proud of you, mom." Aurora welcomed Caytor's embrace. "You're amazing."

"Thank you. It's not at all what I would have anticipated returning to the surface, but the challenge has been good for me actually. Helped me develop a confidence in myself I didn't know I had. I never really considered myself a leader until now." Aurora shrugged and shook her head. "I still don't count myself a leader. I still feel like I'm just making it up as I go along. But as I look back on all that's happened, I see it's all part of a plan." Aurora recounted her thoughts about God and his plan and the ancient earth stories.

Barna and Caytor both nodded at the end.

"I can see how you would think that," Barna said.

"It's a lot more comforting to know that none of this is all random, but actually meant to happen so even though you don't always feel like you know what you're doing, or even wonder if you're making the right choices, the way things are ultimately working seems to suggest that's the way things were supposed to be," Caytor said.

"So you're not upset with me for pursuing this?"

"Not at all, mom. You did the right thing. We were all going to die down there. You at least gave us a choice. Live a potentially healthier, longer life up here, or live out the rest of our days as we'd always done."

"You said you wouldn't come up until your father was gone. Is he ... ?" Despite how their relationship had ended, and her newfound love with Den, Aurora's heart panged at the thought of Merrick's death.

Barna and Caytor hung their heads.

"What? What's happened?"

"They're all gone, mom."

Aurora sat up straight in shock. "What do you mean, they're all gone?"

"There is no more Egerton."

"What are you talking about?"

Caytor looked at Barna. Aurora looked back and forth between the two of them. It seemed like no one wanted to be the one to tell the story.

Eventually, Caytor sighed and began. "After you and the others left, the town tried to keep things working – the lights, the heating systems, the food production, the medical services. But it was really hard with so many people gone. Within weeks, the quality of life had really started to suffer. At the beginning, there had been more food available, but the few that were left started eating whatever they wanted. There was no more rationing, no more making sure there was enough for everyone else, until we were left with very little and, with the dwindled workforce in the greenhouses, not much ready to eat.

"As systems started to fail, a lot of those who'd decided to remain behind began to change their minds and wanted to leave. But the mayor, dad, and quite a few others remained adamant that they were destined to die there and wouldn't leave.

300

"Those of us who wanted to leave prepared to do so, but we didn't know that the mayor had planned to destroy the city. To bury everyone there rather than let anyone else leave."

Aurora raised her hands to her mouth. She looked from Barna to Caytor and back again.

"Webber caught wind of the mayor's plan only a few hours before we'd been planning to go – although the mayor, to my knowledge, never knew when we were planning to leave. Perhaps he did and that's why he scheduled to execute his plan when he did – I don't know."

Caytor hung her head. "We gathered as many people as we could together outside the door to the surface when we heard explosions around the city. The ground shook and the caverns around us started to collapse. We ran for the tunnel and managed to get everyone inside before everything crumbled and buried whoever was left."

"And Den's daughter?"

Caytor shook her head.

Aurora stared at her daughter in horror; her heart overwhelmed with grief at the loss of those who'd chosen to remain behind, and relief that her daughter and others had reached the light. They could have easily been lost in Egerton's collapse and no one on the surface would have ever known the city was gone. Four hundred years of history destroyed by one mad man's need for control.

Aurora stood and walked to the other side of the structure. She couldn't sit any longer. She resisted the urge to run away. She hadn't put on winter clothes and it was too cold outside the structure to hide away on her crag until Dom came and found her.

"How many came with you?"

"Fifty."

Aurora fell to her knees under the weight of grief. One hundred and fifty people crushed to death. It was several minutes before any of them spoke again. Aurora rubbed her thighs as she struggled to process the reality of Caytor's story.

"It's my fault."

"No." Caytor said.

"Yes, it is. It's my fault they're gone."

"No, it's not." Barna had moved from the rock and stood over Aurora's shoulder; Caytor on the other.

"If I had left well enough alone ..."

"If you had left well enough alone, none of us would be here."

"No, but we would have all been alive down there. Those one hundred and fifty people would still be alive."

"Mama." Aurora looked up at Caytor's use of the name she used as a toddler. "Yes, those one hundred and fifty people would still be alive right now, but there are over two thousand people thriving up here in the light after centuries of mayors who chose to keep us in the dark without offering the people of Egerton the choice.

"You can't blame yourself for other peoples' choices. You gave everyone an option none of us even knew we had. You did the right thing."

"Did I?"

"Yes, you did." The three of them turned and looked at Den in his wheelchair being pushed by Dom.

"I thought you were sleeping."

"I was."

Aurora looked at Dom, his expression telling her he'd read her mind again and had brought Den to her.

"You can't carry the weight of those peoples' deaths on your heart and conscience, Rori. You don't deserve to carry them. The only person that deserves that is the mayor and he's no longer alive to carry it and has, no doubt, answered eternally for his choice that cost the lives of the people he was entrusted to care for."

Dom wheeled Den close enough that he could take Aurora's hand. Aurora laid her head against Den's legs.

"Would you all leave us alone for a moment?"

Silently, Barna, Dom, and Caytor left, but it was a while before either Aurora or Den said anything. Aurora's heart hurt too much to speak.

"You did all you could do. You're not responsible for what those people chose, for what the mayor did, and for their deaths."

"They didn't deserve to die like that. Your daughter, Den. I-I ... ." Aurora dissolved into tears. "I'm so sorry."

"She made her choice. I knew no matter what there'd be no changing it. I accepted that the moment I knew I would need to help you."

"But ... ."

"You're not responsible, Aurora."

"But what a way for it to end. I'm not just talking about the mayor collapsing everything. I mean, people going hungry and all that." Aurora waved a hand. "I never imagined that taking all those people out of the city would eventually lead to that kind of destitution. How it would affect the food supply and all that. We felt the hole when the three groups were separated. Imagine how they must have felt with so many others gone who would never return. We at least had the plan to bring everyone together."

Aurora didn't move from her spot on the ground, her head still resting on Den's legs. Den pet her head.

"I'd had the thought a couple of times of going back to try again to convince those who'd chosen to stay behind to come up," Aurora shook her head, "but I never did. To be honest, I was afraid to go back. Afraid to go back down there. Not because of what the mayor might do or what people would think."

Aurora lifted her head and looked up at Den.

"Then what?

"You'll think it's silly."

Den touched a crooked finger under her chin. "Now, you know me better than that."

Aurora looked down at the ground, still ashamed. "I guess the best way to describe it is that I was afraid of the dark. Just the thought of going back down there almost sent me into one of those panic attacks."

"That doesn't sound silly at all. I would think it was kind of normal. We've been held captive all our lives, never known anything else. Now that we've come out of the darkness, had a taste of freedom, seen the sunlight, I don't think anyone else wants to go back."

"I keep thinking of that ancient earth story, I've been reading a lot while you were healing. There's a story about an ancient earth culture, a nation of people that was in Egypt for 400 years as slaves, a man named Moses led them out of Egypt to the land that God promised them. But even though God saved them when the king tried to hunt them down, led them through the desert and provided food and water for them, they grumbled about wanting to go back to Egypt, instead of trusting God to provide for their future as he had already provided for their past and present.

"Despite all the hardships and struggles to get this civilization settled and healthy before the deeper cold comes, I really feel this is our promised land. It's not really flowing with milk and honey, but it has everything we need, we just need to learn how to use it. But we've been given the foundations we need to restart everything, including the history of a people that seemed to lose sight of this, so we don't make the same mistakes."

"Well, you know what? I know I've been asleep for a while, but I don't think I've ever heard anybody grumble and complain about wanting to go back."

Aurora shook her head and smiled. "No, me neither. Doesn't mean there haven't been any. I really have no idea what the construction guys talk about when they're working together, or what the weaving groups talk about when I'm not there. Perhaps there's grumbling and I'm just not there to hear it."

"Perhaps, but I don't think so. Word travels fast in a group like this. It's pretty hard to keep a secret. Plus, I think everyone realizes what's at stake here and is focused on getting ready for winter. They're pretty well occupied. I'm not sure they have enough time to think about anything else."

Aurora nodded, but she was still uncertain. She sighed and laid her head against Den's legs again.

"A hundred and fifty people are dead because of me."

"Two thousand seven hundred and fifty people are alive because of you. Mayor Goodwin was more interested in keeping his authority and power over everyone. You were more interested in providing everyone with a better quality of life." Den petted her head. "Don't forget, even though you didn't go down to try again, there are fifty people who followed when they realized the hopelessness of their situation because of your original efforts."

"Still …"

"You can't save everyone, Rori. It's not even up to you to save them. It never was. Your only role was to offer them a choice and you did that."

"It makes me wonder how long this peace is going to last now that we're here. Did the new arrivals come willingly or did they feel somewhat forced and came reluctantly? Will they integrate well with the people that are already here? What if … ?"

"Aurora, stop it."

The finality in Den's voice surprised her. She looked up at him and immediately regretted keeping him out so long. He was staying out to help her stay strong, but he was clearly exhausted.

"You'll never do yourself any good playing the 'what if' game. This news is a big shock, and it will be to everyone. Perhaps it's natural to ask ourselves if we could have done more to save the others." Den took a deep breath. "But you can't focus on that. Take tonight and grieve for those for whom you felt responsible that you couldn't convince to come with us, but Imogen will only survive, the new arrivals will only integrate well if you lead with no regrets, no looking back. Everyone is here because they made the choice to live in the light. Yes, we grieve for those who decided not to come with us, but we can't live in that grief. Winter is coming, and we all need each other to focus on building this community. The other group will be coming in a few days, there's no room for regrets to get in the way of rebuilding."

Aurora sighed and stood. She leaned down and kissed Den, letting go of all her emotions in the intensity of the kiss. When it ended, Den raised a hand to her cheek and tried to smooth the grief, sadness and tears. The love in his eyes for her belied his fatigue, like he was giving his last ounce of energy to strengthen her.

"We need to get you back to Dom."

Den nodded, too tired to speak.

Aurora wheeled him back inside.

CHAPTER THIRTY-THREE

Seven light cycles later, the third group arrived. With the extra crews available since the arrival of the second group, work on the residence had progressed to the point where some families had already been moved into the first one and the work crews moved down as new buildings were completed.

There were now enough warm clothes and shoes for everyone, at least one set and the second set of clothes were almost complete. Dom and his science team had successfully thawed out a couple of birds, which UWE people used to use for eggs and meat, and potato plants, peas, beans and tomatoes which much more resembled the pictures in the archives better than what they'd been used to eating out of the Egerton greenhouses.

It hadn't taken long for word to spread about the destruction of Egerton and there were several days of quiet working amongst the crews. The thicker snow falls quickly refocused everyone's efforts with the promise that their hard work would make the cold weather more bearable, and keep peoples' spirits cheerful.

There was enough snow on the ground now for the kids to have snowball fights and build snowmen. Inspired by UWE records, a few of the older kids and adults had constructed sleds and skis and snowshoes.

Even though the climb was somewhat treacherous with the ice and snow, Aurora made the trek to her favourite crag overlooking the settlement a couple times a week, and Den had gained enough strength to join her a couple of times.

He'd recovered amazingly well, and was almost back to normal. There were still a few deep bone bruises that would take longer to heel, he wouldn't be able to join the construction crews for a bit, and he still needed a mid-light cycle nap, but he was able to help in the greenhouses, and spend some time with the kids in school, which they'd started once enough families had cleared out of the main compound. Enough families had moved into the new residences that they'd started a small set of classes there too.

With the re-arrangement of families and sleeping quarters, it was possible to build more private spaces for the remaining families so it didn't quite feel like they were sleeping on top of each other and afforded a little more privacy. Most of the people in the main compound were older and unable to participate in much of the outdoor work. Some still worked in the greenhouses or on weaving, but the cold presented a new problem with their bones and joints and despite Dom's efforts to create a soothing balm, the overall skeletal deterioration after having lived underground for so long meant that there was really not much else he could do.

It would take several generations to begin to see the sun's effects on their bodies. The current generation might be able to see some improvement at least in their longevity, but those who were older, like Mr. Poly and his wife, would not experience that.

Dom's voice squawked over the radio. "Cass."

There was no joviality in Dom's voice, and Aurora had an idea what he was going to say. She turned from her observation of the residence construction and took a few steps back toward the main compound.

"I'm here, Dom."

"Mr. Poly's almost ready, as are the others."

"I'll be right there."

The trek took about ten minutes longer than usual. They couldn't use the bikes in the snow, and she'd forgotten to wear her snow shoes so she had to high step her way through the knee-deep snow back to the compound.

She stomped off her shoes and clothes when she stepped inside, thanking God for the warmth the building offered.

She left her shoes near the door, slid on her indoor shoes and trotted to the back room. There she found Dom standing, looking over several of their older citizens. There were about ten in all -- Mr. Poly, his wife and eight others.

"They're all gone, Cass, except Mr. Poly. He was holding on for you."

Aurora's eyes filled with tears. She knew this day had been coming for a long time, but it was still hard to imagine losing so many at once, particularly Mr. Poly who, despite his age, had been one of her most enthusiastic supporters.

Aurora walked through the group, who all looked peaceful and asleep. Her heart took comfort in that. At Mr. Poly's place, she knelt down beside him and took his hand which rested on his chest.

"I'm here, Mr. Poly."

His eyes fluttered open as he turned his head.

"Ah, Miss Aurora. Thank you for coming. I just wanted to say thank you."

Aurora smiled. "You're welcome. You've been so sweet to me; I had to come say goodbye."

"No, no, Miss Aurora. I don't mean that." He took a deep breath as he tried to draw strength for this last exchange. "I mean for the sunlight.

For bringing us out of the darkness and letting us see the light. It's more beautiful than we could have ever imagined."

Aurora looked down at the floor as tears coursed down her cheeks.

"I-I'm sorry you weren't able to enjoy more of it."

"No, no, Miss Aurora. All of us were blessed just to have seen it. We would have been cursed to die in the darkness, but you gave us a chance to see what we never even thought possible."

"But ... ."

He raised a finger to her lips to quiet her. "You gave us life, Miss Aurora. A life we never would have had." His hand dropped to his side and his eyes started to droop. "Thank you, Miss Aurora."

As his eyes closed and his lungs expelled their last breath, Aurora sobbed by his side. She didn't know how long she sat there before she felt Dom's hand on her shoulder.

"I have to take them."

Aurora nodded. "I know." She stood and took the EOL scanner from Dom's hand and walked down to the person on the far end, near the window looking out the back. Within thirty minutes she'd completed all the scans, not that there was any doubt what the cause of death was, but at least they'd be able to trace the progress of their bodies' recovery under the sun as the years progressed.

Aurora met Dom on the other end of the row of bodies, close to the alcove where she used to sleep. With the rearrangement of the sleeping areas, and with Den's recovery, they'd left the radio in the alcove, but moved their sleeping area into one of the former office areas in the main hall.

"I know we don't usually do this, but I feel since these are the first deaths, we need to honor them before their bodies are turned into energy for us. It would give us all a chance to say goodbye to Egerton as well."

"Sounds like a good idea."

By the end of the light cycle, word had spread about the memorial meeting and all had gathered in the freezing cold.

Aurora looked down from the makeshift stage at the people gathered around, and then at the bodies that lay before her.

"Thank you for gathering. I don't know if everyone knew who these people were." She waved her hands over the bodies. "But I just didn't feel like we could let them go without taking a few minutes to honor their lives and remember why we're all here.

"It's been several months now since we emerged from Egerton into the light. We left behind the only world we'd ever known to take a step, really, into the unknown. And you have all worked so hard to make this all work. We wouldn't all be here if it weren't for everyone working together and believing in what we were working for.

"Mr. and Mrs. Poly, Mr. and Mrs. Jarreth, Mr. and Mrs. Kinney, Mr. and Mrs. Singkin, and Mr. and Mrs. Entel weren't able to help much with the work. They did what their bodies were able to do, but they never stopped believing in what we were doing. I'd like to think that they were the bravest of all of us who came to the surface.

"They came knowing that they didn't have much time left and probably wouldn't experience the longer, healthier lives that our grandchildren will experience. Even in his last words, Mr. Poly expressed his thankfulness for having seen the sun and for the opportunity to see and feel it."

As if on cue, the setting sun had reached the crags behind the compound and sprayed orangey-red sunlight across the gathering.

"I know you have all worked hard and perhaps sometimes even became discouraged over how much there was to do and the short time frame we had. I know I did. But that didn't faze Mr. Poly and the others and I have to admit his encouragement has kept me going at times.

"I never set out to be a leader." Aurora shook her head. "Never even imagined myself getting up here like this to talk to you all. But here I am. And Mr. Poly's last words to me reminded me of the family members who chose not to come for whatever reason."

Aurora's voice caught in her throat as she made eye contact with Caytor and her family.

"I thought this would be a time for us all to remember them, to let go of any guilt or regrets we might have had for not being to convince them to come. And then we will send Mr. Poly and the others on their way to be used to help keep this civilization going even in their death. They may not have been able to help the way they would have liked to, but they will still help us live.

"Let us have a few moments of prayer and silence to remember those we're saying goodbye to."

Aurora stepped down from the stage. Immediately, Den was by her side and took her hand. She sobbed as she prayed. Sobbed for the loss of the one of the kindest men she'd ever known. Sobbed for the loss of the people she had tried to save. Sobbed with joy for the fifty who had come afterwards including her own daughter, whom she thought she'd lost forever. Sobbed with thankfulness that Imogen was thriving, and for the blessings that she knew were going to come from their work and that all their needs had been taken care of.

At the end of those silent moments, Aurora swiped the tears from her cheeks and nodded to Dom who waved a hand a group of men. They stepped on to the stage and carried each body down and placed it on a sled that the men would pull to the incinerator. Once the men had disappeared with the bodies, the crowd broke up and Aurora turned and went into the compound to her and Den's room.

Den knew to leave her alone for a few moments to let her process all the emotions coursing through her. She didn't know how long it had been before she heard a knock on the door.

"Come in."

Den slipped in. "You're getting better at that."

"At what?"

Den put his arms around her waist and drew her to him and she surrendered to the warmth of his body, taking hold of his hands.

"Talking to them."

Aurora nodded. "I guess I am."

"I don't know if you know it, but the people are all talking about you being the next mayor."

Aurora let go of his hands, her temper and impatience flaring.

"Oh, Den, do we have to talk about that now? We've just said goodbye to ten people."

"Mr. Poly was one of those who supported the idea."

Aurora couldn't help the smile. "That doesn't surprise me. But, Den, I can't do that. I don't deserve to be mayor. Maybe Dara and the others who've already sat in a leadership role."

"They may have taken leadership of their little group, but they've always looked to you from the very start."

314

Aurora leaned her back against the wall so she could look at Den. Her shoulders drooped.

"Whether you know it or not, you're already leading."

"I guess I am." Aurora nodded then sighed. "I really didn't mean to. I've never really seen myself as a leader."

"Perhaps not, but I've seen a real change in you since before my accident and when I woke up. You were unsure of yourself almost timid and didn't believe you could do it. Now, it just seems to come so naturally to you, and everyone sees it." Den approached her again, and tipped her chin up. "The thing is Dara, Barna, and a few others have been talking about needing something a little more official in terms of city leadership and none of them is talking about them doing anything other than assisting you. With the people split now, you really can't be everywhere."

"No, I guess not." Aurora shook her head and looked him in the eye. "You know, I still can't believe you're standing there in front of me. A part of me is still afraid something's going to happen to you. Dom never knew that one incident was even coming. It was so sudden that we almost lost you."

Den stepped closer and silenced her with a kiss, his hands holding her hips next to his.

"You're not going to lose me, Rori," he growled against her mouth.

"Are you sure you're ready?" Aurora said, breathless, as he started blazing a trail of kisses down her neck and undoing her clothes.

"I've never been so ready for something in all my life."

ABOUT THE AUTHOR

Darlene Oakley is a freelance writer, editor, and transcriptionist based in Canada's Niagara Region. She specializes in writing dentistry, health, and parenting-related articles and has over 200 articles published online to date. She has two sons, 18 and 6, both with learning disabilities, who are the source of inspiration for many of her articles.

Darlene has been writing short stories and books since she first learned how to put pen to paper. This book is a culmination of a life's pursuit and comes out of a love for words and writing.

SOURCES

1. Benefits of Sunlight: A Bright Spot for Human Health. Mead, M. Nathaniel. <u>Environ Health Perspect. 2008 May; 116(5): A197</u>. Web. Dec 5, 2013.

Made in the USA
Charleston, SC
11 September 2015